TITANS

- BOOK 2 -
THE MISSING

KATE O'HEARN

Aladdin
NEW YORK LONDON TORONTO SYDNEY NEW DELHI

ALADDIN

An imprint of Simon & Schuster Children's Publishing Division
1230 Avenue of the Americas, New York, New York 10020
First Aladdin paperback edition June 2021
Text copyright © 2020 by Kate O'Hearn
Cover illustration copyright © 2020 by Clint Cearley
Also available in an Aladdin hardcover edition.
All rights reserved, including the right of reproduction in whole or in part in any form.
ALADDIN and related logo are registered trademarks of Simon & Schuster, Inc.
For information about special discounts for bulk purchases, please contact
Simon & Schuster Special Sales at 1-866-506-1949 or business@simonandschuster.com.
The Simon & Schuster Speakers Bureau can bring authors to your live event.
For more information or to book an event contact the Simon & Schuster Speakers Bureau
at 1-866-248-3049 or visit our website at www.simonspeakers.com.
Cover designed by Karin Paprocki
Interior designed by Mike Rosamilia
The text of this book was set in Adobe Garamond.
Manufactured in the United States of America 0521 OFF
2 4 6 8 10 9 7 5 3 1
The Library of Congress has cataloged the hardcover edition as follows:
Names: O'Hearn, Kate, author.
Title: The missing / Kate O'Hearn.
Description: First Aladdin hardcover edition. | New York : Aladdin, 2020. |
Series: Titans ; book 2 | Audience: Ages 8-12. | Summary: "Astraea, Zephyr, and their friends travel
to a dangerous jungle world in this second book of the Titans series"— Provided by publisher.
Identifiers: LCCN 2020009724 (print) | LCCN 2020009725 (ebook) |
ISBN 9781534417076 (hardcover) | ISBN 9781534417090 (ebook)
Subjects: CYAC: Titans (Mythology)—Fiction. | Animals, Mythical—Fiction. | Mythology, Greek—
Fiction. | Jungles—Fiction. | Adventure and adventurers—Fiction. | Fantasy.
Classification: LCC PZ7.O4137 Mis 2020 (print) | LCC PZ7.O4137 (ebook) | DDC [Fic]—dc23
LC record available at https://lccn.loc.gov/2020009724
LC ebook record available at https://lccn.loc.gov/2020009725
ISBN 9781534417083 (pbk)

For my family—the center of my universe

THE MISSING

ASTRAEA OFTEN THOUGHT THAT STEPPING into the Solar Stream must be like stepping onto the surface of the sun—but without the heat. The bright lights of pure energy blazed so brilliantly that she had to shield her eyes. The whooshing in her ears from the Solar Stream left her unable to hear much of anything else.

Astraea's best friend was traveling at her side. Zephyr extended a large white wing and wrapped it around her. She only ever did that when she was nervous. Astraea was nervous too. In such a short time her life had changed completely. She had thought going to school would be the biggest change. But that was nothing compared to the discoveries they had made.

A race of shape-changing monsters they called the Mimics were secretly attacking Titus. To distract her grandfather Hyperion and his security teams, the Mimics were bringing humans from Earth and creatures from other worlds to Titus. With Titus security occupied rounding up the newcomers, the invaders were slowly abducting the Titan and Olympian leadership and replacing them with their own look-alike kind.

These stealth attacks would have gone unnoticed if a human boy hadn't arrived from California. His appearance in the Arcadia nectar orchards changed everything.

With the help of their friend Tryn and a herd of centaurs, Astraea, Zephyr, and Jake had traveled to the dreadful prison Tartarus to free the abducted Titans and Olympians and then gone to Earth to hide them.

Now they were going to another new place—Zomos. The world that Nesso the snake came from. All Astraea knew about Zomos came from Jupiter, who said Zomos was a wild place.

The one thing she did notice was just how long it was taking to get there. Going to Tartarus had been very fast. Even going to Earth wasn't that bad. But now it felt like they'd been in the Solar Stream for ages.

Astraea looked around her. She saw Jake and Tryn shadowed in the blazing light just in front of her, while beside her were three young centaurs, Cylus, Render, and Darek. If she was honest, she hadn't wanted the centaurs to come along . . . especially Cylus, who was a big bully. But Jupiter had insisted. And since his word was final, they didn't have a choice.

They discovered that moving within the confines of the Solar Stream was next to impossible. But Astraea had to manage only a single step in order to be pressed against Zephyr's side.

"This is taking forever!" she shouted up to her friend's ear.

Zephyr tilted her head back to Astraea. "What?"

"I said, it's"—halfway through the statement, the journey ended, and they exited the Solar Stream into a dense jungle—"taking forever!"

Zephyr looked at her and winked a large brown

eye. "There's no need to shout, Astraea. I'm right here." She tightened her wing to pull Astraea closer.

"Whoa," Jake said, gazing around. "This place is awesome. I've never seen so many colors! Look, the leaves on the trees, they aren't even green—there's red and blue—and look over there; that one has purple leaves!"

Tryn was standing beside him. "It looks a lot like my home, Xanadu. But the colors are different and the leaves on Xanadu's trees are much bigger." He walked forward and bent down to study a strange-looking multilegged insect.

Jake joined him and reached for the bug, but Tryn caught hold of his hand. "No, don't. Remember, Jake, this isn't your world. Things here may be poisonous. My mother always said that's the first rule of exploration. Don't touch anything until you are certain it's safe."

Jake pulled back his hand. "But how are we supposed to know what's safe? It's not like we have any equipment or anything."

"*It isss sssafe,*" Nesso said. The colorful snake was coiled around Jake's neck. "*Alssso deliccciousss. They are my favorite food.*"

Jake reached up and invited the snake onto his hands. "So this is your home?"

"It wasss," Nesso said. *"Now my home isss with you. But it isss niccce to feel the warmth again."*

"Warmth?" Jake laughed. "You're not kidding; this place is boiling! It's much hotter than LA on a summer's day."

Cylus was standing with his centaur friends Render and Darek and nudged them. "Look how stupid humans are, complaining about the heat when we're on an important mission."

"Hey!" Astraea charged up to Cylus. "If you're just going to start trouble, you and your herd can go right back to Earth. We have a lot to do here, and we don't need you bullying Jake anymore."

"I'm not bullying him," Cylus said. "But can I help it if he says stupid things?"

"Oh, and you never say stupid things?" Zephyr asked.

"Never!" Cylus challenged. "Tell me one time I said something stupid."

Zephyr stepped closer to the centaur and looked down on him. "How about every time you open your mouth?"

"Everyone, that's enough," Tryn said. "Jupiter and the others are counting on us. This constant fighting isn't helping."

When Cylus crossed his hands over his chest and opened his mouth to speak, Zephyr bent even closer. "Don't say one word. He's right. . . ." She looked over at Jake. "Would you tell Nesso to start asking her friends to join us?"

Jake looked at Tryn. "I know Zephyr was talking to me. What did she say?"

Zephyr snorted in irritation but said nothing.

"She said it's time to tell Nesso to ask her friends if they will join us."

Jake nodded and pulled Nesso closer. "Did you hear that? Will you call your friends?"

"Yesss," Nesso said. *"Put me down on the ground."* When Jake bent to put the snake down, Nesso raised herself higher. *"You won't leave me, will you?"*

"Never." Jake looked at the others and explained what Nesso had said. Astraea came closer and lightly stroked the snake. "We're friends, Nesso. We'd never leave you behind. We'll stay right here waiting for you."

Behind them, Cylus harrumphed, but with a warning whinny from Zephyr, he didn't say more.

Jake put Nesso down on the ground, and they all watched the colorful snake slip into the undergrowth.

"Now what are we supposed to do?" Cylus said. "Just stand here waiting for the snakes to come to us?"

"I'd like to look around a bit," Render said as his eyes took in the whole area. "I'd never been anywhere but Titus. Now I've been to Tartarus and Earth. I really like seeing new places."

Tryn looked over to the centaur. "You sound like a true explorer."

Cylus shoved his friend and snorted. "Render the explorer, yeah, that would work."

"Why not?" Tryn said. "Why can't he be an explorer?"

"Because he's a centaur," Cylus said. "We are fighters, not explorers. It's you weaklings that should be the explorers."

Jake frowned. "Says who? Why can't he be what he wants?"

"Because that's the way it's always been," Cylus

answered. "You're just a human that doesn't understand."

"But things can change, can't they?" Jake said. "If Render wants to explore, he should be allowed."

Cylus trotted over to Jake and poked him in the chest. "Now you're telling us what we can do?"

"I—well, I mean . . . ," Jake stuttered.

"Enough!" Zephyr snorted. "Cylus shut up and leave him alone. Jake is the only one who can talk to the snakes. I won't allow you to hurt him."

Cylus huffed and walked away from the group. When he was gone, Render approached Jake. "Thanks for trying. But Cylus would never allow me to do what I want."

"I don't understand why you need his permission," Jake said. "You're free to make your own decisions, aren't you?"

"Not really," Render said.

Darek clopped forward. "Cylus is the leader of our herd. We have to do what he tells us."

"Why?" Jake asked.

"Because," Render said. "He is our leader."

"Jake, you don't understand," Astraea said. "Centaurs live as a herd, and as a herd there must always be a leader. That's Cylus. They aren't like us—there's an order to follow. If Cylus tells them to do something, they must."

Jake shook his head. "This makes no sense. If Render wants to explore, why can't he? What if Darek wanted to be an inventor or something? Are you telling me that he couldn't because Cylus says no? That's not freedom."

Astraea looked from Jake back to the two centaurs. They were both looking down and appeared almost sad. As though they realized for the first time just how much control Cylus had over their lives. Thinking about it, Astraea realized how unfair it was for them.

Tryn cleared his throat. "We can argue the difference between herd life and the individual later. Right now we need to find something to hold all the snakes in to take back with us, or there won't be any of us left to argue about anything."

"I've got my backpack," Jake offered. "That will hold a few."

Tryn nodded. "That's great, but we need more.

When you consider that Nesso can give venom only twice a day and even then, it's not a lot. There are a lot of Mimics. . . ."

"Meaning we need a lot of venom," Astraea added.

"Which means a lot of snakes," Jake finished. "My pack is definitely too small."

Astraea started to look around. The trees were tall, but the small leaves meant they couldn't use them to make any kind of container.

Zephyr approached a tree and reached for a vine, but when she pulled it, it broke easily. "There's nothing here. Everything is either too small or too brittle to weave together."

"We need something," Darek said.

After a few minutes, Astraea had a thought. "Wait, I know what we can use." She walked over to Jake and turned her back to him. "Jake, would you tear off the fabric covering my wings? We can make a sack from it."

As Jake started to tear away the cape-like fabric, Zephyr came over. "But, Astraea, you hate showing you wings. We must find something else."

Astraea looked up into Zephyr's dark eyes.

"Thanks, Zeph, but it's all right. We need it."

"All done." Jake held up the large piece of blue silken cloth. He pulled the corners together to form a kind of sack. "This should work great if you hold it closed, or maybe we can find something to tie it. Next we have to ask the snakes if they would go in it."

"Speaking of snakes," Zephyr said, "Nesso has been gone some time. I wonder if the others said no."

Tryn repeated Zephyr's comment to Jake. "She's right; it has been a fairly long time. I hope she's all right."

"Maybe she was eaten by something," Render added.

"No!" Jake said quickly. "Nesso!" he started to shout. "Nesso, where are you?"

Tryn slapped his hand over Jake's mouth. "Haven't you learned anything about traveling to alien worlds? You can't go around shouting at the top of your lungs. You don't know who or what is going to answer."

Jake nodded, and Tryn pulled his hand away.

"Jake," Astraea said. "You and Nesso have a connection. Take a deep breath and close your eyes. Tell me if you can feel her."

Jake did as Astraea suggested. After a moment, his eyes flashed opened and he looked at her in shock. "You're right. I can actually feel her!" He pointed into the dense jungle. "She's that way."

"Let's go!" Zephyr said.

"Wait," Astraea said. "I'll go get Cylus."

"Do you have to?" Zephyr called.

Astraea glanced back at her friend, but then jogged in the direction that Cylus had gone. She found him standing alone looking down into a stream. The water was bright yellow and there were little red and blue fish swimming around.

"Cylus, we're going to go get Nesso."

"So?"

"So, do you want to stay here, or come with us?"

Cylus looked over to her but pawed the ground with a hoof. "Why should I? You and Zephyr will just yell at me again."

"We yell because you're always being mean—"

Cylus opened his mouth to speak, but Astraea held up a hand. "Don't speak; listen. Just because you're a centaur doesn't mean you have to be cruel. I've met your mother. She isn't cruel, and neither are the centaurs working with my parents. The only reason Render and Darek are mean is because you encourage them to be. Can't you see that you would have more friends and a lot more respect if you'd stop being a bully and tried being nice?"

"But . . . ," Cylus started.

"But what? Do you actually like being mean?"

"No," Cylus said, but he made it sound like a challenge.

"Well, then, why don't you try being a little nicer? You can start by not being so awful to Jake. Can't you understand what he's going through? He's never seen anyone like us before. All he's known is Earth, with no idea we even existed. We at least knew humans existed. It's all different for him. But every time he opens his mouth around you, you say something cruel to him or you threaten him. That's why we yell at you. It's bad enough how you treat Tryn—but he's strong enough to take it. Jake is different."

"Yeah, he's weak!"

"See, that's exactly what I mean!" Astraea insisted. "Yes, he's human, yes, they are weaker than us, but that doesn't mean we're better than them. We're just different." Astraea took a step closer. "Look, instead of seeing our differences, why don't you try seeing what we have in common?"

"What's that?" Cylus snorted.

"The Mimics. They want to take Titus from us and then Earth. They are more powerful than us, so you being stronger than Jake means nothing if a Mimic can hurt all of us equally."

Cylus looked at Astraea for a long moment. Then he nodded. "I'm coming with you."

They made it back to the group and nothing further was said. Instead, Jake closed his eyes again and pointed into the dense jungle. "Nesso's that way."

Cylus finally spoke. "Darek, you take the left side. Render, you take the right. I'll take up front." He paused and looked over at Jake. "You come up front with me to lead us."

"Um, sure," Jake said as he cautiously took his place beside Cylus.

Zephyr was walking beside Astraea and looked at her in shock. "What did you say to Cylus?"

Astraea shrugged. "Nothing really. I just reminded him that the Mimics made us all equal."

Zephyr nodded. "True. I just hope it works."

Astraea nodded. "Me too."

They started pushing through the jungle, but the going was slow. The trees grew densely together, and there were vines everywhere. Though the vines were easily broken, their number alone made movement difficult. Added to that was the high heat and humidity.

"I feel like I'm breathing underwater," Astraea complained. "It's so hot here."

"And if one more tree catches my wings, I'm going to scream!" Zephyr added as she tried to push through a thick bush.

Tryn wiped his silver brow. "My mother always told me our home world, Rhean, was hot, but because our sun evaporated most of the water, it was dry heat and didn't really feel too bad. But this is hot and humid and very uncomfortable."

Cylus looked back at Astraea and she saw that he was about to make a comment, but then he stopped. He frowned and looked around. Finally, he turned to Render and Darek. "Do you feel that?"

The two other centaurs stopped and then nodded.

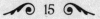

"Something is coming this way," Darek said.

"Something big," Render added.

"I don't hear anything," Jake said.

"Not hear, feel," Cylus said. "The ground is shaking."

Zephyr's ears went back, and she looked at Astraea. "He's right. Something heavy is moving this way."

"Follow me," Cylus said. He caught hold of Jake's arm and started to haul him along to the right.

"But Nesso is that way," Jake insisted, pointing in the direction they had been heading.

"Yes, and that's the same direction the big thing is moving," Cylus finished.

The group tried to hurry through the jungle, but the undergrowth made speed impossible. The struggle was exhausting, and soon everyone was panting and sweating.

"Hurry," Cylus insisted. "It's changing directions."

"Are you saying it's following us?" Tryn asked.

Darek nodded. "It is."

They kept moving but gained little distance. Then a roar sounded—a roar so loud it vibrated right through them.

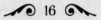

"What was that?" Jake called. "A giant?"

"Giants don't roar," Astraea answered. "Whatever it is, I don't want to know."

Moments later a second roar sounded. This time it was from right in front of them. There were also the sounds of branches breaking and heavy movement.

"There are two of them," Cylus cried. "And we're standing right between them!"

Tryn stopped and turned in a circle. "In all this growth, we can't outrun them."

"So we stand our ground!" Cylus pulled his bow off his shoulder. "Darek, Render, ready your bows. Everyone else, duck down!"

"Duck down, he says," Zephyr muttered to Astraea. "Has he seen me? How am I supposed to duck down? I'm going to be the first eaten!"

Darek and Render loaded their bows and stood facing the direction of the nearest roar. "No one is being eaten today!" Darek called.

"No, it can't be," Jake cried. He was pointing up to the small patch of sky that could be seen between the trees. "It's—it's impossible! It can't be here. It just can't!"

"What are you blabbering about?" Cylus demanded.

Jake was still looking up. "That looks like a T. rex, but it can't be. They're from Earth and went extinct millions of years ago."

Astraea looked up and saw a massive multicolored lizard-like creature. Its head was lifted, and it appeared to be sniffing the air. "What is it?"

"It's a kind of dinosaur," Jake cried. "We are so toast!"

"Look at those teeth!" Tryn called. "It must be a carnivore."

"What's a carnivore?" Render called.

"It means it's a meat eater," Jake said. "And it looks like we're on the menu!"

The immense dinosaur's head tilted to the side and the one huge eye spotted them in the undergrowth. It roared again and started to lunge.

"Shoot for its eyes!" Cylus called as he loosed an arrow.

The centaurs fired arrows at the dinosaur. Most bounced off the scaled head, but one struck the corner of the creature's eye. It roared in pain and raised its head, staggering backward.

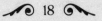

As they watched the first dinosaur, the foot of the second dinosaur crashed down on the ground right beside them, missing Tryn and Astraea by a breath.

Astraea couldn't hold back a scream at the size of the scaled foot beside her. Brutus the giant was big, but somehow his size didn't scare her. This foot was terrifying. Then again, it could have been the huge, sharp claws at the end of the reptilian toes.

No sooner had the foot come down than it was moving again as the creature charged at the wounded dinosaur.

The thunderous sound of the two dinosaurs crashing together was hideous. What made it even worse was how their tails swept across the ground, shearing down trees and brushing everything away as they fought.

"We have to get out of here!" Tryn shouted.

"How?" Jake cried. "Those two are destroying the whole area. Wherever we run, they'll get us." The words were just out of his mouth when a thick, long tail swept over their heads. "Whoa, that was too close!"

"We have to fly!" Zephyr shouted. She looked over to Astraea. "Get on my back, now!"

"What about the others?" Astraea called as she climbed up onto Zephyr's back.

Tryn reached for his skateboard. "Jake, use your board!"

"What about us?" Render cried. "You're not going to leave us here, are you?"

"Of course not!" Tryn ran up to the centaur and looked at him, as though sizing him up. "Vulcan never builds anything weak. If you are strong enough to hold on, my skateboard should be able to carry you. Darek can hold on to Jake's board." He looked at Zephyr. "Are you strong enough to carry Cylus?"

"I don't know!"

A massive foot slammed down on the ground near them again as the dinosaurs moved closer. The roaring intensified as the fight grew more violent. Suddenly the two wrestling monsters fell to the ground and started to roll around.

"Zephyr, please," Cylus called. "Please try. I don't want to die here!"

"Fly, Zephyr!" Astraea cried above the sounds of crashing trees and furious, fighting monsters. "Hurry!"

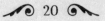

In the tight confines of the jungle, Zephyr opened her white wings. "Cylus, when I take off, catch hold of my back legs. Don't let go!"

Astraea looked over and saw Tryn and Jake were already on their skateboards. She could no longer hear them over the roaring, but as she watched, the two skateboards' wings appeared and started to fly, lifting Render and Darek with them.

"Go, Zephyr, go!" Astraea cried as a dark wall of rolling dinosaurs bored down on them. This was it, the one chance to get away. If Zephyr couldn't fly, they were doomed.

ZEPHYR FLAPPED HER POWERFUL WINGS AS
hard as she could, whinnying. Normally she needed
to run to take off, but with the dinosaurs rolling
toward them, there was no time or space—she had to
launch from a standing position.

Astraea threw her arms around Zephyr's neck and
started to flap her own tiny wings, offering as much
help as she could.

"C'mon, Zeph, you can do it!" she shouted. This
was the first time in their lives that Astraea had ever
been on her best friend's back. How tragic if it was
the last.

The thunderous wall of dinosaurs was right in

front of them. Zephyr's wings beat down harder and faster as they started to lift off the ground. There was a backward jerk as Cylus caught hold of her back legs and his weight pulled them down, but then Zephyr moved again. Higher and higher until they managed to clear the area just as the two fighting monsters rolled through.

Astraea looked down to see Cylus hanging from Zephyr's back legs. "You made it!"

"Yes," he called up. "But I think I'm going to be sick."

"Don't you dare," Zephyr shouted. "Because if you do, I promise I'll drop you!"

Astraea hugged her best friend's neck. "Zephyr, you're amazing!"

"This isn't over yet," Zephyr cried. "Cylus is too heavy for me. I can't carry him much farther."

It was only then that Astraea realized they were still in a lot of danger. Seated high on Zephyr's back, she looked around, hoping to find somewhere safe for them to land. Beneath them, the two monsters continued to wrestle, their unpredictable movements making a large area unsafe. "Zephyr, over here!" Tryn shouted.

Astraea looked back and saw Tryn and Jake on their flying skateboards several lengths behind them. Render was hanging on to the underside of Tryn's board, while Darek clung to Jake's. The boards looked like they too were struggling to carry the added weight of the heavy centaurs.

"There!" Tryn pointed to a rocky plateau rising out of the dense jungle. "Zephyr, turn around. We can land there!"

Zephyr was panting with exhaustion as she tilted her wings and managed to turn around. Astraea could feel her powerful wing muscles quivering and straining to carry Cylus. "You're doing so great!" she encouraged.

Beneath them, Cylus was looking green. Just as Zephyr flew above the plateau, he released her legs and landed on the ground. Going down to his equine knees, he kissed the ground.

Zephyr touched down beside him. Her wings drooped and her head hung low. When Astraea slid off her back, she ran up to Zephyr's head and hugged her tightly. "You saved us!"

"Tha—" Zephyr gulped air. "That was the hardest thing I've ev-ever done. I hurt all over, and my back legs feel like they've pulled out of their sockets."

Cylus regained his legs and trotted over to her. "Thank you, thank you, Zephyr." He threw his arms around her neck. "I am so sorry I called you Pegasus's daughter. I promise I'll never do it again!"

Astraea felt Zephyr tense as Cylus hugged her. Zephyr gasped. "It's okay, Cylus. You don't need to strangle me."

Darek and Render came up to them. Their faces were flushed, and Render had a beaming smile on his face. "That was the best thing ever! I never imagined how exciting flying could be. If we survive this, I am asking Vulcan to make me some wings!"

"You are not going to fly!" Cylus said.

Astraea looked at Zephyr and sighed. "That didn't last long."

"What?" Cylus said to them. Then he considered what he'd just said and cleared his throat. "What I mean is, you really want to fly again?"

"If you'll let me," Render said. "I loved it."

Cylus stole a look at Astraea. "If, um, if you really want to fly, I'm not going to stop you."

"Really?" Render could hardly contain his excitement and reared high on his back legs. "I'm going to fly again!"

Tryn and Jake were standing at the edge of the plateau, looking out over the jungle. The two massive dinosaurs were still fighting. They were crushing a large area of trees as they rolled around. Finally they broke up, and the loser, covered in blood, limped away. The victor threw back his head and roared before heading in the opposite direction.

"Wow," Jake said in shock. "I can't believe what we just saw. How could dinosaurs make it to this planet?"

"It's likely they evolved here," Tryn said. "We had a form of lizard on my old world, Rhean. There are some on Xanadu as well. It is reasonable to assume they evolved here as they did on Earth. With ample food and limited predators, they were able to grow to that size."

"Really?" Render said.

Tryn nodded. "Look at Jake, Astraea, and me. We come from different worlds and yet we have the same shape. Two arms, two legs, one head with two eyes,

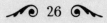

ears, and a nose. Granted there are some difference—I'm silver and Astraea has wings—but they are largely caused by our different environments."

Astraea looked down at the departing creatures. "We don't have anything that big on Titus."

"But you do have lizards," Tryn said. "These are just bigger ones. Besides, Titus has giants. Earth doesn't and Xanadu doesn't, either—as least as far as I know."

Jake shook his head. "I wish my phone worked and I could have gotten a video of that fight. I never imagined that dinosaurs would be so colorful. I thought they'd just be gray like in the movies."

Tryn turned a tight circle. "It doesn't matter what color they are—we're in real danger here. Let's just get the snakes and go before they or their family come back to eat us."

"I'm all for that," Zephyr added. "I would love to go home and soak in a tub of warm water. My back legs are killing me."

They were standing on the flat top of the rocky plateau. The jungle was far beneath them, while above them a clear cloudless sky went on for miles.

Without the trees offering shade, the sun was huge and blazing and the heat was more intense than any of them had ever experienced before.

"We've also got to get out of this sun," Tryn warned. "I'm safe with my silver skin, but you guys are going to burn to a crisp if you stay exposed much longer. Astraea, you're already turning pink."

Astraea looked at her arms. "I know, and my skin is starting to prickle."

"Then let's get moving." Jake shut his eyes and breathed a great sigh of relief. "I can still feel Nesso. She's alive."

"How are we going to get down to her?" Darek asked. "Fly again?"

"I'm happy to," Render offered quickly.

"No way," Cylus said. "I'm not going anywhere but back to Earth or Titus. You guys can fly all you want, but I'm keeping my hooves firmly on the ground."

"I don't think you'll have to fly, Cylus. I have an idea that I think will work." Tryn placed his skateboard down and stepped up on it. "Take me to the snake, Nesso."

The tiny wings on the board appeared and started

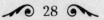

to flap. Tryn was lifted into the air, over the edge of the plateau, and down toward the trees. "Stop!" he called. "Hover."

As the skateboard hovered above the trees, Tryn called to Jake, "The skateboards do work at tracking. Come on. We'll go get Nesso and her friends and come back."

Jake put down his own board and climbed on. He turned back to Astraea. "We won't be long. Try to find some shelter or something. This sun is a killer!"

Astraea looked across the flat top of the plateau. "Where? There's nothing up here but flat rock. Just go get Nesso and her friends and we can leave."

Jake nodded and called to his skateboard, "Take me to Nesso." The tiny wings appeared, lifted the board off the rocky ground, and carried him over the edge.

Astraea, Zephyr, and the centaurs watched them dip down toward the jungle and vanish into the trees. As the moments ticked by, the stinging prickle on Astraea's skin was turning to genuine pain as her skin burned. She looked over at Zephyr and saw that her muzzle was already red and the skin inside her ears was peeling with the sunburn.

The centaurs were not escaping the sun any better. Their bare shoulders and torsos were turning bright red.

Astraea looked around. "Jake's right. We have to find some shade up here or we'll be burned to a crisp."

"Where?" Cylus said. "Look around you. We're at the top of a big flat rock."

"I know," Astraea agreed. "But we can't stay here."

Darek and Render were walking around the edge of the plateau. They stopped at one spot and stared down.

"Hey," Darek called. "Everyone, over here. It's a bit of a climb, but there's a ledge right below us and a cave. If we can make it down there, we can get out of the sun."

Astraea followed Zephyr to the centaurs and peered over the edge. Beneath them were several large rocks jutting out of the side wall, which looked like an uneven staircase down to the ledge. The ledge itself wasn't overly generous, but it was wide enough to hold Zephyr and at least one centaur. Then there was the cave cut into the wall, which looked dark and deep. Though it would be a simple climb for her, Astraea knew it would be tricky for the centaurs with their hooves. She looked at Zephyr. "I'm fine getting down and you are too. But it won't be easy for the centaurs. Would you mind going down first so you can stop the centaurs if they start to fall?"

Zephyr bobbed her head. "Good idea." She trotted a few paces away and then leaped off the edge. Opening her wings, she gracefully glided down the side of the plateau, then circled back and landed lightly on the ledge. She stepped up to the cave and peered in.

"It's really deep. I can't see the back of it. But it's a bit cooler. Come on down."

"You go first," Cylus said to Astraea. "That way you can check for any loose rocks."

Astraea doubted her weight would dislodge many rocks compared to the bigger centaurs. But she was prepared to try. With Zephyr offering encouragement from below, Astraea started to climb down the side. Some of the rocks were sharp and cut into her hands. But after a few minutes, she was grateful to jump the final distance and land safely beside her best friend.

"So, who's first?" Zephyr called up.

Cylus took the lead. "I'll go." The large centaur peered over the side and rubbed his chin.

"Anytime today would be good," Zephyr called.

"I'm thinking," Cylus said. "This isn't easy, you know."

Zephyr looked over at Astraea. "This isn't going to work. They won't be able to do it."

"I heard that," Cylus called. "And I can do anything."

Cylus went down to his knees and maneuvered his equine body around so his back end went down first while his hands clung to the top edge. The centaur looked down for the next step and made it safely. But when his hands released the top edge and reached for a grip on the next rock down, the rock beneath his front hooves broke away. This created a rock slide that pulled Cylus away from the wall as he and the rocks tumbled down the side.

"Cylus, no!" Astraea cried.

"Astraea, get back!" Zephyr shoved Astraea into the safety of the cave and stood among the tumbling rocks, waiting for Cylus to hit the ledge. She was struck multiple times, and cried out, but refused to leave.

"Cylus, curl up," Astraea called. "Pull in your legs!"

The centaur did his best to curl into a ball, but when he hit the bottom, he smashed into Zephyr's waiting legs and his front hoof cut a large gash into Zephyr's shoulder. Despite the wound, Zephyr held true and stopped Cylus from tumbling over the edge.

When the rock slide ended, Astraea ran over to Cylus. She helped him climb to his feet and brushed away the small pebbles that cut into his torso. "Are you all right?"

"A bit bruised, but I'll live."

Astraea looked over to Zephyr and saw the deep gash on her shoulder from Cylus's hoof. "Zeph, you're bleeding!"

"It's nothing," Zephyr said as she inspected her wound. "But if this leaves a scar, I'm going to be really angry."

Astraea pulled up the hem of her tunic and pressed the soft fabric against Zephyr's cut to slow the bleeding. "We need some ambrosia to help you heal."

Cylus was shaking and pale as he reached out to Zephyr. "That's the second time today you've saved my life. Thank you, Zephyr."

Above them, Render and Darek were looking

down in shock. "Cylus, are you all right?" Render called.

Cylus nodded. "But there's no way for you to come down. All the rocks have fallen."

"We can't stay up here; the sun will kill us! We're going to have to jump."

Zephyr shook her head slowly and heaved a sigh. "You're not going to jump. Stay where you are. I'll be right up. . . ." She looked over to Astraea. "I can't believe I'm actually doing this."

"Doing what?"

"You'll see." Zephyr looked at Cylus. "Would you and Astraea clear away the rubble? I'm going to need space to land." She opened her wings and launched off the side of the ledge, then circled up and disappeared out of sight.

"Zephyr, where are you going?" Astraea called.

"She's just landed up here," Render called down.

Cylus grunted as he shoved a large boulder over the side of the edge and then moved over to an even bigger one. "Come on, Astraea, give me a hand."

Only then did Astraea realize what her best friend was planning. She joined Cylus in clearing the fallen debris off the narrow ledge. "She's crazy," Astraea said. "Carrying you nearly pulled her legs off. How can she carry Darek and Render?"

"If she doesn't," Cylus said as they strained to shove another large boulder over the side, "Render and Darek are as good as dead."

"Get ready," Render called from above. "She's taking Darek first. She said there's not a lot of room down there and she'll need your help with Darek when she's closer."

With the last of the debris cleared, Astraea and Cylus looked up and waited.

Zephyr shouted, "Get ready," as she appeared with Darek holding on to her back legs.

Zephyr appeared over the edge, flapping her wings harder than Astraea had ever seen. Darek was holding on to her back legs as she seemed more to float than fly down toward the ledge.

"Please don't drop me!" Darek cried.

"Then don't let go!" Zephyr grunted.

"We're here for you," Cylus called. "Just a bit closer." He reached up and caught hold of Darek's rear hoof to direct him down. "Nearly there . . ."

Astraea caught hold of Darek's front hooves and

guided them down. When he was a few feet above the ground, she called, "Let go."

Darek released Zephyr and landed with a heavy thud on the narrow ledge.

"You're safe," Astraea called as she steadied him.

Zephyr started up again. "I'll be back with Render in a moment."

Darek's face would have been pale if it weren't for the bright sunburn. His shoulders were starting to blister from the burns.

"Get out of the sun," Cylus ordered. "The cave is right here."

"I want to help with Render," Darek said.

"There's no room out here," Cylus said. "Astraea and I will take care of Render. Go inside—now."

Darek did as he was told and vanished into the darkened cave just as Zephyr appeared over the edge to repeat the same maneuvers with Render. Moments later, the centaur was on the ledge.

"Everyone into the cave," Zephyr called from the air. "My wings and legs are killing me. I'm not sure how well I'll land!"

Once everyone was safely inside, Astraea stood at

the entrance and watched Zephyr fly out over the plateau, then turn in the sky and head back to the ledge. When she landed, Astraea ran out of the cave and threw her arms around her.

"You're amazing. I can't believe you just did that! Come inside. It's much cooler."

Zephyr was panting heavily, and her wings were drooping as she limped into the cave. "I—I deserve a medal for that," she muttered as she followed Astraea inside.

"Two medals," Astraea said.

"Three!" Cylus agreed. He approached Zephyr and patted her neck. "When this is over, you have your choice of anything I own."

"Me too," Darek said.

"Anything—or—or even all of it," Render finished. "Thank you for saving us."

"I'll just be happy to get back to Titus and soak in a lake," Zephyr said tiredly. "Until then, I'm going to lie down. My back legs feel like they've been pulled off."

The centaurs stepped back and allowed Zephyr deeper into the narrow cave. With Astraea beside her, Zephyr settled down on the stone floor and heaved a

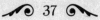

great sigh. "Remind me to never do that again."

Astraea sat beside her and combed her fingers through Zephyr's mane. "You were so amazing. I never knew you could hover like that."

"Neither did I," Zephyr admitted. "But I couldn't risk flying them out farther in case they fell."

"You realize you just saved their lives."

Zephyr nodded. "Guess so." She turned her white head to Astraea. "You know, if you'd told me before Arcadia opened that I would be carrying two—no, three—centaurs to safety, I'd have said you were crazy."

"It makes you wonder what else is going to happen," Cylus said as he walked past them and explored deeper into the cave.

"Or what might be about to happen," Astraea added.

"Let's hope that's the last of the excitement," Zephyr finished. "I'm too tired for more."

3

JAKE AND TRYN SOARED THROUGH THE
jungle on the flying skateboards, heading toward
Nesso.

Jake lifted his baseball cap off his head and wiped
away the sweat. California had nothing on the heat
of this world. He looked over at Tryn and saw that
his silver skin had a light sheen, but he showed no
signs of suffering from the heat.

"Aren't you hot?" Jake called. "I'm baking!"

Tryn shook his head. "Not really. I don't like this
humidity, but it's better than Earth. I was freezing
there."

After a while, they touched down on the ground

in an area covered with leaves and undergrowth. If Nesso was here, he still couldn't see her.

"Nesso," Jake called softly. "Are you here?"

The jungle around them was alive with sound. There was light rustling from the undergrowth, and the sounds of insects calling one another, while the canopy of trees was filled with movement and birdcalls.

"Jake," a small voice sounded.

Jake went down to his knees. "Nesso, I can hear you, but I can't see you. Where are you?"

"I am here. . . ."

A moment later Nesso appeared from under some leaves and slithered up to Jake's foot. He reached down, and she slid onto his outstretched hand, followed by two other snakes that looked just like her.

"Well, hello there," Jake said.

The two snakes hissed, but Jake couldn't understand what they said. "Nesso, did they just say something?"

"Yesss," Nesso answered. *"They asssked if you were my big thing. I told them you were."*

Jake looked at Tryn. "I thought I would be able to understand them all, but I can't."

"This is fascinating," Tryn said. "Because of the bite, you can understand Nesso, but not all her kind." He looked at the other two snakes. "Can you understand me?"

"Can you undersssstand the other big thing?" Nesso asked the two snakes.

Jake heard more hissing but had to wait for Nesso to translate.

"No, they can't undersssstand you. But I have told them why we are here. They will help usss if we promissse to take them away with usss."

Jake checked the ground, but there were no other snakes. "Where are the others? I thought there would be more."

"They are gone," Nesso explained. *"It isss too dangerousss for them to ssstay. They are being hunted, ssso they have left."*

"Who is hunting them?" Jake asked.

Nesso stood higher on Jake's hand. *"Everything here isss changed. There are ssso few of usss now. The othersss don't know who isss hunting them, only that it isss too dangerousss to ssstay. Everyone isss leaving. We mussst leave too."*

Jake explained to Tryn what Nesso said.

"Of course we'll take them with us," Tryn said to Nesso. "But we need more of your kind to help us. Do you know where the others have gone?"

"They have gone far away. Far from the danger."

Jake again repeated the message and then asked, "Can they tell you anything about the hunters?"

After a moment, Nesso said, *"They don't know. Only that it isss bad. They hear the othersss ssscream and then they are sssilent. They are gone-gone."*

"Does gone-gone mean dead?" Jake asked.

"Yesss."

Jake turned to Tryn. "Something is killing the snakes. There aren't many left here now."

Tryn looked at Nesso. "Have you ever had this trouble before?"

"No," Nesso said. *"But it'sss bad. I called and called but could find no more."*

"Three aren't enough," Jake said. "We need to find more." He looked at Nesso. "Can they tell you what direction the others traveled in?"

"Yesss. They went toward the sssun when it goesss dark."

When Jake repeated the message, he added, "Let's go get Astraea and the others and try to follow them."

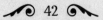

He held Nesso up to his neck so she could take her place. When she did, the other two followed, and the three settled down together.

Tryn looked at him and laughed. "I thought one snake around your neck was funny. You should see yourself now."

"Yeah, but at least it keeps my hands free." He called down to Nesso. "You guys ready?"

"Yesss," she hissed in reply.

Jake and Tryn climbed onto their skateboards and called down, "Take us back to Astraea and Zephyr."

The two skateboards rose in the air and carried them above the canopy. The plateau was some distance away, and it was only then that Jake realized just how far they'd traveled. In the opposite direction, Jake saw a herd of tall, long-necked dinosaurs grazing on the highest trees. "Tryn, look over there!"

"They are amazing," Tryn said. "I must tell my mother about this world."

As they flew closer to the plateau, Nesso called, *"Where are we going?"*

"To that big flat rock," Jake said.

"No. You mussstn't!"

"Why not?" Jake asked. "We had to go there when the two dinosaurs were fighting. There's nothing there."

"Lergo livess there," Nesso cried. *"Lergo eatsss everything. Even thossse really big thingsss."*

Jake called the message over to Tryn, and he maneuvered his skateboard closer. "We have to, Nesso," he started. "Astraea and the others are there. What is Lergo?"

Jake could feel the three snakes trembling around his neck. "Whatever it is, it has these guys freaked out."

"It isss like usss," Nesso said. *"But big. It livess in a cave on that mountain. It huntss and it eatss. None of usss go near it."*

"A cave, you say?" Jake said. "No problem. The others are on the top of the plateau. There wasn't a cave there."

"There isss!" Nesso insisted.

As they approached the top of the plateau, the skateboards skimmed over the surface but kept moving. When they reached the opposite side, they sailed over the edge and started to descend.

"Tryn," Jake called fearfully. "I see a cave."

"So do I."

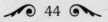 44

"And the skateboards are taking us there. . . ."

"That's probably because Astraea and the others are inside."

"Yeah," Jake cried. "So is Lergo!"

4

ASTRAEA LEANED AGAINST ZEPHYR, FANNING
herself with the hem of her tunic. Even in the shade
of the dark cave, it was still hot. "I hope they come
back soon," she commented. "I want to leave here."

"Me too," Zephyr agreed.

Cylus, Render, and Darek were lying down across
from them with their hooves tucked neatly beneath.
Their bows were leaning against the wall and their
arms were crossed over their chests as they rested.
Render and Darek were both dozing, but Cylus kept
looking deeper into the cave.

"If you're so curious, why don't you go explore?"
Astraea said to the centaur.

Cylus looked at her and shook his head. "It's not that. I think I hear something. I've been hearing it for a while."

At those words, both Darek and Render became alert. Darek climbed to his hooves and looked deeper into the cave. "Now that you mention it, I do hear something, but I'm not sure what it is. It's like hissing." He reached for his bow.

"I don't hear anything," Astraea said. She looked at Zephyr. "How about you?"

Her head was down, and her eyes shut. "I'm too tired and sore to hear anything."

Render rose and stood beside Darek. "It is hissing." He took two steps deeper into the cave just as Tryn and Jake arrived at the entrance and started to shout.

"Get outta there!" Jake cried.

"Hurry," Tryn shouted. "There's a serpent in there!"

Render looked back at Jake just as two blazing red eyes appeared from the darkness. Then a red tongue flicked in and out of an unseen mouth and the hissing became louder.

"Run!" Jake howled.

Cylus was on his feet in a flash and reaching for his bow. Astraea rose and helped Zephyr up.

"Don't waste your arrows. Just run!" Tryn cried.

"Where?" Darek called. "We're too high."

"We'll carry you," Tryn called. "Just like before. Hurry. Its moving!"

The hissing intensified as the huge serpent slithered out of the darkness and into the light. It opened its mouth, revealing rows of sharp teeth, including two very long fangs.

"C'mon!" Jake shouted. "Jump. We'll catch you!"

The serpent snapped at Darek and missed the centaur by a hair. Then it opened its mouth wide and tried to snatch Cylus.

There was no time to think. Astraea ran beside Zephyr and leaped up onto her back.

Zephyr called back to Cylus, "Run and get ready to grab my legs again!"

The entrance to the cave was right in front of them, but it felt like the longest run in Astraea's life as the deadly serpent slithered quickly behind them.

"Faster!" Astraea shouted.

Render was the first out of the cave, and he leaped

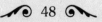

straight off the ledge. He cried in terror as he flew out over the vast openness high above the jungle canopy and started to fall.

"I'm coming," Jake shouted, then commanded his skateboard to follow Render down and scoop him up.

Tryn did the same the moment Darek made it out of the cave and jumped off the ledge.

Cylus reached the ledge first, then turned and waited for Zephyr. His eyes were huge as he pointed. "Zephyr, it's right behind you!"

Astraea stole a glance back and gasped. All she saw was a wide gaping mouth and rows and rows of sharp teeth and fangs.

"Get ready!" Zephyr shouted.

They were just reaching the cave entrance when Zephyr shrieked and fell to the floor. Astraea was still seated on her back and cried out when Zephyr's full weight came crashing down on her right leg.

They slid together out of the cave, across the ledge, and right over the side. After that, everything started moving too quickly for Astraea to follow accurately. All she knew was that her right leg was in agony, while a great heavy weight was pulling on her left.

Astraea screamed as she started to slip off Zephyr's back. She reached for her best friend's mane and tried to hang on, but it wasn't working. She was still being pulled off. It was only then that she understood what was happening. When she and Zephyr fell off the ledge, Cylus leaped into the air and caught hold of Astraea's left leg and was now hanging from it.

Somehow, Zephyr managed to right herself in the sky. But with Cylus's heavy weight pulling down on her leg, Astraea was sliding off Zephyr's back.

"I've got you!" Tryn shouted as he caught hold of Astraea's right arm and pulled her back onto Zephyr. "Zephyr, take us down!"

"No," Nesso hissed to Jake. *"Don't land yet. Lergo will follow usss. Fly for asss long asss posssible."*

Jake repeated the warning, but he knew they couldn't stay airborne for long. The skateboards were never intended to carry the weight of the centaurs. And now Tryn's was carrying even more as Darek hung beneath him while he held on to Astraea to keep Cylus from pulling her off Zephyr.

Astraea tried to hold on, but it was getting harder. Her left leg felt like it was being pulled out of the socket by Cylus hanging on for dear life.

"I know where we are," Nesso called to Jake. *"Hold out your hand and I will direct you to sssafety!"*

Jake did as Nesso suggested, and the snake left his neck and crawled out onto his hand. "You'd better hurry, Nesso. We aren't going to last long!" He stole a glance down and saw the tiny wings on his skateboard starting to fail.

"Go thisss way," Nesso called as she faced left.

"This way!" Jake shouted. "Zephyr, follow us if you can."

Astraea heard Zephyr's strained voice but couldn't understand what she said over the sound of her own screams. She did however feel Zephyr change direction.

Astraea's right arm was being wrenched by Tryn to keep her on Zephyr and her left hand was tangled in Zephyr's mane. She could feel her friend's hair being pulled out. "Faster, Zeph!"

"Over there. I see it!" Tryn called. "Come on, Zephyr. Just a bit farther. You can do it!"

Astraea felt like she was being split in half. Her head was spinning and every part of her hurt. She could no longer see where they were going. All she knew was pain.

Then Tryn released her arm and Astraea was pulled off Zephyr's back by Cylus. Before she could scream again, she splashed down into cool water and slipped beneath the surface.

5

ASTRAEA TRIED TO SWIM, BUT HER LEGS were like stone and wouldn't move. As she drifted down into the depths, she felt arms wrap around her waist and draw her back up. She broke the surface and gratefully gulped a mouthful of air.

"I gotcha," Jake said calmly. "Just relax and breathe."

Astraea coughed up water and floated on her back as Jake drew her to the shore. But when they reached the shallow edge and her right leg touched the ground, she howled again.

Tryn came forward. "Lift her up. That leg looks really bad."

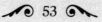

Jake and Tryn slid their arms beneath Astraea and made a kind of cradle to carry her out of the water. She winced with each movement. When she was settled on the ground, she looked down and saw the mess the cave's rocky floor had done to her leg. Her skin was peeled and bleeding.

Zephyr limped up to her and pressed her muzzle to her. "I'm sorry, Astraea. It's my fault you were hurt."

"No it isn't," Astraea said as she reached up to stroke her friend. "It was an accident. I'm all right, just a little bruised. But that was some fall. What happened?"

"I'm not sure," Zephyr said. "I was running and then I was down. I don't remember what happened between the two."

"That serpent was right behind you. I think it knocked you down." Cylus was standing at Zephyr's rump and inspecting her side. He started to brush off bits of rock and debris. "There are some deep cuts here from sliding on the floor."

"Trust me, I know," Zephyr said tiredly. She lifted her head and looked around. "I really hate this place. There are too many things wanting to eat us. The sooner we get out of here, the better." She looked down at Astraea. "Do you think you can walk?"

Astraea tried to stand up, but when her leg moved a bit, she cried out and fell down.

Jake knelt beside her and looked at her leg. "Yep, that's what I was afraid of. It's broken, all right. One of my friends broke her leg when we were boarding, and it looked all bent and funny just like yours does. Only she had a bone sticking out."

Tryn frowned. "I've never heard of a Titan breaking a bone before. You're usually too strong." He rubbed his chin. "However, it has been some time since you last ate ambrosia."

Astraea tried to think of the last time she'd eaten anything, let alone ambrosia. She couldn't remember. "True, but I did have some nectar back on Earth—wait, I also had one of those doughnut things."

"That's not enough," Tryn said. He looked at all the Titans. "You must all be on your guard. You need ambrosia to keep up your strength and we don't have any. You may not feel it, but you're all getting weaker. So be extra careful. You can get seriously hurt now."

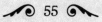 55

"What are you talking about?" Cylus challenged. "I'm just as strong as ever."

"No, you're not," Tryn insisted. "Please don't make me prove it to you."

Cylus looked at Tryn for a moment and then shook his head. "I won't."

Jake stood up and looked around. "Okay, this is going to be really gross, but we have to set Astraea's leg and then put some kind of splint or brace on it."

Astraea didn't like the sound of that. "What do you mean, 'set' my leg? You're not going to touch it, are you? It *really* hurts!"

"We have to," Jake insisted. "I've taken first aid at school and I've seen it on TV all the time. If you're out in the wilderness and you break your leg, you have to set it and brace it, or there could be permanent damage."

Tryn nodded. "It make sense. We need to find something solid to make the splint. Like a branch or something."

The three centaurs started looking around and gathering branches. A few minutes later, there was a large stack beside Astraea.

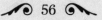

"What are you going to do with all of those?" she asked in alarm.

"We don't need all of them," Jake said. "Just a couple." He selected two strong branches and pulled all the twigs and leaves off them. Next he reached into his backpack for the fabric from Astraea's tunic, which they had planned to use as a sack for the snakes. He handed it to Tryn. "Would you tear this into a few strips so we can use them as ties?"

When everything was prepared, Jake knelt beside Astraea again. "I don't know how to tell you this, so I'll just say it. We are going to have to pull your broken leg until the bones realign. Then we're going to tie two of these sticks to it so you can't move it. I'm sorry, but it's really going to hurt."

Astraea shook her head. "Oh, no you're not. No one is touching my leg!"

"Astraea, we must," Tryn insisted. "Look at it. It's already starting to swell up. If we don't do this now, who knows how badly it could damage your leg. You might even lose it."

Zephyr leaned down again. "Please let them do it, Astraea. You can't lose your leg."

Astraea looked up into Zephyr's eyes and saw a shadow lingering there. Her friend was suffering but was still more worried about her than herself. Finally Astraea nodded. "All right, but I won't promise not to scream."

"Scream all you want," Tryn said. "Just try to keep it soft so we don't attract monsters." He looked up. "Cylus, Darek, come here. I need you to hold on to Astraea's arms. Don't let her move."

The two centaurs came forward and each caught hold of Astraea's upper arms. Jake knelt beside her broken leg while Tryn took a position at her feet.

"All right," Tryn said. "I'm going to pull as carefully as I can. Jake, you squeeze Astraea's leg and let me know when the bones feel aligned. Then we can bind it."

Jake nodded. "Wait!" He reached for another branch and handed it to Astraea. "Here, bite down on this. It might help with the screaming."

"Why should I bite a stick?" Astraea asked. "Is it part of the treatment?"

"You'll see," Jake said softly. He looked at Tryn. "I'm ready when you are."

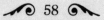

Tryn took a deep breath and smiled weakly at Astraea. "All right, everyone. We'll do this on my count of three. One . . . two . . ."

Astraea couldn't remember hearing three. The moment Tryn said it, he lifted her broken leg and started to pull while Jake gripped it and squeezed. Pain blazed through every part of her. She bit down on the branch until it broke in two. She never imagined anything could ever hurt so much.

With the centaurs holding her arms, Astraea tried her best not to scream—but as the pain intensified, she couldn't hold it in any longer. Once she started, she didn't think she would ever stop.

"Just lie back and relax," Tryn said gently as he helped settle Astraea against a tree.

Her heart was pounding, and she felt dizzy. But she had to admit, after the terrible pain of setting her leg and putting on the splint, it was starting to feel a bit better. It still hurt to move, but at least she *could* move it.

"There's no time to rest," Astraea said. "We have to find the snakes and go."

"Yes, we do," Tryn said. "But it's still bright day out there. We don't know which direction the sun sets in. So we have to wait for it to start to go down if we hope to find out where the snakes went."

"Besides," Jake offered. He pointed to his bare neck. "Nesso and her two friends are out looking for others. I promised we'd stay here and wait. And there's water right here that's safe to drink."

"How do you know it's safe?" Astraea said.

Jake grinned. "Because you swallowed loads when you fell in. If it wasn't safe, you'd be sick by now. I've had some too and I'm okay and look over there. . . ." He pointed to the centaurs as they splashed in the water. Their equine bodies were completely submerged and all she could see was from their chests up. If she didn't know better, she'd swear they were human boys playing. "They're all fine."

Zephyr was also in the water, standing shoulder deep. She was fluttering her wings and looked like a bird in a bird bath. The dirt and dried blood washed off her side, revealing the cuts from the fall in the cave.

"I think Zephyr needs to rest too," Tryn said.

"She's had a rough day and could use the break."

Astraea watched Zephyr in the water. To the others, everything looked fine. But Astraea knew her better than anyone. Her best friend wasn't moving normally, and she'd lost some of her glow. There was something in her posture that showed she wasn't feeling well.

"Carrying the centaurs really took it out of her," Astraea said. "She's exhausted."

"That's why we're staying put for a while," Jake said. He sat down beside her and leaned against the thick tree trunk. "This place is unreal. I can't believe what we've seen."

There was rustling in the leaves beside Jake. Moments later, Nesso reappeared with the two snakes from earlier and three more.

"We found a few more," Nesso said as she rose. *"But that isss all. The othersss have left the area. Thessse two are very young and too weak to make the journey. Can they come with usss?"*

"Of course," Jake said as he held out his hand to Nesso. "Do you think they'd mind traveling in my backpack?"

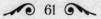

"*Not if it meansss ssstaying sssafe,*" Nesso said.

Jake opened his pack and arranged his skateboard helmet at the bottom to make a small nest for the snakes. "That should keep you safe," he said as he laid down his pack for the snakes to crawl in. "Nesso, please tell them not to bite me or anyone here if we reach in for something."

"*They know not to bite anyone in our group,*" Nesso hissed. "*Even if you hit them like you did me.*"

"I didn't hit you on purpose!" Jake protested. He looked at Astraea. "I hit her once by accident and she'll never let me forget it."

Astraea looked at Nesso and smiled. She never thought she could ever care about a snake, but after knowing Nesso, she realized just how much she liked them. "I won't let him hit you again, Nesso. I promise."

Astraea laid her head back, shut her eyes, and listened to the sounds of the jungle and the centaurs splashing in the water. She couldn't remember ever being more tired in her life. Before long, she drifted off to sleep.

6

ASTRAEA WOKE WITH HER CHEEK BEING lightly tickled. She opened her eyes and saw Zephyr's white muzzle right beside her.

"The sun's going down," Zephyr said softly. "It's time to get moving."

Astraea reached up and stroked her friend. Zephyr's soft muzzle was warmer than usual. "Are you feeling all right?"

Zephyr snorted and shook her head. "Are you kidding? My head hurts, my side hurts, my back flanks hurt, my wings hurt, my legs feel like they've been pulled off, and I'm burning up in this heat. Beyond that, I'm doing just great."

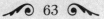

"Well, at least you didn't break your leg," Astraea said. "I don't know how I'm going to walk."

"You're not going to."

"In case you hadn't noticed, my wings are too small for me to fly."

"You're not going to fly either," Zephyr said. "I'm going to carry you."

"What?" Astraea cried. "Zephyr, no. I could never ride you. You're not a horse. Besides, I know how you feel about Emily Jacobs riding Pegasus. You said it's demeaning. You're my best friend. I would never do that to you."

Zephyr pawed the ground with a golden hoof. "Yeah, well, about that. I might have been a bit wrong. I think I understand why Pegasus carries Emily. You've been on my back twice now, and if I'm honest, I like carrying you. It brings us even closer."

"But . . ."

"Astraea, don't you realize you're more than a friend to me? You're my two-legged sister. My family. I love you and I want to do it. Not because you can't walk, but because I just really want to."

Astraea sat back stunned. She and Zephyr had been together all their lives, and it was true Astraea considered Zephyr more than a friend. She was her sister. But Zephyr had always been so tough and hated to show emotions. When she did, it was usually anger at Pegasus for letting Emily ride him.

For as touched as Astraea was, Zephyr's comment caused more concern. She gazed into Zephyr's dark eyes and saw something there. She just wasn't sure what. Could it be the lack of ambrosia?

Jake and Tryn approached the tree. "Hey, look, Sleeping Beauty wakes," Jake teased.

"Who?" Astraea asked.

Jake grinned. "Never mind. Are you ready to get moving?"

"I guess so. I was just wondering how."

"I told you," Zephyr whinnied. "You're going to ride on my back, and that's the end of the discussion."

"Whoa," Jake said. "Don't know what Zephyr just said to you, but she sounds really angry."

Zephyr turned on Jake. "And you shut up, human," she said irritably.

"Hey, Zeph, calm down." Astraea reached up and

stroked Zephyr's muzzle again. "Thank you. I'm grateful to you for giving me a ride."

Zephyr harrumphed. "Good. It's settled." She looked at Tryn. "Help Astraea get up onto my back. Just watch out for her leg. We're losing daylight, so let's get moving."

Tryn stole a glance at Astraea, and she shrugged. Zephyr wasn't behaving like herself at all. She used to make a show of not liking Jake, but that's all it was. A show. Deep down she did like him. Why, then, had she snapped at him?

Tryn moved closer to pick her up. "I'm sorry, but this might hurt a bit."

"It can't hurt any more than setting it did." Astraea wrapped her arms around Tryn's neck while he put his arms around her and lifted her gently off the ground.

"Jake, grab her bad leg and move it slowly with me."

Astraea had never been this close to Tryn before. But with his face right next to hers, she looked deeper into his blue eyes with the silver specks and was surprised to see even more colors hidden inside. There were flecks of red, green, and a trace of purple. They were the most beautiful things she'd ever seen. Like some kind of precious and rare jewels.

"Are you all right?" Tryn asked softly.

Astraea nodded. "Uh-huh."

Under her stare, Tryn started to blush. But his silver skin didn't blush red; it became an even deeper, sparkling silver.

"Tryn, you okay?" Jake asked. "You face has gone all shiny and a funny color."

"I—I'm fine," Tryn said quickly as he easily lifted Astraea higher and over Zephyr's back.

Astraea tried not to wince when Jake settled her broken leg beneath Zephyr's folded wing. "All set."

"Finally," Cylus said. "Can we go now? The sooner we get the snakes, the sooner we can leave this awful place. I'm tired, I'm hungry, and I just want to be where things aren't trying to kill us all the time."

"I agree," Zephyr said as she started walking. "The sun is setting in this direction. Let's go."

7

MAKING THEIR WAY THROUGH THE JUNGLE was long and hard as the denseness of the trees made walking difficult.

Astraea was seated on Zephyr's back and she felt her friend straining. As the sun moved farther across the jungle, Zephyr's movement became more stilted and she started to shiver.

"Zeph, what's wrong?" Astraea leaned forward and stroked Zephyr's neck. Her skin was hot to the touch and wet with sweat. "And don't tell me it's nothing."

Tryn and Jake came forward. "What's wrong?" Jake asked.

Astraea was studying the back of Zephyr's head.

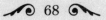

Her friend was looking straight ahead, not glancing left or right, and didn't seem to react when branches hit her in the face.

"Something's wrong with Zephyr, but she won't tell me what," Astraea said.

Standing right next to her, Tryn started to sniff the air. Then he leaned closer to Zephyr's side and sniffed again.

"What are you doing?" Cylus demanded. "Are you actually sniffing her?"

Tryn looked at Jake. "Help me get Astraea off her back."

"What's happening?" Astraea asked. "What's wrong?"

Tryn called forward, "Zephyr, stop so Astraea can get down." But she kept walking. "Zephyr, stop!" he yelled.

"Zeph . . . ?" Astraea called. Fear crept into her voice as her friend kept moving. "Zephyr, talk to me!"

Cylus charged forward and blocked Zephyr's path. But she kept moving until she walked straight into him. Cylus had to push against her chest to get her to stop.

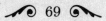

"Hey, she doesn't look good." Cylus waved his hand in front of her face. "Her eyes are glazed and it's like she doesn't even see me."

Tryn caught Astraea around the waist and helped to lift her down. When she was standing on her good leg, Render came forward to support her while Jake and Tryn went back to Zephyr. Tryn lifted her left wing.

"Whoa!" Jake cried as he plugged his nose. "What's that terrible smell?"

Tryn looked at him with a grim expression. "It's Zephyr. Look . . ."

"What is it?" Astraea asked. "Let me see."

Tryn looked at Render. "Don't let her come any closer."

"What are you talking about?" Astraea demanded as Render held on to her. "Let me go. I need to see what's wrong with Zephyr."

Tryn put Zephyr's wing back down and shook his head. "Those cuts on her side aren't from sliding on the floor," he said grimly. "They're bites."

"Bites?" Jake cried.

Tryn looked at everyone in the group. "Back in the

cave, that serpent didn't just knock Zephyr down. It bit her. Now her wounds are badly infected. There may have been venom as well."

"Zephyr!" Astraea shouted. "Zephyr, please, talk to me."

When Astraea called again, Zephyr turned her head slowly toward her. "Astraea . . . ?" she said softly just before she collapsed to the ground.

8

"ZEPHYR!" ASTRAEA SCREAMED. SHE PULLED away from Render and fell to the ground beside her best friend. Beneath her hand, she felt Zephyr struggling to breathe. "She's so hot!"

Tryn nodded. "It's a fever. Her body is trying to fight the infection, but she hasn't had ambrosia and is too weak. If there's also venom, then that's a whole different problem."

"What are you saying?" Astraea cried. "That Zephyr is going to die?"

"Could be," Tryn said darkly.

"Hey," Cylus said angrily. "Don't you go around saying things like that. You don't know anything, freak!"

Nesso was around Jake's neck and started to hiss. *"Jake, Zephyr isss in big trouble. That isss how Lergo huntsss. It bitesss and then waitsss for itsss prey to die. It will follow usss to get to her."*

When Jake gasped, Astraea looked at him. "What? What did Nesso say? Tell me the truth!"

Jake repeated Nesso's message. "It's just like Komodo dragons back home. They bite something, and the bacteria in their mouth kills their prey with infection. Then they follow it and eat it."

"No!" Astraea shouted. "Zephyr isn't going to die, and that serpent isn't going to eat her!"

"We won't let it happen," Cylus said. He pulled his bow off his shoulder and loaded an arrow. "If that thing comes after us, we'll kill it!"

Render and Darek also loaded their bows.

Tryn knelt beside Zephyr and felt her neck. "Her pulse is racing, and her breathing is getting ragged. At the very least, she needs ambrosia."

"Uh, Tryn," Jake said. "We're in a jungle. There's no ambrosia here."

"I know," Tryn said. "The only place that has it is Titus."

"Then go!" Astraea cried. "Or give me the ring and I'll go. We can't let Zephyr die!"

Tryn got up and started to pace the area. "None of us can go back to Titus. Not now. With the Mimics there, it's just too dangerous. I wish there were some on Earth."

"Where else is there ambrosia?" Jake asked.

Tryn sighed. "There's lots on Xanadu. But the ring won't take us there."

"What are you talking about?" Darek said. "You don't need that ring anymore. You've got your skateboards from Vulcan. They should take you anywhere you want to go. They found Nesso here in the jungle, didn't they?"

Tryn's mouth fell open and he slapped his head. "How could I be so stupid! He's right. We have our boards. We can go to Xanadu and get all the ambrosia we need!"

"And tell Emily Jacobs, Pegasus, and Riza what's happened," Astraea added. "They can heal Zephyr and stop the Mimics!"

"You can tell them yourself," Tryn said to Astraea. "You're coming with us."

Astraea could hardly believe what she was hearing. "You don't actually expect me to leave Zephyr?"

Jake came closer. "You have to come with us. You're hurt. What if that serpent comes back for you? How will you run away?"

"I won't run away," Astraea insisted. "I'll stay here and fight along with the centaurs. I won't leave Zephyr—not now, not ever."

"But . . . ," Tryn started.

"You heard her," Cylus said. "She's staying right here with Zephyr. So stop arguing and get going!"

9

JAKE AND TRYN WASTED LITTLE TIME GETTING ready. Before leaving, Jake asked Nesso to tell two snakes to stay with Astraea and to call out to any other snakes that might be passing in the area. He would take the juveniles with him.

When they were freed from his backpack, they settled around Astraea's neck and promised to get anyone else they found to join in the fight. After that, they said brief good-byes.

"Hurry!" Astraea called as she lay beside Zephyr. Her face was a portrait of pain and fear. "Please hurry."

"We will," Jake promised. He looked at Tryn. "You ready?"

Tryn nodded. "But I hate leaving you in case Lergo comes."

Cylus charged up to him, still holding his bow at the ready. "We'll take care of Lergo. Just stop talking and go!"

Tryn nodded and looked down at his skateboard. "Take me to Xanadu."

Jake repeated the message to his own skateboard and its tiny wings appeared and started to flap. He looked back at Zephyr collapsed on the ground. "Hold on, Zephyr. We'll be back soon."

Jake faced forward as the skateboard climbed up over the trees and high into a sky of blazing reds and greens of sunset. Soon his eyes were watering from the speed and he couldn't speak. Faster and faster, higher and higher they flew until there was a sonic boom and a bright flash as they entered the Solar Stream.

Jake was still surprised by the experience of traveling within the Solar Stream. He looked around at the swirling, blazing light and was reminded of all the sci-fi movies he'd ever seen where starships entered light-speed or wormholes. The one thing the movies never addressed was just how loud it was.

He'd never noticed before, but as he rode his board, the hair on his arms was standing up with the static electricity. He was also curious why he could still breathe. There had to be air because he could breathe. But where did it come from?

Experience in the Solar Stream had taught him that trying to speak was just as futile as trying to walk or run. All you could do was stand and wait.

Jake became aware of time's passage. It appeared that the more urgent the situation, the longer it took to get anywhere. Leaving Earth to go to Nesso's world had seemed to take forever because the Titans and Olympians hiding on Earth were counting on them. But now that Zephyr's life was at stake, the trip to Xanadu felt endless.

Eventually they burst free of the Solar Stream and appeared above another lush jungle.

"Yes!" Tryn cheered as he punched the air. "I'm home!"

Jake moved his skateboard closer to Tryn. "How can you tell? It looks the same."

"No, it doesn't. Look around you, Jake. The trees are different colors and the leaves are much bigger. Smell the air. It's so much sweeter and it's not nearly as hot." Tryn looked around and gathered his bearings. "Okay," he said, "I know where we are. If we go that way, we can reach the continent of the Rhean. My home." He pointed in the other direction. "Or we go that way to reach the Temple of Arious, where we'll find Riza, Emily, and the others." He looked down at the skateboard. "Take us to the Temple of Arious."

Jake called down to his own board, "Follow Tryn."

As they zoomed across the sky, they were soon joined by a flock of strange-looking birds. Their feathers were fluffy orange and they were as big as dogs. Jake wondered how it was possible for them to fly. He was also stunned by how tame they were. They flew right next to him and kept their green eyes on him. One even lightly pecked at his skateboard.

"Have you seen this?" he called over to Tryn. "I bet I could reach out and touch them. This is freaky!"

"No, this is Xanadu," Tryn called back. "Every living creature here is at peace. There are no predators, so none of the wildlife has reason to fear. Even if an animal was once a predator, it changed when it was brought here. You need to be careful and not hurt anything or you could disturb the balance, and that will really upset Riza."

"I keep hearing that name. Who exactly is Riza?"

"You'll see," Tryn said. "But try not to stare when you first meet her."

"Why? Does she have two heads or something?"

Tryn shook his head. "No, just the one, but she's the most beautiful being you'll ever meet. You'll just want to stare. Riza finds it funny, but the Olympians think it's rude."

"I'll be careful," Jake said. "I just hope she can save Zephyr."

"She will," Tryn said confidently. "There isn't anything that Riza and Emily can't do."

The skateboards brought them lower in the sky as they flew closer to a clearing. A flat-topped building stood in the center of the clearing, surrounded by multiple white marble houses. Jake leaned forward and gasped when he saw the center building. "Hey, are those helicopters on the roof?"

Tryn nodded. "Many years ago, Emily's powers

were unpredictable, and she accidentally sent them here. Riza thought they were cute, so she put them up there as decoration. That's where we're headed. That's the Temple of Arious."

They were soon touching down in the clearing. Tryn picked up his skateboard and looked around as a frown crossed his brow. "Hello!" he called.

"Is it always so quiet?" Jake asked.

"No," Tryn said. He pointed to the closest marble house beside the temple. The vegetable garden was untended and overgrown by vines from the jungle. "That's Emily's house. Her aunt loves that garden. She'd never let it get overgrown."

Tryn ran toward the house and didn't stop when he reached the front door. He threw it open and entered. "Emily? Pegasus? Steve? Are you here?"

Jake followed him inside and saw a strange mix of furnishings. Some were like what he'd seen at Zephyr's house on Titus, but there were definitely some pieces from Earth—including a large entertainment center with a flat-screen television, a stereo system, and racks full of music CDs and movie DVDs.

"Emily!" Tryn shouted. "Are you here?"

Jake followed Tryn out of the house and into the main clearing. "Hello? Diana? Apollo? Chiron? Is anyone here?"

The only sounds they heard came from the jungle. Soon there was loud crashing and sounds of branches breaking as a massive two-headed creature—that was easily double the size of an elephant—came charging up to them. It had multiple legs, long purple fur, and mouths full of teeth.

"Brue!" Tryn cried as he ran up to the animal and disappeared in her long shaggy coat. "I've really missed you!"

Brue started dancing on her feet like an excited puppy.

"You know what that is?" Jake asked fearfully, looking up at the animal.

Tryn looked back at him through all the purple fur. "This is Brue—she's the Mother of the Jungle. She's kind of like a guardian. But she shouldn't be here alone. She's always with Paelen." Tryn scratched Brue's chest. "Where is Paelen, girl? Take us to Paelen."

Brue shuffled on her feet, threw back her two

heads, and let out a mournful howl. She caught hold of Tryn's arm and tried to pull him into the trees.

Tryn patted Brue and pulled his arm free. "I've missed you too, but I don't have time to play." He looked back at Jake. "Something's wrong. Even if Riza and Emily are off world on a rescue mission, there are always Olympians here." He trotted away from Brue and shouted, "Is anyone here?"

Again, all that came back to them was the sound of the jungle.

Tryn caught Jake by the arm. "Come with me. If anything has happened, I know who can tell us."

"Who's that?" Jake asked as he jogged behind him.

"Arious," Tryn answered. "She's a huge super-computer that helps run this world."

Jake gasped. "This world is run by a supercomputer?"

Tryn nodded. "But she is unlike any computer my people have ever encountered before. She has a consciousness all her own—and has independent thought."

"Like AI?"

"AI?" Tryn repeated.

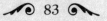

"Yeah, it means artificial intelligence."

Tryn shook his head. "There is nothing artificial about Arious. You'll see."

Jake followed Tryn into the Temple of Arious. The entrance was immaculate, and as they entered, unseen lights came up. Images were carved into the walls, and Jake wanted to explore, but the desperateness of the situation kept him on Tryn's heels.

He followed Tryn to a deep staircase and was forced to run to keep up with him as they descended. When they reached the bottom, Tryn ran down a long corridor and stopped before a stone wall. He looked around as a deep frown set on his face. "This door is never closed."

"There's a door here?" Jake asked.

Tryn nodded. "Something is definitely wrong." He banged on the thick stone wall. "Arious, it's me, Tryn. Can you hear me? Run a scan and you'll see it's me. Please open up!"

After several seconds, there was a hum and the whole stone wall moved to reveal it was a door. Tryn and Jake entered the control room.

"Whoa," Jake said as his eyes tried to take in all the

polished metal. The walls, floor, and ceiling shone brightly. In the center of the room was a large consul with a step and a platform. "This place is awesome."

Tryn nodded and walked up to the consul. "This is where the Xan would deposit and receive their collective knowledge. If you were to stand on that platform and touch those two posts on either side, your mind would be scanned for its memories, but also, you would gain the shared knowledge of everyone who ever stood there before you. I've been on there and it's amazing. Through it, I saw when the Xan first visited my world long before the sun went supernova. I also saw it destroyed."

"Trynulus," Arious called. "I am so pleased to see you. We are in trouble."

"Arious, what's happened?" Tryn asked. "Where is everyone? We really need to speak with Riza and Emily."

"They have all been taken. The attack was fast and brutal, and we couldn't defend ourselves. The last thing Riza did before she was disabled was to seal me to protect me from the invaders."

Tryn's face turned pale silver in shock. "Riza has

been disabled? How is this possible? She and Emily are Xan, the most powerful beings in the universe."

"They are, but those that took them came disguised as friends. With one touch, Riza and Emily were weakened and then rendered unconscious. The others tried to fight, but they too were defeated with a touch."

Jake was standing beside Tryn and whispered, "That sounds like the Mimics."

"Mimics?" Arious responded.

"Arious," Tryn said. "This is Jake, a human from Earth. Please, I must link with you and share what we've encountered." He crossed to the center consul and stepped up on to the platform. When he put his hands on the two pillar receivers, he looked back at Jake. "I'm going to link with Arious. It's the fastest way to share what we've experienced. Stand back and don't touch me, no matter what you see or hear. Arious has been set to receive and share with humans, but not a human and a Rhean at the same time. It would be dangerous for you."

Jake held both his hands up and took a step back. "Gotcha. I won't move. Just hurry."

Tryn nodded. "All right, Arious. Initiate upload."

The moment he said that, the room started to hum. Tryn threw back his head and became stiff as he linked with the supercomputer.

Jake watched in fascination as his friend communicated with Arious. This was right out of a science fiction movie. But usually the supercomputers in them were evil. In this case, Tryn trusted Arious. Jake just hoped he was right.

After a moment the humming stopped. Tryn shook his head and stepped clear of the platform.

"Well? Did you see what happened here?" Jake asked.

Tryn nodded. "It was the Mimics, all right. But they're not what we thought. They've been around for millennia and are the ancient enemy of the Xan."

"Now that they have taken Riza and Emily, the Phirril, or Mimics as you call them, will spread through the known universe," Arious said.

Jake still couldn't understand. "What do they want with Riza and Emily? Just to stop them from defending Titus? Did they kill them?"

"No," Arious answered. "It is worse than that."

Tryn nodded. "Riza and Emily aren't the first Xan to be taken by the Mimics. Arious just showed me. Every thousand years or so, they would come here and abduct a Xan. They are then taken back to the Mimic world. No one knows exactly what happens to them there. . . ."

"But we speculate the Mimics feed off their power," Arious finished.

"They're going to eat them!" Jake cried.

"We do not know what they do," Arious said. "Though the ancients speculated that they didn't; otherwise they would be back more often. It was reasoned that the Mimic queen fed off the Xan power when she was preparing a big division. A kind of species spawning."

"Only now they've taken the last two Xan in existence," Tryn said. "This will be their last chance to divide on a large scale, so they're probably going to make it a big one."

"That's seriously dangerous," Jake said. He looked over at the computer. "What about the others? The Olympians and Emily's family? What about Pegasus? Why did they take them as well?"

Arious hummed and then spoke again. "I must assume they took the others as hostages to control Riza and Emily. Especially Emily. She may be Xan, but she has all her human emotions. She would surrender herself to the Mimics if it meant keeping those she loved safe. With two Xan under their control, the Mimics will spread farther than ever before with no one able to stop them."

"But we have the snakes," Jake insisted. "Their venom is deadly to the Mimics. We're gathering them up now."

"Yesss," Nesso said. *"We will ssstop them."*

"I am sorry, young Nesso, but even you will not be able to stop the queen."

Tryn frowned. "Wait, Arious, you can understand Nesso?"

"Of course," Arious answered. "I understand all. And we are grateful to Nesso and her kind, but the Mimic queen never leaves her world. After millennia of searching, we never discovered where it is. Now, because of my link with you, Tryn, I have seen what Mimic Vulcan told you. That the Mimic queen's name is Langli and their home world is Tremenz in the Zolcar system. But that knowledge is of little use now that the Xan are gone. It would be too danger-ous for anyone to attempt a rescue. So the queen will divide, and the Mimics will overrun the universe."

"What are you saying?" Jake asked. "That we give up and wait for the Mimics to take over?"

"What choice do we have?" Arious asked.

"We fight. That's what we do," Jake insisted. "Look, Nesso has venom that kills the Mimics. We've been to Nesso's world and there are other snakes that are willing to help us. So we get a team together, take a lot of weapons and snakes, and go to Tremenz to free everybody."

"You are prepared to do this?" Arious asked.

"Well, duh, of course. And don't say I'm too young. I've seen what the Mimics can do, and I'll do anything to stop them from reaching Earth."

All the lights on the mainframe flashed. "You remind me of Emily. You have the same spirit. Come, link with me, Jake. Let me know you and add your memories to my collective."

"Um, what?"

"Yes, that's a great idea." Tryn caught Jake by the

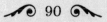

arm and pulled him over to the center consul. "Just in case anything happens to you, there will be a record of your existence."

Jake shook his head. "But you said it was dangerous for me. . . ."

"No, I said it was dangerous if you touched me while I was in. It's safe if you go in alone. Arious will be set up for a human."

"Yes," Arious said. "I have linked with humans before and you will be perfectly safe. Join me, Jake. Let me know you, the one who is prepared to fight for the last Xan."

Jake looked at Tryn. "You're sure this is safe for me?"

"I promise."

Jake didn't feel the same confidence. He'd seen too many movies where things went bad. But it was kind of cool to think that all his memories— his family, friends, and all the skateboarding tricks he'd learned—would be recorded. Kind of like a big library with a book called *Jake* in it. "All right," he said finally. "But if my brains get scrambled, I'm going to be really angry."

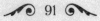

"You'll be fine," Tryn said. "Just step up there and place your hands on those columns. Arious will do the rest." He reached up to Jake's neck. "Nesso, come to me. I don't want you hurt while Jake is linked with Arious."

Nesso slid away from Jake and rested in Tryn's hand.

"I am ready," Arious said. "I will also set to retrieve only. So you need not worry about seeing the history of the Xan until after this is over. Then, if you want to know more, you will be welcome back."

"Ah, I was kinda hoping to see the Xan," Jake said. "Especially if they are as beautiful as Tryn says."

"You'll see Riza for yourself when we go get her," Tryn promised.

Jake nodded and placed his hands on the receivers. "Okay, I'm ready."

"All done," Arious said.

Jake shook his head. "Wait, you haven't started yet."

"Yes, I did," Arious said. "You are but a young child. Viewing your memories took only a millisecond."

Jake looked at Tryn. "That sucks. I thought it should at least take an hour. I've done a lot of cool stuff."

Tryn nodded and returned Nesso to Jake. "My first time was quick too."

Arious's lights flash. "You have led an interesting life, Jake Reynolds, and are a credit to your family. Thank you for sharing."

"No problem," Jake said. "But I do want to come back and see what you've got stored in there."

"You will be welcome," Arious said.

"First we have to save Zephyr and stop the Mimics," Tryn said. "Then maybe I can take you to meet my family as well."

"Indeed," Arious agreed. "There is plenty of ambrosia for Zephyr in the Olympian homes here. Take as much as you need. It would have been helpful if you had brought a sample of the infection that is endangering her life so I could produce medication. I do not even have a record of her physiology."

"She's the daughter of Pegasus's clone, Tornado Warning. Isn't that enough?" Tryn said.

"No. She has a Titan mother, Lampos. I do not

know her, either, so I cannot produce anything to help her."

"Then we've got to hope that the ambrosia is enough. Thank you, Arious. We'll take the ambrosia to Zephyr and gather the snakes." Tryn looked over to Jake. "We have to move. It's a long journey back."

"Tryn, wait," Arious said. A drawer in the main-frame opened. "Here, take these."

Tryn and Jake peered inside and saw several rings. "Are these . . . ?"

"Solar Stream gems," Arious answered. "Take two. They will open to Xanadu. Once you have collected enough snakes, gather everyone from Earth and bring them here. Then we can plan the rescue of Riza and Emily."

Tryn reached into the drawer and pulled out two rings. He handed one to Jake. "In case we get separated, get to Earth and give this to Jupiter to bring everyone here."

Jake nodded and put the ring on.

"We'll be back as quickly as possible, Arious," Tryn called as they ran out of the control room.

"I will be waiting."

10

ASTRAEA WAS LYING ON THE GROUND leaning against Zephyr. As the minutes ticked by, her fever was rising. "She's so hot."

Render clopped closer. "She's also changing color. Look, she's going yellow, and her black blaze is fading."

Astraea was lying too close to notice, but as she sat up and looked again, she saw Render was right. Zephyr was turning a sickly yellow, and the black blaze on her chest was now pale gray. There was also a rattle in her chest with each shallow breath she took.

"We have to do something," Astraea said helplessly. "We can't wait for Tryn and Jake."

"What do you suggest?" Cylus said.

Astraea looked around. "How far back was the water?"

"You want to go swimming?" Darek said. "Now?"

"No!" Astraea said. "If there is any way we can get Zephyr there, I want to put her in the water to cool her down. Maybe if we wash her wounds, it will help."

Astraea waited for Cylus to say some sharp retort or call her stupid. Instead he shoved Render. "You stay here with Zephyr. Darek and I are going to go gather some strong branches."

"What are you planning?" Render asked.

"We're going to make a sled to carry Zephyr back to the water." Cylus approached Astraea and handed her his bow and quiver of arrows. "If that serpent comes for Zephyr, go for its eyes. They will be the weak spot. Use as many arrows as you need."

"I will," Astraea promised. "Cylus, thank you."

Cylus nodded his head but didn't say anything. He turned and, together with Darek, vanished into the trees.

Astraea settled down beside Zephyr again, stroking her friend's hot head. "I can't believe this is happening to you. Please hold on, Zephyr. I can't lose you."

Render bent down and touched her shoulder. "You won't. She's strong. She will recover."

Astraea looked up at him, but she was too miserable to speak. Her throat was constricting, and her eyes were filling with tears as she stayed at Zephyr's side listening to her struggling to breathe.

In all of Astraea's life, no one she cared for had fallen ill, let alone been in such danger. Even though her parents had been weak when they were found in Tartarus, they weren't going to die. But as she touched Zephyr, she could feel her friend slowly slipping away.

A while later, Cylus and Darek returned with what looked like half the trees in the jungle. They were covered in deep, bleeding scratches.

"What happened?" Render said.

"We finally found some strong vines," Darek said. "But they've got really sharp thorns."

Astraea looked at the pile of thick branches and thorns. "What can I do?"

Cylus reached for the first branch. "You can keep

that bow at the ready." He looked at Render and Darek. "You two, with me. Let's build a sled."

None of them had ever constructed anything before. They'd never had to. But although the centaurs had a few false starts, Astraea marveled at their cleverness. She had never imagined that Cylus would have any idea what to do. He liked to hide his intelligence under an exterior of anger and brutality. But he worked with the other two, weaving the branches together and binding them with the thorny vines, and their makeshift sled was soon taking shape.

What especially surprised Astraea was how Cylus ensured the sled was covered in a thick layer of soft leaves so Zephyr wouldn't feel the branches beneath her. Astraea feared Zephyr was too far gone to feel anything, but she was grateful for the consideration.

"Okay," Cylus said as he brushed a long strand of chestnut hair out of his eyes. "We're ready. Astraea, move away from Zephyr. We're going to have to lift her."

Astraea crawled out of the way as the three powerful centaurs approached. Cylus looked at the stricken Zephyr with an analytical eye. "All right, Render, you take the front legs. Darek, you take her rear legs. I'll lift her back right behind her wings. Just be careful and don't drop her!"

As the three centaurs took their positions, Astraea feared they wouldn't be strong enough to lift Zephyr. She was stunned as they bent down and, with loud grunts of strain, heaved Zephyr into the air and carried her over to the sled.

"Easy," Cylus said through clenched teeth. "Take her down easy. . . ."

If Astraea hadn't seen it with her own eyes, she would never have believed it. In just a few moments, Zephyr was secured on the leaf-covered sled. The centaurs had made it look easy, but the heavy film of sweat on their bodies revealed that it was anything but.

Cylus approached Astraea and bent down to lift her.

"What are you doing?" she asked.

"Can you walk?" Cylus demanded.

"No, not yet, but—"

"Then you ride." Cylus carried her over to Render and settled Astraea on the equine part of his body.

"Keep the bow up," he ordered as he moved over to the sled.

"Am I too heavy for you?" Astraea asked Render.

"Don't be silly," Render responded as he twisted his boy torso back to look at her. "I hardly feel you. Just grab hold of my shoulders if you feel you are going to fall."

"I will," Astraea promised.

Cylus and Darek then took a position at the front of the sled and reached for the long poles at the end. With a great heave, they lifted up the front where Zephyr's head was, while the rear part of the sled remained on the ground.

"Let's go," Cylus said.

The trip back to the pond was a slow-but-steady trudge through the jungle. The sled got caught on trees or bushes several times, but the centaurs put their heads down and used their brute strength to push through. All the while, Astraea and Render kept their bows at the ready.

"There it is." Cylus grunted as he strained to pull the sled through another dense cluster of overgrown of bushes.

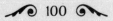

When they burst through, Cylus and Darek reached the shore and kept walking into the water. They went out deeper and then turned the sled around, so Zephyr's body was in water, while her head remained above the surface at the shallow shore.

Astraea slid off Render and crawled into the water. She looked back at him. "Would you hold Zephyr's wing up so I can clean her wound?"

"I'll do it," Cylus said tiredly. "I'm already wet."

"No," Render said, facing Cylus. "You've worked hard enough. Sit and rest awhile. It's Astraea's and my turn to take care of Zephyr."

There was a flash of anger on Cylus's face at Render's defiance of his orders. But then it faded, and he waded back into the water to cool down and relax.

Render entered the water and walked up to Astraea, lifting Zephyr's wing out of the way to reveal her wounds. If anything, the stink was even worse than before. "Oh—oh, that's bad," Render said as he scrunched up his face and looked away.

Astraea hadn't seen the wounds the first time, but now, as she lay in the water and inspected them, she wondered how Zephyr had made it this long. The deep fang punctures were red, swollen, and angry. The skin around the marks was turning black and festering.

"Oh, Zeph," Astraea wept. She gently brushed water over the wounds. "Please hold on."

Cylus swam over to Zephyr and touched her head. "She's not as hot as she was." He looked at Astraea. "The water was a good idea."

Astraea glanced at him in misery. "But are we too late? She's so sick and weak." She leaned against her best friend and didn't try to hide her tears.

At her neck, the two snakes moved. They slid down Astraea's arm and crawled onto Zephyr. They approached the nearest tooth mark, and their forked tongues flicked in and out of their mouths.

"That is disgusting!" Cylus cried. "If we didn't need them so much, I'd squish them for that. Get them away from her."

Astraea went to reach for the snakes, but they slid off Zephyr's side and into the water. Before she could catch them, they swam smoothly to shore and slid up onto dry land. Moments later they vanished in the undergrowth.

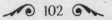

"Where are they going?" Darek cried. "We need them!"

"I—I don't know," Astraea said. "Nesso said they would stay behind to look for more snakes. Maybe while we're here, they've gone looking for them."

"That's just perfect," Cylus complained. "Not only is Zephyr getting worse, but we've lost the snakes."

"They'll be back," Astraea promised. "Nesso said they would help. We must believe her."

Nightfall arrived with a whole new set of sounds in the jungle. Even with the sun down, it was still just as hot as during the day. Everyone was in the water trying to stay cool. Astraea sat beside Zephyr, stroking her and trying her best to keep the wounds flushed.

Above them the sky was filled with bright stars. None of the them looked at all familiar, and Astraea wondered just how far they were from Titus. It felt like it had been a lifetime since she'd seen her home sky.

"Hey, they're back," Cylus called.

The two snakes slithered back into the water and approached Astraea. Each had a red berry in its mouth.

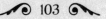

"They just went to get some food," Astraea said. "Remember, Nesso said she would eat anything."

Astraea held out her hands in the water, and the two snakes slid up onto them. But instead of going up to Astraea's neck, they crawled back onto Zephyr. They approached the nearest wound.

"What are they doing now?" Cylus asked.

"I'm not sure," Astraea said.

Everyone gathered and watched the two snakes sitting on Zephyr. They rose up high, and then each bit down on the berry they were holding. Bright red juice trickled out of their mouths and onto Zephyr's puncture wounds. Immediately the infected area started to smoke and sizzle.

"Hey!" Cylus cried. "They're trying to kill her!"

The centaur raised his hand to swat the two snakes away, but Astraea caught it as it came down. "No, Cylus, stop. Look!"

Where the juice touched the wounds, the swollen skin was going down. The snakes were spreading out the juice as far as they could. When they finished, they slipped back into the water and swam ashore.

"I think they're trying to help her," Astraea said.

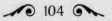

"Why would they?" Cylus demanded.

"Because Nesso told them we were going to save them. So they are trying to save Zephyr."

On the shore, the two snakes stopped and turned back to the water. They hissed before they started moving again. After a few feet, they stopped and looked back at them.

"I think they want us to follow them," Astraea said.

"Oh, so now you speak snake?" Cylus said.

"No, but I don't have to. Look."

Once again, the snakes moved and then stopped and turned back.

"I'll go," Render offered as he swam toward the shore. He clambered out of the water and started to follow the snakes. "If I don't come back, don't look for me. Just save Zephyr and get out of here."

Darek followed him to shore. "I'll help too."

When they were gone, Cylus stayed at Zephyr's head. "She's going to be fine."

Astraea could hear the doubt in his voice and knew he said it as much for himself as for her.

"She has to be," Astraea said.

Little more was said as they sat in the water and waited for the others to return. After a while, they heard movement in the trees, and the two centaurs returned.

"There's a big bush full of these berries," Darek said. "There were actually three snakes there too. I think your two told them what's happening. One left, but these two wanted to come with us." He pointed to his neck and Render's. They each had a snake coiled around them. "Now we've got new friends too."

The centaurs entered the water and approached Zephyr. Astraea received her two snakes back and then started to work with the berries. She squeezed them in her hands and let the juice run into Zephyr's wounds. Like before, the wounds sizzled where the juice hit them. But with each drop, the stink lessened.

Over the course of the night, Render and Darek made several journeys back to the bush. Astraea worked tirelessly to crush the berries and spread the juice over Zephyr's wounds. Her hands were dyed scarlet, but she didn't care even if the color was permanent.

Just before the centaurs started on another berry run, Cylus held up his hand. "Everyone, stop—quiet!"

Astraea had now spent enough time with Cylus to know that he had fantastic hearing. Much better than everyone else. He heard things long before they did.

Cylus waved at Darek and Render and motioned them back into the water. They gathered around Zephyr. "Something's moving out there," Cylus whispered.

"Is it Lergo?" Astraea whispered.

Cylus shrugged. "Could be." He reached for one of the poles to the sled and indicated to Darek to grab the other. They turned Zephyr around and pulled her into deeper water while keeping her head above the surface. They swam across the pond to the opposite shore and ducked beneath some large overhanging branches.

Just as they closed the curtain of branches behind them, Astraea slapped her hand over her mouth to keep from screaming. In the darkness, her keen vision saw an all-too-familiar shape appear on the shore where they had just been.

"It's not Lergo," Render uttered. "It's a Shadow Titan!"

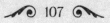

11

THE SHADOW TITAN WAS CHASING SNAKES
to the water's edge. Before the unfortunate snakes
could make it, the Shadow's large, black foot came
crashing down on them, killing them instantly.

Astraea didn't think she could ever be more horrified than watching the brutal murder of the gentle
snakes. In that same instant, Lergo crashed through
the trees and arrived on the shore. Its massive body
slithered past the Shadow Titan as though it didn't
see it. It sniffed the same route they had dragged
Zephyr along on the sled, stopping at the water's edge
where Zephyr had spent most of the day.

This was the first time Astraea and the others saw

all of Lergo. In the confines of the cave, they had seen only its eyes and mouth. Even though it was dark, everyone could clearly see the truth.

"Look at the colors," Cylus whispered. "Lergo is just an overgrown Nesso."

Lergo's head panned along the surface of the water, and its forked tongue flicked in and out, as though tasting the air.

"It's looking for Zephyr," Astraea whispered. She was crouched in the water beside her unconscious friend. She looked at Zephyr and saw her wounded rear flank was floating above the surface on the sled. Struggling with her broken leg and hoping to be as quiet as possible, Astraea grabbed the bottom edge of the sled and pushed down until Zephyr's haunches were beneath the surface.

On the opposite shore, the Shadow Titan was standing beside the immense snake. Its armored head peered down at the dead snakes at its feet, and then it studied the massive snake beside it, back to the dead snakes, and finally back to Lergo. It drew its sword and started to hack at the snake, but each blade swipe only bounced off Lergo's thick scales.

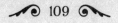

The immense snake looked back at the Shadow Titan and changed color. Instead of the multicolored rings like Nesso, the snake was now black. It hissed at the Shadow Titan, but the Shadow didn't stop whacking it with the sword.

Moments later, a second and then a third Shadow Titan appeared on the shore. The newcomers also drew their weapons and attacked Lergo. Despite their combined efforts, they were causing little damage to the snake.

"How many Shadows are here?" Astraea said softly.

"Too many," Darek said. He motioned everyone closer and dropped his voice. "I think the Mimics sent them here to kill all the snakes because they're the only things that can stop them."

Astraea realized Darek was right. Nesso said the snakes had fled the area because they were being hunted. They were trying to get away from the Shadow Titans and Mimics who were killing them.

"Astraea," Cylus said softly. "Hand me my bow. When I tell you, let Zephyr's wounds rise above the surface."

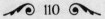

"If I do that, Lergo will smell her and come after us!"

"I know, but I have an idea." He looked at Render and Darek. "Get your arrows and bows ready. The moment Zephyr is up, do what I do. But be fast."

Astraea realized she was putting all her trust in Cylus. Cylus the bully. Cylus the centaur who cared only about his own kind. But also Cylus who had built a sled for Zephyr and would now do anything for her after she saved his life and the lives of Darek and Render.

"Get ready," Cylus called softly. "Now . . ."

Astraea stopped pushing down on the end on the sled and let it rise to the surface. She was still unsure what Cylus planned. She looked back at the snake and then to Cylus and nearly shouted "no" when she watched Cylus start rubbing the points of his arrows in Zephyr's deepest wounds. He sniffed the arrowhead and his face contorted. "Ugh. It still stinks." He looked at the other centaurs. "Do it."

When they finished, Cylus said to Astraea, "Push her down again—it will hide the smell."

Astraea was too stunned to do anything other

than what Cylus told her to do. Beside her, the centaurs loaded their bows. Across the pond, Lergo rose up higher as its tongue flicked the air. Suddenly its head turned in their direction. It had picked up on Zephyr's smell again.

"Aim only for the Shadow Titans," Cylus ordered softly as he let his first arrow fly.

Darek and Render soon followed. All the arrows struck their marks and stuck into the Shadow Titans' armor.

"Arrows don't hurt them," Astraea said.

"They're not supposed to," Cylus said. "I just hope this works."

The Shadow Titans didn't seem to notice the arrows sticking out of their armor. But within seconds of them being struck, Lergo stopped looking in Zephyr's direction and focused on the Shadows.

"We put the smell of Zephyr's infection on them," Cylus explained softly. "If we're lucky and it's still potent enough, it will draw Lergo away. Otherwise . . ."

Before Cylus could finish, the snake opened its mouth wide and bit down on the nearest Shadow

Titan. Lifting its head high in the air, it swallowed the Shadow whole.

The two remaining Shadow Titans didn't seem to notice or care as they continued to hack at the immense snake. But after the first Shadow Titan was swallowed, Lergo attacked and ate the remaining two.

When all the Shadow Titans were gone, Lergo's tongue flicked out several more times, tasting the air. Cylus joined Astraea in holding Zephyr's flank beneath the surface so the massive snake couldn't smell her.

Finally Lergo returned to its normal color and slithered back through the jungle.

Though the danger had passed, everyone was too frightened to move. They all took turns holding Zephyr's wounds under the water all night in the hopes of keeping Lergo away.

12

BRUE WAS STANDING OUTSIDE THE TEMPLE and followed them to the Olympian homes as Jake and Tryn gathered two large sacks of ambrosia. It was more than enough for Zephyr, Astraea, and the centaurs, as well as the others waiting on Earth.

"Let's get moving," Tryn said.

Just as they were about to step onto their skateboards, Brue caught hold of Tryn's right arm in one of her mouths.

"Brue, I don't have time to play. Let me go." Tryn tried to pull his arm free, but this time Brue refused to release him. Instead she started to drag him away.

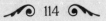

Jake stepped back fearfully. "I thought you said nothing here is dangerous."

"Nothing is," Tryn insisted as he tried to free his arm. "Really, Brue, we have to go save Zephyr!"

Brue's second head caught hold of Tryn's other arm, and together they lifted him off the ground and started to carry him into the dense jungle.

"Tryn . . . ," Jake called. "For not being dangerous, she looks awfully dangerous to me. Fight her."

"No," Tryn said. "The Mother of the Jungle is peaceful. She's trying to tell us something—it's like she wants to take us somewhere."

"Yeah, to a nice safe place to eat!"

"If Brue really wanted to hurt me, all she has to do is bite down, or even pull her heads apart. But she isn't. Whatever this is, it's important."

Jake shook his head and followed behind the Mother of the Jungle. "What is it with these crazy jungle planets and their giant monsters!"

After a few minutes Brue stopped. She put Tryn down on the ground and whined.

"What is it?" Jake asked.

The Mother of the Jungle took another step

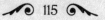

forward and lowered her heads to the ground before a large mound of dead leaves and vines. She started to brush away vines.

"You're kidding," Jake said. "She does want to play."

"I don't think so." Tryn approached the mound. "It looks like something's buried here." He started to pull away the vines and then gasped, stumbling backward.

"What is it?" Jake stepped closer and saw what looked like the tip of a white wing.

He bent down and brushed more vines away, then looked at Tryn. "It's a dead animal. Actually," he said as he uncovered more, "it looks like Zephyr or even Tornado Warning."

Tryn nodded. "That's because it's Pegasus."

13

ASTRAEA AND THE CENTAURS SPENT THE whole night in the water. When the sun finally started to rise, they risked letting Zephyr's hindquarters float to the surface.

The moment her infected flank broke the water and they lifted Zephyr's wing out of the way, Astraea couldn't believe her eyes. The wounds were still there, but they were much smaller and scabbed over. The foul odor was gone.

"Look at that," Render said. "She's healing. Those berries cured her."

Astraea didn't know whether to laugh or to cry. She wanted to kiss each snake that had brought the berries to her friend and then Darek and Render for their help.

"Are you crying again?" Cylus asked.

Tears were streaming down Astraea's cheeks. "No. I'm just so happy Zephyr's still alive."

"Me too," Cylus finally admitted.

Render brushed the branches aside and looked across the pond. "I don't think anyone's here," he said. "But I see something glinting over there." He looked at Cylus. "Can I go see what it is?"

"I'm not stopping you," Cylus said abruptly. Then his tone softened. "I mean, yes, if you want to. Just be careful. There could be more Shadow Titans, or Lergo might come back."

"I will be." Render pushed free of their cover and swam across the pond. When he climbed out of the water, he reached for something and held it up.

"It's a sword," Darek said. "The Shadow Titan must have dropped it when it when Lergo attacked it."

Render reached for a second sword and finally the third one. He held them in his arms and entered the water again. When he arrived back at their hiding spot, he ducked beneath the branches, approached Cylus, and

handed him one of the swords. "This is all that's left from the Shadow Titans. I think that snake must have spit them out. I never saw the Shadows drop them."

Cylus held up the sword and inspected it closely. "I don't recognize the metal." He looked at Darek and Render. "Do you?"

Render studied the sword and shook his head. He handed his to Astraea and the other to Darek.

Astraea looked at the strange weapon. There were almost iridescent rainbows swirling in the metal. The edge was still lethally sharp, even after all the blows the Shadow Titan had levied at the giant snake. "They still look brand-new."

Render was frowning. "Weren't the original Shadow Titans created by Saturn?"

Astraea nodded. "In the war against the Olympians."

Render said. "If that's true, where did they get these swords? I've never seen anything like this before, and my dad works with metals just like Vulcan."

"You're right," Darek said. "Titus doesn't have anything like this." He was turning the blade around, inspecting it all. Then his eyes went to the handle. "Look at the pommel and hilt. They're not from Titus. We don't have this kind of wood."

"What's it mean?" Cylus said.

Darek continued. "I think it means that these were made by Mimics using materials from their world, not ours. Maybe even the Shadow Titans themselves aren't really Titans. What if they made them, too?"

"Why would they?" Cylus asked.

After a moment, Astraea had a thought. "I think I know. It's fear. Think about it. The Shadow Titans were the most fearsome fighters in the war. Everyone was scared of them because they couldn't be defeated and showed no mercy. It took the special flame-swords to destroy them. Maybe whoever the Titan traitor is, he told them about the swords and they designed new ones to scare us."

"It worked," Render admitted. "They scare the life out of me!"

"So if the Mimics' Shadow Titans aren't *real* Shadow Titans," Darek mused, "then we might not need those special flame-swords to defeat them. These might even work."

"There's only one way to find out," Cylus said. "We have to find another one and try these swords."

"You want to go looking for Shadow Titans?" Astraea gasped.

"If we want to find out the truth, we have to," Cylus said.

Zephyr stirred in the water and lifted her head. "Would you all please shut up—my head is killing me!"

"Zephyr!" Astraea squealed. She swam up to Zephyr's head and hugged her tightly.

"Astraea, please, headache, remember? Squeezing my head really isn't helping!"

"I'm sorry," Astraea said excitedly. "But I can't help it. We thought you were going to die."

Zephyr snorted. "It's going to take more than a giant snake to kill me."

"That same giant snake just ate three Shadow Titans," Render said.

"What?" Zephyr cried. Then she shut her eyes. "Ouch, my head."

"Just take it easy," Cylus said softly. "You've had a bad night. Lie back and relax for a while."

Instead of lying back down, Zephyr looked around. Finally her eyes settled on Astraea. "Where are we? Why am I wet? How did I get here? I can't seem to remember anything after they set your leg."

"Wow, you missed a lot," Render said.

They briefly explained the events right after Zephyr collapsed. When they finished, Zephyr looked at each of them. "Thank you for making this sled and saving me."

"You saved us first," Cylus said.

"I think we must be even now," Zephyr said.

"Not hardly," Cylus said seriously. "You saved me at least twice."

"And us," Darek and Render said.

"Look," Astraea interrupted. "You can keep track of who saved who the most later. Right now we must figure out what to do next. I personally want to get as far away from Lergo as possible—not to mention that there may be more Shadow Titans around here."

When everyone agreed, Zephyr raised her head again. "That works for me. Let's just find the rest of the snakes and be ready to leave when Jake and Tryn come back." She rose a bit farther. "Move back, everyone. I want to try to get up."

Astraea swam a bit farther away from Zephyr. "Nice and easy," she coached. "You've been really sick, and you haven't eaten anything. You're going to be weak."

Zephyr looked back at her. "Weak? I passed weak ages ago. Right now I'd be happy to be able to stand up without falling over."

Zephyr made it to her feet, but as she feared, her legs buckled, and she splashed back down into the water. Her second attempt was the same. On the third try, Cylus and the two centaurs surrounded her and helped support her as she climbed shakily to her hooves.

"Just stand there for a moment and get your balance," Cylus said he stood pressed against Zephyr to keep her upright.

Zephyr shook her head and snorted. "I really feel like Brutus has stomped on me."

"I wish Brutus were here," Astraea said. "We sure could use a giant that's on our side on this world."

After a while, Zephyr took her first unsteady step as she climbed out of the pond and up onto the shore. Once she was settled on solid ground, she stretched her wings and gave them a good flapping before settling them down.

"Are you all right?" Astraea called.

"You're kidding, right?" Zephyr said.

"I know you feel terrible," Astraea finished. "But I mean, do you think you can walk?"

Zephyr nodded. "If it means walking away from here, yes, I can walk." She took a step and then stopped. She looked down at her chest, then to Astraea, and down to her chest again. "Um, Astraea, would you mind telling me what you guys did to my black blaze? It seems to be missing."

Astraea had wondered how long it would take for Zephyr to notice her blaze was mostly gone. All that remained was the tiniest hint of gray. "We didn't do anything, Zeph. Your fever did it, or the venom from Lergo. You were turning yellow and then it faded away."

"So, let me get this straight. I got bitten by a big snake and now my blaze is gone, and I look like Pegasus. *Just like Pegasus!* Is that what you're telling me?"

Astraea shrugged. "Um, yes . . ."

Zephyr threw back her head and whinnied furiously. "Noooooo!"

"Zephyr, calm down," Cylus said. "It's just a bit of color. You're alive. That's all that matters."

"It's more than just a bit of color!" Zephyr cried. "That blaze is what set me apart from Pegasus. It was my identity. Now it's gone and the teasing is going to get even worse!"

"No, it won't," Cylus insisted. "I swear if I hear one person compare you to Pegasus, it will be the last thing they ever do."

"Zeph, please," Astraea said. "You're just getting over something terrible. You can't waste your energy like this."

Zephyr turned to her, and the pain in her eyes was clear. "How would you feel if you woke up and all your hair was gone?"

Astraea leaned over and reached for one of the Shadow Titan swords. Then she pulled her long hair forward and put the blade to it. "I will cut it all off right now if it would help. Zephyr, you are not defined by your blaze any more than I am by my hair. You are you. The rest is just extra."

Astraea started to cut her hair when Render caught hold of her arm and stopped her. "Astraea, don't. For one, your mother will kill you, and for two, it won't help Zephyr."

"No, it won't," Zephyr agreed. She tilted her head to the side. "But I do appreciate the gesture. Please put the sword down. I'll be all right. I just have to get used to it."

"Maybe the color will come back when you eat ambrosia," Darek offered.

"Or we could dye it once this nightmare is over and we're back on Titus," Astraea offered.

"Yes, I guess." Zephyr sighed. She looked over at Cylus. "Would you put Astraea on my back, and we can get moving?"

"I'll carry her," Render offered.

Zephyr snorted. "Oh no, we're not starting this again. I carry Astraea and you keep those swords and bows ready. If there were three Shadow Titans here last night, who knows how many more there could be."

Astraea hated to admit it, but Zephyr was right. With her broken leg, she couldn't walk, and if she was honest, she wasn't great with a bow. The centaurs were natural warriors. Finally she nodded and allowed Render to carry her over to Zephyr and lift her onto her back.

When she was set, Astraea leaned forward and wrapped her arms around Zephyr's neck. Saying nothing, she hugged her best friend tightly.

Zephyr turned back and nodded. "I feel the same." She looked at the centaurs. "Lead on. Let's go get some snakes."

They traveled in the same direction as the previous day. As they walked, they quietly laughed at the rumbling of each other's empty stomachs.

"I don't think I've ever been so hungry in all my life," Cylus complained.

"I'm so hungry I could eat a tree," Render said. "I wanted to eat some of the berries we used on Zephyr, but I wasn't sure if they'd be poisonous."

"We can't trust anything here," Astraea said as her own stomach churned and complained about the lack of food. "I just hope Riza and Emily get here soon with some ambrosia."

They passed the time describing the banquet they were going to have once this was over. Not one item or dessert was left off their extensive list.

Several times they had to stop to let Zephyr rest. Though she tried to keep going, she was exhausted. It was a good opportunity for the others to rest as well. It seemed like it had been ages since they'd slept or eaten.

Other stops were made when the sounds in the jungle changed. On two occasions they had to hide as best they could while enormous dinosaurs passed through the area.

After one particularly gigantic, four-legged creature moved within shooting distance of them, Darek shook his head. "Not even Brutus could beat that one! Why is everything here so big?"

"I don't know," Astraea said. "Jake seemed to recognize them, but to me they're all just big and scary."

Throughout the day, Cylus would stop and look back. When Astraea asked him why, he would frown and say it was nothing. But the fact that he kept doing it was starting to spook her.

"What?" she finally demanded. "Cylus, tell me—why do you keep looking back? You've been doing it all day!"

Cylus paused. "I haven't said anything because I'm not sure."

"Not sure about what?" Zephyr said.

"I don't know," the centaur said. "But I keep feeling like we're being followed. I haven't heard or seen anything. But the feeling won't go away. Actually, it's getting worse."

"I've been feeling it too," Render offered. "But considering everything here wants to eat us, I thought it was just me overreacting."

"Then I'm overreacting too," Darek finally said.

"Maybe it's Lergo again," Astraea said fearfully as she looked around, including up in the trees.

Cylus shook his head. "I don't know how I know, but it's not. Lergo slithers. I'm not hearing that."

"What are you hearing?" Zephyr asked.

"Nothing," Cylus said. "That's what's so strange. I feel it, but I can't hear it."

"Then let's keep moving," Astraea said. "If something is following us, all this stopping is giving them a chance to catch up."

Despite agreeing not to stop to listen, they all did as they followed the setting sun. Just before it vanished completely, they reached the end of the jungle and were faced with a golden beach leading up to a deep green ocean. Tall, choppy waves broke the surface and crashed to the shore as the sun lit golden on the surface.

At the very opposite end of the beach, they saw

a rocky cliff face climbing high into the sky. At the base of the cliff, the ocean's waves pounded against all the fallen boulders, casting great plumes of ocean foam into the air.

"It's beautiful." Astraea sighed as Zephyr stepped onto the sand. Apart from their visit to the plateau, this was the only other time they had been free of the dense jungle, and Astraea celebrated being able to see the wide-open sky again.

"Look out over the ocean," Zephyr said. "I can't see the end of it." She looked back at Astraea. "Do you mind if I walk into the water? It looks so cool and inviting. I could use another good soak."

"Me too," Astraea agreed.

Zephyr treaded into the water until it covered her back and was up to Astraea's waist. She sighed at the relief it offered from the heat. "Oh, this is wonderful. I could stay here all night."

Astraea sighed at the relief the cool water offered her broken leg. "It sure is. Finally, there's something good about this world."

Cylus and the centaurs waited on the shore as Astraea and Zephyr cooled off. After a few minutes, Zephyr walked back to shallower water.

"Feeling better?" Cylus asked.

"Much," Zephyr said. She looked around. "Now where are we supposed to go? The sun's going down over the water. We can't swim out there."

"I don't know." Astraea reached up to her neck and gently pried the two snakes away. She peered into their red eyes. "I hope you two can understand me. Where do we go now?"

She held the snakes out to Render. "Would you put them down on the sand. Maybe we can follow them."

When Render lowered them to the sand, they slithered out a bit and then looked back, as though saying they understood. Then they started crossing the sand.

"I guess we follow them," Astraea suggested.

Zephyr treaded in the shallow water following the snakes while the centaurs stayed on the shore. Just before they'd crossed half the beach, Cylus stopped and looked back toward the jungle. "I still keep feeling we're being followed!" He looked at the two other centaurs. "Do you feel it?"

They both nodded and raised their bows. Darek frowned. "I think it's more than one thing following us."

"Me too," Render agreed. "I'd offer to go back and check, but in this place, I'm likely to get eaten."

"We stick together," Cylus said. "It's safer for all of us."

Astraea looked back toward the jungle. She wasn't sure if she was now feeling something, or whether she was reacting to the centaurs' nerves. Whatever it was, she was becoming very uneasy. "I don't think I like it here on the beach. We've very exposed."

"Then let's keep moving." Cylus was now walking backward with his bow raised while Darek and Render looked to the side, up the beach, and into the jungle around them.

Zephyr's ears were constantly flicking and listening to everything. Then her eyes settled on the water farther out and she tilted her head to the side. "Astraea, does it look like something's moving out there?"

"It's the waves, isn't it?" Astraea said.

Zephyr snorted and shook her head. "I don't think so. Look again. There's definitely movement."

Everyone stared at the water. Cylus took two steps into the surf. "She's right. There is something moving out there. You can see the ripples on the surface. And if you look carefully, you can see it's kind of glowing. . . ." He squinted his eyes and then they went wide. "And it's coming this way! Zephyr, get out of the water, now!"

Zephyr opened her wings and launched into the air while Cylus galloped out of the surf and up the beach. An instant later, a massive blue ocean creature launched itself onto the shore and snapped its tooth-filled mouth shut in the area they'd just been standing.

When it failed to catch them, it wiggled and rolled back into the pounding surf. But instead of moving into deeper water, it stayed there, waiting and watching.

"I hate this world!" Zephyr cried as she touched down on the sand again. "And I hate constantly saying how much I hate it!"

"Why does everything here want to eat us?" Darek panted. "Doesn't anything eat plants?"

"Did you see that thing?" Render cried as he paced the area. "I've never seen anything like it! It had scales and fins like the sea creatures on Titus, but so many teeth! If we had anything like that back home, Neptune wouldn't stand a chance even with his trident."

Astraea was looking at the water and shaking her head. "How can anything survive here? All these creatures want to do is eat each other."

"Look at it out there." Zephyr pawed the sand. "It's just waiting for us to make another mistake." She clopped closer to the shore, but still far enough away from the ocean creature. "Forget it, fish face. You're not making a meal of us!"

"Let's get moving," Cylus said, looking nervously around. "I really don't like it here."

"No kidding," Zephyr agreed.

Astraea peered down to the sand and saw the two snakes waiting for them. She nodded. "All right, you two, we're ready."

As though they understood, the snakes slithered across the sand. Everyone followed keeping a keen eye on the jungle behind them and to their left and the ocean at their right. It seemed that danger could come to them from any direction.

Eventually they crossed the beach and were

approaching the cliff face on the opposite side. They stopped and peered up.

"I hope they don't expect us to climb up there," Darek said, peering up the sharp cliff face. "It's really high."

"They'd better not, because I just don't have the energy to carry you all," Zephyr said. She took a step closer to the snakes. "Wait, look, behind those boulders—there's a cave in there."

"Oh no!" Cylus cried. "No more caves. Remember what happened last time we went in one."

The snakes hissed up at them and then moved between two large boulders and disappeared into the cave.

"Those two can just forget it. I'm not going in there," Cylus said.

Moments later they returned, followed by more snakes than they ever expected to see. Some were smaller than Nesso, but some were much larger, and one was longer than all the centaurs put together in a line and reached up to the top of Zephyr's legs.

"So this is where they've all gone," Astraea noted. "Look at the size of that one! I guess it's true that they do grow into Lergo. Do you think we should tell Jake, considering how devoted he is to Nesso?"

"Nah, don't tell him." Zephyr chuckled. "Let's keep it a surprise for him."

"Yeah." Cylus laughed. "A really *big* surprise!"

They all laughed as more snakes came out of the cave and formed a kind of slithering carpet around them.

Zephyr took a cautious step back. "Hey, you know something? I don't think I like this. In fact, I'm sure I don't like it. I mean, Nesso is fine, maybe even kind of cute in her own scaly way. Even the others are okay. But this is a lot of slithering snakes!"

"Too many," Cylus said.

The original two came forward and lifted themselves up as high as they could. Render bent down and offered his hand and they slid on. He handed them up to Astraea. "I've already got one; these two are yours."

Both Darek and Render each had a snake around their neck and weren't too pleased about it. Astraea accepted them and smiled. "I don't know what you're all worried about. I think they're sweet."

"Hello?" Zephyr said. "Have you forgotten about

that big one in the cave? You know, the one that nearly killed me!"

"No, I haven't," Astraea said. "But have *you* forgotten it was these two and the ones with Darek and Render that brought the berries that saved your life?"

When they were settled around Astraea's neck, the two snakes hissed. Immediately the others on the ground parted, creating a trail leading into the cave.

"Let's go," Astraea said.

"Go where?" Cylus said suspiciously.

"Into the cave," Astraea said.

Cylus shook his head. "I told you, no more caves for me."

Astraea's leg was throbbing, and she was more tired than she imagined possible. The last thing she wanted was to fight with Cylus. "Fine. Stay out here if you like with all the things that want to eat you. But Zephyr and I are going in. I'm exhausted, my leg hurts, and I need to rest. If there were any danger in there"—she pointed up to the snakes at her neck—"I don't think these two would let us go in." She leaned forward to Zephyr. "What do you think?"

"Well, I . . . ?" Zephyr said hesitantly.

"Fine," Astraea said. "You can stay out here too. But I am going in." She started to slide off Zephyr's back.

"Astraea, stop." Zephyr tightened her folded wings and locked Astraea on her back. "If you really want to go in, we'll go in. Don't get down. It'll only hurt your leg even more."

"But I don't want to force you to go where you don't want to!"

Zephyr burst out laughing. "It's too late for that. We came to this world, didn't we?" She started to walk forward between the snakes. "But if I go in there and get bitten again . . ."

"I know," Astraea said, patting her neck. "You'll never forgive me."

"Just so long as that's clear," Zephyr finished.

Once inside the cave, they found the air was much cooler and it was easier to breathe. There was a lot of sand on the ground, as well as large clumps of washed-up ocean grasses. Render helped Astraea off Zephyr and lowered her to a pile of dried grasses.

Zephyr settled beside her, and the three centaurs lay down near the entrance. Once they were comfort-

able, the wave of snakes entered and made their way to the very back of the cave.

Despite their large quantity, they were oddly silent. No hissing or communication of any kind. It was obvious the snakes were terrified and were seeking a safe hiding place.

As they moved past Astraea, the giant snake paused. Their eyes met and held for a moment. Then the snake leaned closer to her, it's tongue flicking in and out.

Astraea reached out her hand and tentatively pet the snake's wide snout. At her touch, it shut its red eyes and tilted its head to the side. Instead of joining the others at the back, the large snake coiled up at her side.

"I think you've made a new friend," Zephyr teased.

"I do too," Astraea agreed as she continued to stroke the snake.

"I can't believe this," Cylus said to her. "And I doubt anyone back home would either if we told them about it."

"I know," Render agreed. He yawned loudly. "I'm so tired. I feel like I haven't slept in an age."

"Me too," Darek agreed.

Once all the snakes were inside, Cylus rose and walked over to the entrance of the cave. "You all rest. I'll keep watch."

"You need to sleep too," Astraea said.

"I know, but whatever is following us is still out there. One of us should stand guard. I'll take the first watch, and then we can switch."

"I'll take the second watch," Render offered.

"And I'll do the third," Darek put in.

Astraea knew there was no point arguing with the centaurs. They all needed rest, but their warrior training meant they would keep watch, despite their exhaustion. She nestled against Zephyr and dosed off, feeling grateful to them.

It felt like Astraea had just closed her eyes when a warning shout from Cylus and the clanking sounds of swords startled her awake. With the moon shining brightly into the cave behind them, it wasn't long before Astraea realized what she was seeing. Cylus was fighting two Shadow Titans. With a sword in one hand and his dagger in the other, he was a true warrior.

As their weapons clanked against each other, wild sparks flew into the air. Cylus was brave and unflinching as he took on the attackers. With a quick, swiping undercut, he skillfully struck one of the Shadows in the arm and sliced it off at the shoulder. But the creature didn't feel the wound and kept fighting.

Just as Render and Darek rose to their hooves, Astraea watched in horror as a third Shadow Titan charged at Cylus and knocked his sword away while the other lunged forward and thrust his weapon into the centaur. With a single cry, Cylus collapsed to the cave floor.

"Cylus!" Render howled as he raised his weapon and charged into battle.

Like Cylus, both Render and Darek fought bravely and with more skill than Astraea could imagine. Their swords moved so swiftly, she couldn't see the blades anymore. Just the sparks as they struck the Shadow's blades.

But despite their efforts, Render was wounded and fell to the ground, while Darek was struck in the head with a cracking blow that Astraea and Zephyr heard at the back of the cave. He collapsed

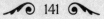

and became still. When they were hauled out of the cave, more Shadow Titans entered.

Astraea stole a glance back at the snakes and saw them disappearing into cracks and crevices. There was no time for anything more as a Shadow Titan charged forward, caught hold of Astraea, and hauled her to her feet. She screamed when her broken leg touched the ground. "Stop!" she begged. "My leg is broken!" Unable to stand, she fell to the floor of the cave again.

"Leave her alone or I'll stomp you!" Zephyr whinnied. She reared up and kicked the Shadow Titan away from Astraea. The massive bird Shadow collapsed to the ground and fell to pieces as Zephyr stomped it to oblivion. More Shadow Titans charged forward and tried to subdue Zephyr. Finally, when a large green turtle Shadow raised its weapon to Zephyr's neck, Astraea shouted, "Zephyr, stop, please. They'll kill you!"

Seeing she was surrounded, and feeling the blade at her throat, Zephyr stood down. Though her nostrils flared and her ears went back, she allowed herself to be captured by the Shadow Titans.

With Zephyr subdued, Astraea was hauled up

again by a Shadow Titan. Despite her pained cries, she was dragged along the sandy floor and out of the cave, past Cylus, Darek, and Render.

The ocean's waves were pounding on the rocks, casting salty spume in the air and making a voice sound very soft and far away. "Bring them to us."

Astraea and Zephyr were taken over to a line of Mimics. Standing in their true, blubberous form. With the moonlight reflecting on their wet-looking gray skin, they were even more terrifying.

Astraea had only ever seen one from behind in the cells of Tartarus, or when they were melting from Nesso's venom. But standing before her were four healthy, horrifying Mimics. Their eyes were dark and bulbous and the skin on their faces was drooping into deep folds. There were no noses that she could see, or lips on their wide, thin mouths.

One of them brought its hand to its mouth and spoke. "Bring those still alive closer."

Astraea was dragged forward and deposited at the feet of the creatures, with Zephyr right behind her. The three centaurs were deposited outside the cave. Astraea looked back at them, but they weren't moving. Were the centaurs dead? Could it be true?

The Mimics each held a torch, yet they seemed to be straining and had to squint to see her as they bent down and peered closer.

One of them gasped or made a sound that could have been a gasp. "These *are* the Titan spawn that have caused us so much trouble."

"Indeed," mused another. "But where are the rest? There are two biped spawn missing." It looked at the first Mimic who'd spoken. "Ask your Shadows to tell us how many they killed in the cave."

The first Mimic held up its hand to its mouth again and started to speak. "How many Titans did you kill in the cave?"

One of the Shadow Titans held up three fingers and pointed back to the cave entrance and the centaurs.

"Those are the centaurs," said the first Mimic. "Where are the bipeds?"

"Perhaps they separated, and our Shadows only followed this group," said a new Mimic.

Astraea realize Cylus and the others were right. They had been followed. She was sickened to realize they had led the Mimics directly to the snakes' hiding place. She just hoped they'd managed to escape deeper into the cave, where the Mimics and Shadow Titans couldn't reach them.

The Mimic standing above Astraea raised its hand to its mouth again. It was then she noticed the small, round silver device it held. "Hold her up. I wish to see her better."

Astraea winced as the Shadow Titan lifted her off the ground by her wrist and held her out to the Mimic.

"So, Titan, where are the two bipeds that were always with you?"

"I don't understand," Astraea said. "What is a biped?"

"You are a biped, as you walk on two feet. That one behind you is a quadruped, as she uses four."

Astraea looked back at Zephyr and then back to the Mimic. She realized they were talking about Jake and Tryn. She lowered her head. "They were eaten by a big serpent. It tried to get me too and broke my leg."

The four Mimics looked at each other and spoke in a strange language. Then the one in front of Astraea spoke again. "We know you are here for the snakes, to use them against us. Did you really think we would allow you to collect them? We have been following you since you arrived. You never had a chance against us."

Astraea knew they were lying. If they had been followed from the moment they arrived, the Mimics would have known that Jake and Tryn had left and not been devoured by Lergo. "I don't know what you're talking about."

"Of course you do," the Mimic said calmly. "But what you don't realize is what you're up against. If you encounter one of us, you encounter us all. If you kill one of us, we all know it. So we know what you did on Titus with our Vulcan and Lyra and in the nectar orchards. We also know it was you on Tartarus who freed the others. You have taken the Olympian and Titan leadership and hidden them away from our grasp. You and your spawn friends have disrupted our plans, but you have not stopped us. However, even that is over. You will tell us where Jupiter and the others are, and then you will die."

"Why should I tell you if you're just going to kill me?" Astraea said.

"Because your answer will determine how you and your friend die. Either fast and painless or slow and very uncomfortable. The choice is yours."

"I'll take slow and uncomfortable, please," Zephyr said.

Astraea looked back at Zephyr. She was surrounded by Shadow Titans. But her eyes weren't on them. They weren't even on Astraea or the Mimics. They were watching the ocean.

Astraea followed her gaze and saw the glow rising from the shoreline. The creature that had tried to attack them earlier in the day was still there. Only now that it was night, its glow had increased.

Astraea looked from the ocean back to the Mimics. They didn't seem to notice it. Or if they did, they didn't care. "If I tell you what you want to know, can I choose how I die?"

"Is this some kind of trick?" the Mimic demanded. "If it is, you would be a fool to try it. There is no escape for you, and should you attempt anything against us, your end would be more unpleasant than you could imagine."

Astraea shook her head. "How could it be a trick? You have all the power, and I am just a spawn with a broken leg. But I want to ask: If I must die, can it be in the water? My mother's family were water nymphs. In fact, I am only the second generation out of water. You seem to care so much about family; you must understand that I want to die in the home of my people."

"You did not originate on this world," the Mimic said.

"True, but water is water. If you let me die there, I will tell you where Jupiter is."

"Astraea—no—you—can't," Zephyr called. "You—can't—betray—Jupiter . . ."

Astraea looked back at her friend. Zephyr was the worst actor ever. If they somehow managed to survive this, she was going to ask the Muses to teach her how to act.

"What's the point of trying to trick them?" she said. "They are more powerful than us. If I must die, I want it to be in the water!" Astraea looked back at the Mimic. "Well, do we have a deal?"

The Mimics looked at each other and spoke in their unfamiliar language. Finally the one before her nodded. "All right, spawn. If you tell us what we want to know, we will end you swiftly in the water."

"Hey, I want the same deal!" Zephyr cried. "If she gets to go into the water, I want to go too. My grandfather is Neptune, and he's from the ocean."

"I see no reason not to grant your request," the Mimic said cordially. It lifted its hand to its mouth and spoke into the metal device again. "Carry this spawn into the water up to your knees and allow the other to follow."

The Shadow Titan started to walk, holding Astraea up by the arm.

Zephyr was still surrounded by Shadow Titans but was led to the shore beside her.

Astraea looked out at the water and saw the glow of the ocean monster waiting just offshore. The Mimics still hadn't noticed the glow. This convinced her even more that they couldn't see very well. Perhaps it was only at night that their vision was weak, but in any case, she hoped she could use it against them.

When she was carried into the surf, the Shadow Titans turned to face the beach. The Mimics had walked closer but stayed out of the water.

"All right, spawn. We have done as you asked. You will die in water. Now, tell us, where are Jupiter and the others?"

Astraea knew this was it. Life or death. She was

gambling with her life and Zephyr's. She wasn't even sure this would work. "Use your talking device to tell the Shadow Titan to release me. You know I can't run or swim away, so there's no need for him to hold me up."

The Mimic eyed her suspiciously. "So you know about our communicators. Fine, but it will gain you nothing. The Shadows are ours to command." It raised its hand to its mouth. "You may release the Titan. She can't run anywhere."

The Shadow Titan released Astraea's arm. She landed in the ocean on her good foot and kept the broken leg raised. Putting her hands behind her back, she started to wiggle her hands and fingers at the water, hoping to attract the monster.

"Well?" the Mimic said.

"Oh yes," Astraea mused, wiggling furiously. "You want to know where Jupiter and the leadership are?"

"You know we do," said the Mimic.

"Astraea—wait—stop—don't—tell—them . . . ," Zephyr called flatly.

"I must," Astraea said to Zephyr. "So now, my dearest friend, a friend I have had all my life, that

I consider a sister. Now we must both prepare for what's coming. We have lived a short life, and now our end is almost *here*. . . ."

"You are wasting precious time," the Mimic cut in. "It will gain you nothing. Just tell us where Jupiter is!"

Astraea paused and turned toward Zephyr. But her eyes weren't on Zephyr. They watched the water behind her. The glow was intensifying. "Yes, um, Jupiter, well, he's is on Rhean. That's another world the Olympians used to visit."

The four Mimics looked at each other and spoke. Then the one said, "You are lying to us. Everyone knows Rhean was destroyed in a supernova. Did you really think you could trick us, you foolish little spawn?"

"Well, I had hoped . . . ," Astraea said. "But if you seriously expect me to betray Jupiter, you're not only ugly, but you're crazy as well!"

The four Mimics moved closer to the water's edge, and the one who was doing all the talking stood before her. "It could have been so quick and painless for you. But now you will understand fully what we are capable of." It raised its hand, and a tendril appeared and shot out toward Astraea.

 151

14

"ASTRAEA, NOW!" ZEPHYR REARED UP AND kicked the closest Shadow Titan into the path of the deadly tendril. Then she bucked and kicked several more Shadows with her back hooves. She charged at Astraea just as the ocean creature rose out of the water and swam straight at them.

Astraea reached out, caught hold of Zephyr's mane, and swung up and onto her back as her friend opened her wings and took off into the dark sky. Beneath them, the ocean creature burst onto shore. With its massive mouth open, it caught hold of three Mimics and then slithered back into the water. The fourth Mimic stood in stunned silence, as though it didn't quite understand what had just happened.

"Zephyr, I have an idea. Swoop down on the Mimic!" Astraea reached up to her neck and pulled the two snakes free. "I'm so sorry, you two, but we really need your help—please, if you can understand me, bite the Mimic!"

"It won't work," Zephyr called. "They haven't bitten Jake. Their venom hasn't been changed."

"I know, but I've been trying to figure out how biting Jake can change them. It doesn't make sense. I just need to try. Get us down low enough for me to do that."

When Zephyr swooped in low, Astraea dropped the two snakes on the Mimic's bulbous head. A tendril shot out of the Mimic and reached for Zephyr's hoof, but she was faster and pulled away.

Zephyr turned in the sky and headed back. "I told you, it won't work, not without Jake."

Astraea's heart sank. The snakes did need to bite a human to be deadly to Mimics. But as Zephyr soared over the Mimic's head, she watched the Mimic start to melt.

"Zeph, Zeph, wait, turn around again, go back, I think it's working!"

Zephyr swooped around again and looked down on the melting Mimic. "Whoop, whoop! That's fantastic!" She landed in the sand. "Hey, look, the Shadow Titans aren't moving."

Zephyr was right. Without the Mimic to tell them what to do, the Shadow Titans stood like statues on the sand.

"Take us down," Astraea called. "I have to get the snakes out of the Mimic goo before it kills them."

Zephyr landed and kept a watchful eye on both the stationary Shadow Titans and the ocean. The glowing monster was still onshore, but not moving.

"I think eating the Mimics killed it," Zephyr said. "Look, its glow is fading."

Astraea looked at the massive monster and felt a tinge of guilt. They had caused its death. "I'm sorry," she called softly to it.

"What?" Zephyr cried. "That thing would have eaten us if it got the chance."

"Yes, but that's its nature," Astraea said. "We can't blame something for its nature. It is a predator—we are its prey. I'm just sorry we're responsible for its death."

"I don't think I'll ever understand you," Zephyr said.

Astraea slid off Zephyr's back and landed on her good leg. She lowered herself down to the sand and crawled over to the Mimic puddle. "There are the two snakes. We have to get them out of there."

"Wait here." Zephyr galloped up to the edge of the jungle and returned with a stick. She dropped it beside Astraea. "This should do it."

"Thanks, Zeph." Astraea used the stick to pull the two unconscious snakes out of the puddle. She also reached for the metal cylinder that the Mimic used to control the Shadow Titans.

Crawling to the ocean's shore, she rinsed off the snakes. When they were clean, she held them in her hands and looked down on them sadly. "I feel so bad about doing that."

"I don't," Zephyr said. "We now know that the snakes are deadly to Mimics without needing to bite humans."

Astraea looked up at Zephyr. "Do you think the

Mimics were telling the truth? That they can feel when other Mimics die and they know who caused it?"

Zephyr snorted. "Well, they recognized us easily enough. I do believe it."

Astraea nodded. "Then others will be coming here to see what happened to them. They'll know it was us."

Zephyr nodded. "We'd better go."

Astraea shook her head. "We can't. We have to check on the centaurs."

"Astraea please, no," Zephyr said sadly. "Don't make me go back there and see what the Shadow Titans did to them. It will hurt too much, especially after everything the centaurs have done for us. Just let them be. I'm so sorry I never got to say goodbye or even a proper thank-you after they built that sled for me."

"I know," Astraea agreed. "But Zeph, I have to check. We don't know for sure if they're dead. Maybe they're just hurt. We can't leave without checking."

Zephyr dropped her head. "You're right. We owe them that much."

Astraea rose and leaned heavily on Zephyr as she hopped toward the cave. Just outside it, they found

Darek where the Shadow Titans deposited him. But Cylus and Render were gone.

She dropped to the ground and checked on Darek. He had a huge lump on his head but was breathing. "Zeph, he's alive!"

"Thank the stars!" Zephyr lowered her head to Darek. "That's some lump. He's going to have a terrible headache when he wakes up." She looked around. "Where are Cylus and Render?"

The giant snake appeared at the entrance to the cave. It approached them, hissed, and then vanished inside. "That's what happened," Zephyr said. "It's taken Cylus and Render inside to eat."

"I don't think so. Look, it wants us to go in there."

"How do you know?" Zephyr said. "It could have been a warning to stay out. Or maybe it's mad at us because it couldn't have Darek."

"You're just saying that because you don't like the snakes."

"No, it's because they all turn into monsters like Lergo when they grow up. And it likes to eat big things like us."

"Well, I don't agree with you," Astraea said. "And I'm going in there."

"Are you crazy? What if they're still hungry?"

"Trust me, Zeph, the snakes aren't dangerous."

Zephyr sighed heavily, but let Astraea lean on her as they started to pick their way around the rocks and into the cave. Once they were in, they saw Cylus and Render toward the back, surrounded by snakes.

"I told you," Zephyr said. "They plan to eat them."

"No, they don't," Astraea insisted. "Look at them; they're protecting them." She went down to her knees, and the snakes cleared a path for her to go to the centaurs. "See? I was right. They were protecting them."

"That's impossible. They're just snakes. Why would they?"

"Because they're intelligent and sensitive. Look at Nesso. She'd do anything for Jake."

"Yes, because she bit him, and they're connected."

"Maybe it wasn't the bite. Maybe they're all sweet. The centaurs were in trouble, so they helped them." When she reached Render, she saw the large wound that pierced his shoulder, but his chest moved regularly. "Zeph, look, he's alive too!"

"But—but I don't understand," Zephyr cried, "the Shadow Titans said they were dead."

"Maybe they can't tell the difference between unconscious and dead."

"Go check on Cylus," Zephyr said excitedly. When Astraea was beside the fallen centaur, Zephyr called. "Please tell me he's alive too."

Cylus was covered in blood, and there was a large wound that went from his stomach through to his back. At first Astraea didn't feel anything, and her heart crashed. But then there was a very weak breath. "He's alive, but barely."

"How?" Zephyr cried. "I saw that Shadow's sword go right through him."

"I don't know. It got him right were his torso joins the equine part of his body. He's still bleeding." Astraea tore a large piece of her tunic off and pressed it to both sides of Cylus's wounds. "He needs help. He's alive now, but he won't be for long." She looked at the centaur's pale face. "Just hold on, Cylus. Please, hold on. . . ."

"He needs ambrosia," Zephyr said. "Stay here with them. I'm going to check on Darek again."

Zephyr walked forward and reached for something on the ground. She carried it to the back of the cave and dropped it beside Astraea. It was Cylus's bow. She then carried over his quiver of arrows. "You may need to fight the Mimics if they come back." Zephyr paused. "Better yet, just throw more snakes at them; that seems to work."

Astraea didn't say anything to Zephyr's comment. She felt guilty enough dropping the two snakes down onto the Mimic. It felt like a betrayal.

Time seemed to stand still as Astraea stayed with Cylus, pressing fabric to his front and back wound. Beside her, Render stirred and moaned. "Take it easy, Render. You've got a bad wound. It's stopped bleeding, but it could start again."

"Wha-what happened? There were . . ."

"Shadow Titans," Astraea said. "You fought very bravely, but you were stabbed."

"What about Cylus and Darek?"

"Cylus has been badly hurt. I can't get his bleeding to stop. Darek is still outside the cave. They hit him in the head and he's unconscious. Zephyr's with him."

"No, she's not," Darek appeared at the entrance

with his hand pressed to the back of his head. He clopped in and made it to the back of the cave. "Zephyr told me what happened—that's great news about the snakes."

"What about the snakes?" Render asked weakly.

Astraea told him about their discovery that the snakes didn't need to bite humans to be deadly.

"That is good news," Render said. "I just hope we live long enough to share the information with the others."

"Me too." Darek knelt beside Astraea and checked on Cylus. "This isn't good."

"I know," Astraea said. She looked back to the entrance. "Where's Zephyr?"

"She's gone to check something. She said she'll be right back."

"Gone where?"

"I don't know. She said something about Mimics not seeing very well in the dark, and then flew off. I think she might be doing a patrol to make sure more aren't coming after us."

"Hand me my bow," Render said weakly. "We have to be prepared for more."

"You're not moving!" Astraea said. "You lost a lot of blood. Just stay still for a bit. I'll watch the cave."

Darek reached for his bow, loaded an arrow, and pointed it at the entrance of the cave. "You take care of Cylus. I'll keep watch."

As the time passed, the two unconscious snakes in Astraea's lap stirred. "I'm so sorry I did that to you," she said to them. She expected them to leave her after what she'd done. Instead they slowly made it up to her neck and settled down. This was the best thing they could have done to ease her guilt.

They soon heard movement outside the cave. "It's just me. Don't panic," Zephyr called. She trotted in. "All right, I've got good news and bad news. What do you want first?"

"Bad news," Darek said.

"There is a Mimic camp not far from here, back in the direction we came from. It's inside the jungle right before the beach starts. So it was Mimics and Shadow Titans that Cylus was feeling. Probably waiting for us to lead them to the snakes."

"Which we did," Astraea said glumly.

"True," Zephyr said. "There are about six or

seven Mimics left there and a few Shadow Titans."

"So what's the good news?" Render asked.

Zephyr looked at him. "That you three are alive."

"That's the best news," Astraea agreed.

"And," Zephyr continued, "the Mimics have a campfire."

Astraea frowned. "I don't understand. Why is that good news?"

"Fire!" Darek said; then he grasped the back of his head. "Ouch! Remind me not to get excited." He looked at Cylus, then back to Astraea. "Fire is very good news. The jungle around here is too wet for us to make our own fire. I saw a couple of torches on the beach, but they were extinguished."

"They were from the Mimics," Zephyr said. "But the ocean monster put them out when it got them. The melting Mimic put out its torch too. But there are torches and a big fire in their camp."

"That's great." Darek said. "All we have to do is sneak in there and light one of them and bring it back here. Then we can save Cylus."

Astraea shook her head. "I don't think I'm understanding. What does fire have to do with saving Cylus?"

"We'll use the fire to seal Cylus's wounds closed so he doesn't bleed to death," Darek said. "My father told me that's how they used to treat wounds on the battlegrounds."

Astraea finally understood. "So fire could save his life?"

"Yes," Darek agreed.

Astraea looked over at Zephyr. "What are we waiting for? If Cylus needs fire, let's go get him some."

15

RENDER WAS TOO WEAK TO JOIN THEM BUT offered to stay with Cylus and keep pressure on his wounds.

"Hopefully we won't be long," Darek said.

"Be careful," Render called. "Those Shadow Titans are fierce warriors. I never imagined they could be so strong."

"We will be," Astraea said. She was back on Zephyr, and as they headed out of the cave, she looked over at Darek. "Are you all right to go? You look almost as pale as Cylus and Render."

"Cylus, Render, and I have been friends all our lives," Darek said. "Just like you and Zephyr. There is nothing I won't do to save them. Even with this headache, if I must march into their camp and fight all the Shadow Titans, I will."

Astraea looked at Zephyr and nodded. "Me too."

"And me," Zephyr agreed.

They crossed the beach, walking past the stationary Shadow Titans. Astraea looked at the tall, dark, terrifying fighters. They looked like black marble statues standing in the sand. "Zephyr, stop. I have an idea." She called to the centaur, "Darek, wait . . ."

Darek was several paces ahead and picking up one of the Mimic's extinguished torches. "If you don't want to come, I understand. But I'm going to the Mimic camp to light this torch."

"It's not that. I have an idea." Astraea briefly explained what she and Zephyr learned from the Mimic about the metal controller for the Shadow Titans. "I pulled the Mimic's controller out of the goo. It should still be in the sand if we can find it."

They made their way over to the puddle of dead Mimic. After a bit of searching, Darek found the controller and cleaned it off. He handed it to Astraea. "How does it work?"

"I'm not completely sure." Astraea inspected the small silver cylinder. There was a button on the side. At first she did as the Mimic had done, putting it up to her mouth and saying, "Shadow Titans, turn around." But nothing happened. Then she pressed the button and repeated the command. Four Shadow Titans on the beach turned.

Darek yelped and raised his bow at the Shadows.

"Darek, you idiot!" Zephyr said. "You heard Astraea tell them to turn around. She controls them." She looked at Astraea. "I think that Shadow Titan hit him harder than we realized."

Darek lowered his bow. "Uh, sorry. It was a reflex."

"It's a good one," Astraea said. "But this time, I'm controlling them." She spoke into the controller again. "Shadow Titans, stand on one foot."

Immediately the four Shadow Titans stood on one foot.

"This is perfect!" Darek said as he trotted around the four Shadow Titans. "We control these warriors." He pointed at an unmoving Shadow standing farther away. "What's wrong with this one?"

"Maybe the controller only works on a few," Zephyr

suggested. "Those other Shadows must work with a different one. The trouble is, the Mimics were swallowed by that giant ocean creature."

"Maybe it didn't get their controllers." Darek trotted closer to the shore and started to search. "Here!" he cried excitedly. "I found another one!"

Darek did as Astraea had done and managed to get four more Shadow Titans working. There were three left unmoving. After a full search, they couldn't find their controller.

"At least we have eight fighters now," Darek said. "Wait here. I'm going to take my four back to the cave. I'll show Render how to use this controller in case the Mimics or Shadow Titans get past us and come after them."

Darek spoke into the controller and ordered his four Shadow Titans to follow him. While he was gone, Astraea sat on Zephyr, gazing out over the water of the alien world. "This has all gone wrong, hasn't it? My broken leg, you nearly dying from Lergo's bite, and now Cylus and Render. If we're not careful, we won't survive this world long enough to get the snakes back to Jupiter."

Zephyr nodded. "I miss the days when all you and I had to do was think about how to have fun. Your mom and dad were home. I had my little house with my parents in the stable. We didn't know anything about Mimics. Shadow Titans were just scary fighters from the past." She sighed. "It feels like such a long time ago. I wonder if we'll ever get back to that life."

"I sure hope so," Astraea agreed. "I never imagined that we'd ever have to fight—or think about war or even dying." She looked back at the cave. "But now I'm terrified we won't be able to save Cylus."

"Me too," Zephyr agreed.

Darek returned a few minutes later. "Render nearly passed out when I walked in there with the Shadow Titans. But he's all right now. I showed him how to use the controller." He looked toward the trees. "We'd better get going. Cylus isn't good."

Astraea ordered the Shadow Titans to lead them to the Mimic camp. Just before they entered the jungle, Zephyr looked over at the centaur. "Darek, do you think your arrows still have Nesso's venom on them?"

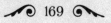

Darek shrugged. "I hope so, but they got wet when I was in the water with you. It might have washed off. Why?"

"You know why," Zephyr said.

Astraea looked down on Zephyr. "You think we're going to have to fight the Mimics to get to their fire."

"I don't think—I know," Zephyr said. "If they are linked, and we pretty much know they are, by now they'll know the others are dead and that we did it. They might even be moving against us right now. We have to be ready to fight."

Darek pulled two arrows out of his quiver and handed them to Astraea. "If the Mimics try to touch you or Zephyr, stab them with these. If they still have venom, they should work."

Astraea accepted the arrows. Then, as a precaution, she held up the controller. "Shadow Titans, stop." When they did, she continued. "When we enter the camp, if anyone tries to hurt us, you will defend us. Even if someone else gives you a command not to. You will do only as I say. Raise your right hand if you understand."

The four Shadow Titans raised their hands.

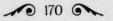

"Thank you," Astraea said into the controller. "You may lower your hands and proceed." Immediately the Shadow Titans started to walk again.

Zephyr looked up at Astraea. "Do you think that will work?"

"I sure hope so," Astraea said. "We need all the help we can get. Even if it's from Shadow Titans."

They stopped talking and entered the trees. Without the moonlight showing overhead, the jungle was dark. Almost too dark for Astraea to see. Titans had excellent night vision, but this was testing it.

Darek took the lead and treaded carefully through the trees. He held up his hand to stop them. Astraea whispered into the controller, "Shadows, stop." The four large Shadow Titans stopped and stood still.

They listened to the sounds of the jungle. Once they got used to all the natural calls of wildlife, they realized they weren't hearing anything else moving through the trees. Darek nodded and motioned them forward again.

It wasn't long before they saw a glow in the distance. Walking a bit farther, Astraea was stunned to see how close the Mimic camp was to the beach. She quietly ordered the Shadow Titans to stop again.

"They were right behind us," she whispered to Darek.

He nodded. Then he handed the unlit torch to Astraea. "Light this as soon as you can and get it back to Render. Don't wait for me."

Astraea shook her head. "Oh no. We stick together. We've got our Shadows. If there's a fight, we fight together. No running or flying away."

Darek looked exasperated, but finally he nodded. "Fine, but stay behind me."

"Ahem," Zephyr said softly. "Are you telling us to stay behind because we're girls and you don't think we can fight as well as you? Is that what you're suggesting?"

"No—well—yes," Darek finally admitted. "But I've been trained to fight since I was little. All centaurs—boys and girls—are. How much training have you had?"

"All right, not a lot," Zephyr admitted. "But I have a temper and I like to stomp things. I did bring down a Shadow Titan in the cave, and I knocked Cylus down at Arcadia."

Darek nodded. "Great, if I need someone stomped,

 172

I'll send them to you. But for now, do as I say and stay behind me."

Astraea remained silent. She also resented being told to stay behind the centaur, but at the same time, Darek was right. He had training, and they didn't. But she resolved to change that. When this was over, she was going to learn to fight like a centaur.

Darek crept closer to the clearing that had been made for the Mimic camp. Astraea lay down along Zephyr's back and peered through the trees.

Up ahead she saw what Zephyr had seen from the air—seven Mimics were standing around a campfire. They each had a container of the flattened animals beside them and were steadily cramming whole animals into their horrifying mouths.

Astraea remembered Jake telling her that Tryn had turned a different shade of silver when he'd seen them eat. Astraea now understood.

"That is disgusting," Zephyr said softly.

"Yes, but it's also great," Darek said. "If this is all of them, they're in the one area." He pulled several arrows out of his quiver and stuck them in the ground beside him for easy reach. Then he loaded an arrow into his bow. "If the venom is still good, I should be able to get most of them before they find us." He looked back at Astraea. "This is going to be fast and ugly. The moment I fire the arrow, they might figure out which direction it came from, so get ready to move and keep moving. We'll try to confuse them. When I call 'now,' I want you to order the Shadows to attack."

Astraea listened to his instructions and nodded.

This was real.

This was war.

16

DAREK RAISED HIS BOW, STOLE ONE MORE look back at Astraea and Zephyr, and nodded. He released the first arrow. It shot into the camp and then vanished.

"You missed," Zephyr said softly.

"No, I didn't," Darek said. "It passed right through the leg of the one closest to us. But I don't think it felt it."

"Then the venom's not working," Astraea said. The words were just out of her mouth when the Mimic started to gurgle and melt. "Forget what I said. It's working."

As the Mimic melted, the others in the group turned

and tried to look around. Their squinting eyes and uncertain body movements confirmed what Astraea suspected. The Mimics couldn't see well in the dark. Two of them put controllers to their huge mouths and gave a command. Instantly the Shadow Titans moved, forming a protective wall around them.

"Now!" Darek whispered. "Send in our Shadows to get theirs away from the Mimics!"

Astraea commanded her Shadow Titans to charge in and fight the Shadows protecting the Mimics. Instantly her four drew their swords and charged into the camp, taking on the Shadow Titans protecting the Mimics.

The sound of clanging swords filled the air as Shadow Titan fought Shadow Titan. The Mimics huddled together, blindly sending out tendrils in all directions, hoping to touch their attackers.

Astraea clutched the torch, ready to move when the way was clear, while Darek picked up another arrow and loaded his bow. When there was a free shot, he took it, and another Mimic went down.

The fight around the campfire was a terrifying sight as the Shadow Titans fought and the Mimics continued to cast their tendrils in all directions to try to hit them. All directions but one.

"Zeph, I've got another idea," Astraea said. "We can get them from the air. Look, they're not shooting their tendrils up. Just around."

"That's until we attack from above," Zephyr said. "Then they will."

"Maybe, but we can get one or two before they do. All we have to do is graze them with the arrow."

Darek was still waiting for his next clear shot. But with the Shadow Titans fighting all around the Mimics, it was difficult. "That's a good idea," he said. He handed several more arrows to Astraea. "You've got the two I gave you. Take these as well. Head back to the beach and then launch from there. We don't want to give this location away."

"You're actually considering this?" Zephyr whispered.

Astraea nodded. "We don't stand a chance in there. Not with those Shadows going at it and the Mimics shooting their tendrils. We need fire to save Cylus. There's no other way."

Zephyr snorted. "You two are going to be the

death of me." She turned quietly and headed back through the jungle toward the beach.

When they were free of the trees, Zephyr stopped. "I can't believe we're doing this. We're actually *attacking* Mimics!"

"There's no other way. Darek is great with his bow, but it's difficult for him to get a clear shot. It will be sunrise soon. It's better if we do this in the dark."

Zephyr snorted and started to run. "Well, if we're going to do it, let's do it. But for the record, I think it's a bad idea!"

She launched into the air, then turned back toward the Mimic camp. They flew over it and saw that Darek had managed to bring down another Mimic. There were only four left.

"Get ready," Zephyr called. "I'm going to fly in close. Throw your arrows at them and see if you can hit them."

Astraea felt the nerves bunch in her stomach. She clutched three arrows tightly in her hand. Just as Zephyr swooped down on the camp again, she threw them as hard as she could at the group of Mimics.

Before Astraea could see if she hit her targets,

Zephyr was veering away. When they turned in the sky and passed over the camp again, Astraea saw that two of her three arrows had struck Mimics.

"Zeph, it worked!" Astraea cheered. "We got two of them!"

"How many arrows do you have left?" Zephyr called.

"Four."

"Four arrows and two Mimics, that should work." Zephyr said. "Get ready. I'm going back in."

Astraea prepared to throw the arrows the way she had last time. But when Zephyr started her dive toward the remaining two Mimics, a tendril shot out from one of them and wrapped around Zephyr's front hoof. She gasped and then collapsed, falling uncontrolled to the ground.

Astraea was thrown free of Zephyr and landed hard on her broken leg. She cried in agony as the bones in her leg snapped apart again.

With the wind knocked out of her, Astraea was barely aware of the two Mimics moving around the fighting Shadow Titans and coming toward her.

"So, Titan spawn," one of them called. "You

 179

believed you could defeat us! So many have tried, but none succeeded."

Astraea was in too much pain to speak as she tried to drag herself away from the advancing Mimics. Her arrows and the Shadow controller were scattered on the ground several feet away. But they may as well have been a world away.

The two Mimics looked at each other. "I am going to enjoy this," one said as it reached out to touch Astraea. "But you, spawn, you definitely will not."

Just as the Mimic's hand reached for Astraea, one of the snakes at her neck sprang forward and bit the Mimic's wrist. The creature stumbled back with the snake still dangling from it.

"Noooo . . . ," it slurred as it started to melt.

The final Mimic watched its companion melt. Then it turned its bulbous head back to Astraea. "That will be the last of my kind that you kill."

"No, it won't," Darek called as he charged forward with his bow raised. He released his poison arrow and shot it through the Mimic. "This is just the start!"

17

TRYN THREW HIMSELF TO THE GROUND and started to uncover Pegasus. "Jake, help me!"

Jake worked at the stallion's head and pushed away all the vines, while Tryn uncovered his torso and wings. Before long, all of Pegasus was exposed. His once-white coat was filthy and covered in dead leaves and mud. His eyes were shut, and he wasn't breathing.

Tryn's voice caught in his throat. "Pegasus is dead. Those monsters killed him." Tears rimmed his eyes as he fell across Pegasus's body.

"Jake, put me down on the big white thing," Nesso hissed softly.

"He's dead, Nesso," Jake said softly.

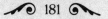

"I don't think ssso. I ssstill sssee heat from hisss forccce. It isss fading, but it isss there."

"Tryn," Jake said excitedly. "Nesso thinks he may not be dead!"

Tryn rose and pressed his head tightly against the stallion's chest. After a moment, he gasped. "There is a heartbeat! It's faint and it's slow, but it's there! We've got to get him to Arious. She'll know how to save him."

"How are we supposed to move him?" Jake cried. "Tryn, you're really strong. But look at the size of him. There's no way you could lift him, and I'd be lucky to be able to lift a leg."

Tryn stood up and started to run. "Stay with him," he called. "I'll be right back."

"Where are you going?"

There was no answer as Tryn vanished into the trees.

Brue was rubbing Pegasus gently as Jake sat on the ground beside the fallen stallion. "Just hold on there, boy," he said, stroking the stallion's face. "We'll get you some help real soon."

 182

As he waited, he kept speaking, but he wasn't sure if it was for Pegasus or for himself. "I know Zephyr, and she looks an awful lot like you. She's been hurt too. We came here to get you guys so you could help her." He sighed heavily. "Those Mimics are sure causing a lot of trouble. But don't you worry. We'll go to their world and get Emily back."

At the mention of Emily's name, Pegasus's breath caught. Then it became weak again. "That's right, Pegasus. We'll rescue Emily. Tryn has told me all about her. How you two are always together. I'm really looking forward to meeting her. And Riza, too. I hear she's beautiful."

After what seemed an eternity, there was loud rustling in the trees again. Tryn crashed through and ran over to them. He knelt beside Pegasus and pressed a silver vial to the stallion's neck.

"What's that?" Jake asked.

"I haven't a clue," Tryn said. "It's some kind of injection. Arious was talking too quickly, and most of what she said didn't make sense. But she produced this and said I had to get it into Pegasus immediately."

"Okay, you got it into him," Jake said. When there was no change, he shrugged. "Now what?"

Tryn sat back on his heels. "I don't know. Arious said it should restore some of the energy that's been drained out of him."

"Did she say how long it would take?"

Tryn shook his head. "He's very weak. It will take some time."

Jake and Tryn settled down beside Pegasus to wait. While they did, Tryn stroked the stallion. "When I was a child, Pegasus told me the story of how he and Emily met. I was reminded of that when Zephyr collapsed. It felt like history was repeating itself."

Jake shook his head. "Nope, I haven't got a clue what you're talking about."

"When Zephyr collapsed and Astraea crawled over to her, she was lying beside Zephyr with her broken leg in a splint."

"Yes," Jake said. "So?"

"So, not long after Emily met Pegasus in New York City, they were both wounded. Emily's leg had been hurt by a Nirad and Pegasus had been shot by the CRU. Pegasus told me that Emily lay with him while the CRU agents interrogated her. In doing that, she saved his life."

Jake started to nod. "Astraea has a hurt leg just like Emily had, and she was stroking Zephyr just like Emily stroked Pegasus."

"Exactly," Tryn said. "It doesn't really mean anything, but I saw the bond between them. Astraea will be destroyed if anything happens to Zephyr."

"Nothing is going to happen to Zephyr," Jake said. "Pegasus will recover, and then we'll get the ambrosia to her."

As they spoke, the stallion's breathing grew stronger. "I think it's working," Tryn said. "Pegasus, it's me, Trynulus. We're here. Try to wake up."

One of the stallion's wings fluttered.

"He moved!" Jake cried. "Did you see that? His wing moved!"

Tryn nodded. "That's it, Pegasus. Come back to us. We need you."

"Yeah, Zephyr needs you too!" Jake added.

Little by little, Pegasus started to wake. He was soon moving a hoof, then another wing. He nickered weakly.

 185

Tryn rose and pulled Jake up. "He told us to stand back. I think he's going to try to get up."

Jake sighed heavily and stood up. "I'd hoped I could understand him since he's older than Zephyr and has been hanging around with Emily. But all I heard was a neigh."

Tryn stepped back. "Pegasus cannot speak English. Emily could understand him only once she became a Xan. Before then she was just like you. Humans can't understand him."

It took several more minutes before Pegasus was strong enough to climb to his feet. Even then he needed Tryn's help to stay up.

"Arious said to bring you down to her when you are strong enough," Tryn explained.

Pegasus's head was low, and he nickered again. Tryn looked at Jake. "He's asked us to help get him there."

Jake, Tryn, and Brue struggled to assist the large stallion through the jungle and into the clearing. By the time they reached the Temple of Arious, Pegasus had recovered a bit more and was able to walk on his own, though he was very weak and slow.

Getting into the temple was fairly easy. However, the stairs leading down to the supercomputer were a different matter completely. As Brue was too large to fit in the stairwell and Jake wasn't strong enough to help hold him, it took all Tryn's considerable strength to keep Pegasus from falling down the stairs. He stood in front of the stallion and braced him with each step.

Tryn was out of breath and panting heavily when they finally reached the lower level. Pegasus nickered softly.

"You've very welcome," Tryn panted.

They made their way down the long corridor and found the door to Arious still open. Tryn and Jake escorted Pegasus in.

"Pegasus," Arious said. "I am so pleased to see you! Come closer."

Pegasus clopped closer to the consul. A small door opened on the mainframe, and a tiny speck of red light appeared and started to spin around Pegasus.

"That's Arious Minor," Tryn explained. "It's the mobile version of Arious Major."

When the light finished, it went back into the

mainframe, and Arious said, "Tryn and Jake, please go outside and leave Pegasus with me. He requires additional treatment."

"We can help," Tryn said.

"Yes, you can," Arious said. "You help by going home and telling your family and the other Rheans what has happened. We are going to need their help, along with all the Olympians and Titans, to take on the Mimics."

Jake shook his head. "No! We have to go back to help Zephyr. She's dying."

"I am so sorry, Jake," Arious responded. "But informing the Rheans is critical to combating the Mimics. It won't take long. Then you can take the ambrosia to Zephyr."

"But my people are not warriors," Tryn said.

"Very true," Arious agreed. "And I am not suggesting they fight. We will need help with weapons, caring for wounded, and many other things."

"And milking the snakes," Jake offered.

"Indeed," Arious agreed. "They should at least be notified so they can decide their involvement. The Mimics pose a great threat to them as well. I have no

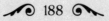

doubt they have their eyes set on Xanadu now that the Xan are gone."

"I understand," Tryn said. He went up to Pegasus and patted his neck. "I hope you feel better soon, Pegasus. Zephyr needs your help, and we have to save Emily and Riza."

Pegasus pressed his head to Tryn and then looked over at Jake and nickered. As they left, Jake asked, "What did he say?"

Tryn smiled. "He thanked us both and says he owes us a debt. Though the debt is to Brue, really. I wouldn't be surprised if she was the one who buried him, to hide him from the Mimics." Tryn paused. "I guess she really is the Mother of the Jungle. She cares for everyone and everything."

Jake nodded. "She sure does. I just hope Pegasus recovers soon. I hate leaving Zephyr alone this long."

"Me too," Tryn said.

They exited the temple and picked up their skateboards. "Come on," Tryn said as he climbed onto his. "It's time you met my family."

18

THE SUN WAS UP, AND THE HEAT OF THE day was already brutal in the Mimic camp. Astraea was lying beside Zephyr where she'd fallen out of the sky after the Mimic's touch.

Zephyr moaned and started to awaken. "Oh, my head is killing me again. I told you this was a bad idea." She looked around. "What happened?"

"You were hit by a Mimic tendril and then you kinda crashed."

"Crashed?" Zephyr cried. "I have never crashed in my life. Not even when I was young and learning to fly."

Astraea chuckled. "I was there, Zeph, remember? You crashed plenty of times."

"Maybe, but it was in water. That was different. I've never crashed on land and hurt myself."

"Well, you crashed spectacularly last night," Astraea said. "I'm fine by the way. Thanks for asking."

Zephyr looked over at her. "Are you all right?"

Astraea was trying very hard not to let the pain from her leg show. "If you're asking if my leg is broken again, the answer is yes."

"I'm so sorry," Zephyr said. "But it was your idea to play hero and try to fight the Mimics from the sky."

"And it worked, too," Astraea said. "They're all gone."

"Really? But we're still in their camp?"

Astraea nodded. "We couldn't go back to the cave. When Darek took the torch back to help Cylus, he found the tide coming in. Apparently, it floods completely during high tide."

"The cave is flooded?" Zephyr panicked. "We have to get Cylus and Render out of there!"

"Calm down. It's already been done." Astraea pointed across the camp to where Darek was helping Render and Cylus. "See? They're safe."

"How long was I out?" Zephyr cried.

"Quite a while," Astraea said. "The Mimic held on to your leg a long time. Then you hit your head. So you were kind of knocked out twice."

"No wonder my head is pounding so much." Zephyr moaned. "But how did you get Cylus here?"

"Once all the Mimics were gone, Darek found the controllers and commanded the Shadow Titans to stop fighting. A couple were too damaged to work again, but most of the others were all right. They repaired themselves and were able to carry Cylus here. We now have twelve working Shadow Titans under our control. They've circled the camp."

Zephyr was still looking at the centaurs. "How is Cylus?"

"Not good," Astraea responded. "Darek managed to seal his wounds, but he's lost so much blood. He needs ambrosia."

"We all do," Zephyr said. She continued to look around and neighed in surprise at the sea of snakes surrounding them. "How did you get all the snakes here?"

"We didn't. They followed the centaurs. I guess they realize it's safer to stay with us than in the cave."

"I'm not so sure about that," Zephyr said.

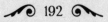

"Sure about what?" Darek asked.

"Keeping the snakes here in this camp. The Mimics must know what's happened by now. They're sure to send more."

"And we're ready for them," Darek said. "We've got our Shadow Titans surrounding the camp, and the snakes are here with us. The Mimics would have to be insane to try to get us. If we can just hold out until Jake and Tryn get back, we'll be fine."

19

JAKE FOLLOWED BEHIND TRYN FOR WHAT felt like half a day. The Rhean settlement was farther away from the Temple of Arious than he'd expected.

"Tryn, why is your home so far from Arious? I thought you would be closer."

Tryn shook his head. "No. Riza told us we could settle anywhere we wanted, and the elders chose this place. It is far enough away from Arious that we can govern ourselves. There are many other regions and species that are refugees from disaster just like we were. Some don't even know that they've been brought here. So even though Riza and Emily visit regularly, most of the Rheans won't leave our area until our

world is ready for us to return." Tryn pointed up at the sky.

Jake looked up and saw the shadow of an immense red moon. Back in LA he used to love it when he could sometimes see the moon during the day while the sun was out. But this moon was a lot bigger and brighter, and it appeared to be close.

"Whoa, what is that?" Jake asked.

"Our home world, Rhean," Tryn said. "Riza and Emily brought it here from across the universe when our sun went supernova."

"They what?" Jake choked. He nearly stumbled off his board. But the board wouldn't let him fall and righted him again. "Are you telling me that two people actually brought an entire planet here?"

"Not people—Xan. Yes, they did," Tryn said. "That's how powerful they are."

Jake was studying the outline of the large planet orbiting Xanadu. He could hardly believe that it was once across the universe. "So you can't live there?"

"Not yet. Rhean is still establishing a stable orbit, atmosphere, and environment. When it's ready, my people are planning to move back. For now we live here. I was born here, so I would prefer to stay on Xanadu. It's my real home."

Jake frowned again. "But if Riza and Emily were powerful enough to bring it here, couldn't they just, you know, snap their fingers and make it livable?"

"They could, but Riza's not like that. She believes in letting it happen naturally. And it is happening, but slowly. When it's ready, the New Rhean will be genuine, and not artificially created."

"That is awesome," Jake said, gazing up at the red planet. "I hope I get a chance to see it someday."

"Me too," Tryn agreed. "But for now our region will have to do. There it is."

Jake could hardly believe what he was seeing. Up ahead, the jungle ended on a glistening shore. Then there was a wide river, and across the river stood a beautiful glistening city that went on as far as his eyes could see. There were tall buildings with slanted roofs lining busy streets. There were also what looked like a lot of parks, as trees grew around the buildings. A long suspension bridge crossed over the river and connected the city to the jungle, but there were no people or vehicles on the bridge as they approached.

"Wow," Jake breathed. "This place reminds me of Los Angeles. But with cleaner air."

They crossed over the water and entered the sky over the city. Tryn directed his skateboard toward the outskirts of the city. Here the buildings weren't so tall and there were more trees, grasslands, and ponds. The streets were wide and homes lined either side.

To Jake it looked like an American neighborhood. At least it did until he saw a group of silver-skinned people looking up at them curiously.

"There's my house," Tryn said excitedly. "And my dad and Fiisha!"

Tryn maneuvered his skateboard until he touched down in the spacious backyard of one of the homes. A tall man was picking fruit off a tree. Beside him a large animal covered in mottled gray fur was waiting to eat any dropped fruit. It was the same animal Jake had seen in one of Tryn's photographs the first night he'd met him. It looked even stranger in real life—like a hyena crossed with a giraffe and a hippo. The animal saw Tryn first and started to grunt and jump around.

"What is it, Fiisha?" the man asked. He turned, and his face lit up. "Tryn!"

 197

"Dad!" Tryn jumped off his board, ran up to his father, and embraced him tightly.

This was the most excited Jake had ever seen Tryn—though he had changed a lot since they'd first met.

"What are you doing here?" his father asked.

Jake touched down and looked at the man Tryn had told him was from Earth and had once been a CRU agent. His hair was long, curly, and black, and his blue eyes twinkled with joy as he embraced his son. Jake noticed that he spoke with a thick English accent.

"Who is this?" Tryn's father asked as he turned to Jake.

"Dad, this is Jake. He's from Los Angeles." Tryn went down on his knees to play with the excited animal. "He was found on Titus." He looked up at Jake. "Jake, this is my father."

Jake offered his hand. "Nice to meet you, Mister . . . ?"

"Just call me Ben," he said as he shook Jake's hand. "What does Tryn mean you were 'found on Titus'?"

Tryn rose and became serious. "Dad, there's big trouble. You must call the elders together. We're all in terrible danger. Titus has been invaded. Jupiter and the council are hiding on Earth, and Riza and Emily have been abducted from here. The Mimics are going to kill them and take over the universe."

"What?" Ben said. "Mimics? What are you talking about?"

"Let's go inside," Tryn said. "I want to see Mom and Triana, and then we have to talk."

When Tryn had told Jake he had a little sister, Jake had never imagined that he meant a beautiful girl just a year younger than him. Triana was bright and outgoing and very excited to meet him. In appearance she was much like Tryn, with dark hair and deep blue eyes with bright sliver flecks. Unlike Tryn, she had double dimples in her silver cheeks and asked a thousand questions.

Tryn's mother was stunning with her silver skin and blue hair. When Tryn first saw her, they started speaking the language of the Rheans, which to Jake was just a lot of excited squeaks, clicks, and grunts.

Tryn pulled away from his mother and brought

her closer to Jake. "This is Jake." Then he introduced his mother. "Jake, this is my mom."

Ben stood beside his wife. "You won't be able to pronounce her name any more than I can, so in English, we call her Tara."

"It's nice to meet you, Tara," Jake said.

"And it is lovely to meet you," Tara said with a strong accent that ended with a click at the end of the sentence.

"Come, sit," Ben said. "Tell us everything."

They all sat around a dining table as Jake and Tryn explained what they'd been through, from Jake's first appearance on Titus to going to Nesso's world and then finding Pegasus near death.

"We never knew," Ben said. "No one reached out to us here."

"I don't think they could," Tryn said. "From what I gather, the attack was fast. The Mimics took everyone."

"Perhaps it was to stop them from warning us or seeking our help," Tara suggested.

While they spoke, Jake asked permission to release the snakes from his pack. They were then settled on the table and joined Nesso in eating some ambrosia.

"So, you can communicate with Nesso, and their venom is deadly to the Mimics?" Tara asked as she studied the small snakes drinking nectar and eating ambrosia.

"We couldn't communicate at first," Jake said. "It was only after she bit me."

"Which wasss after you hit me," Nesso added, spitting out crumbs as she hissed. *"Tell them the truth."*

Jake sighed and glared at Nesso. "Okay. Nesso bit me only after I *accidentally* hit her while going through my pack."

"Thank you," Nesso hissed.

"You're welcome." Jake chuckled and explained their exchange. "After the bite, it kinda connected us," he continued. "I can't understand other snakes and they can't understand me, but Nesso works as a translator."

"And yes," Tryn added. "When Nesso bites the Mimics, or even if we put her venom on a weapon and cut the Mimics, they don't just die. They actually melt."

Tryn's mother gasped. "Trynulus, have you fought? Killed?"

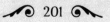

"Fought, yes. Killed, no, not yet." Tryn lowered his head. "Forgive me, Mother, but I will kill the Mimics. I know it will shame our family, but you would understand if you saw them and what they are doing. We have spoken to them. They see us as nothing more than obstacles to their quest. They won't engage with us; they won't negotiate. They just want our worlds and will kill us all to get them."

His mother became silent. Finally she looked at her husband. "Then we fight."

"What?" Ben cried. "But that goes against everything the Rheans stand for."

"No, we stand for peace and have known only peace because we have avoided conflict through negotiation. But if these creatures won't negotiate, if they have tried to kill my son and have taken our two beloved Xan, then I will fight. It will be distasteful, but we will do it."

"You might not have to," Jake said. "Arious said that we will need more than fighters. We need people to make weapons, treat the wounded, and milk the snakes of venom."

"I want to fight with Tryn and Jake," Triana said. "They wounded Pegasus."

Jake saw the same intensity in Triana's eyes that he often saw in Tryn's. But Tryn never looked so pretty doing it.

"There will be no fighting for you, young lady," Ben said. "There will be plenty of other jobs that are just as important." He considered a moment and then nodded. "All right, here's the plan. . . ."

Tryn looked at Jake. "I told you he was a CRU agent. He used to be called Agent B when he was back on Earth."

"I'm not a CRU agent anymore," Ben said. "But I still have all my training and experience—and I have a family and friends I care for deeply. Emily and I went through a lot in the past. I won't let those creatures harm her now."

Tara looked up at her husband. "So, what do we do?"

Ben started. "Tara, I want you to go to the Rhean elders and tell them what has happened." He looked at Tryn. "You linked with Arious, right? She has seen everything?"

Tryn nodded. "She already knew about them. They are old enemies of the Xan and used to take a Xan every thousand years. So Arious knows more about them than we do."

"Fine, I think Rhean groups should be gathered to go to Arious. They must link with her to see what we're up against." He looked at Tryn and Jake. "I want you two to go back to Nesso's world. Help your team gather as many snakes as you can and bring them here. Then it's back to Earth to collect the Olympians and Titans hiding there. Your mother and I will organize things here and start drawing the venom from these snakes."

Tryn stood. "What about Pegasus?"

"Arious will take care of Pegasus," Tara said. "Though I will go and check on him."

A whinny startled them all. Jake turned and saw Pegasus entering the room. The stallion was the spitting image of Zephyr, if not a bit taller. He still looked unsteady and was smudged with dirt, but his head was high and his eyes bright.

"Pegasus!" Triana squealed. She ran over to the stallion and threw her arms around his neck. "Tryn told me what happened. Are you all right?"

All Jake and Ben heard were knickers and whinnies,

but the Rheans nodded. Tryn looked at Jake. "Pegasus says he is recovered enough to come with us to help Zephyr."

"But you're still too weak," Tryn said back to the stallion. "Zomos is a dangerous place filled with immense creatures."

Pegasus's ears went back, and he whinnied and snorted.

Tryn lowered his head. "I'm sorry. I understand."

Tryn's mother explained to Jake and her husband, "Pegasus has linked with Arious and seen everything you have. He is insisting on going with you to help Zephyr, and then to Earth to gather the Olympians and Titans. He will not be stopped."

"Just as stubborn as ever, eh, Pegasus?" Ben said. "It reminds me of old times."

Pegasus nodded.

"All right," Ben continued. "You guys go to Zomos." He paused and looked at the snakes on the table. "Jake, Nesso's venom was only poisonous to the Mimics after she bit you?"

Jake nodded. "I don't know how it works, but it changed her somehow. She said she bit the one that took her from Zomos, but nothing happened. Now her venom is so deadly it melts them."

Ben nodded. "Then would you ask Nesso to ask her two friends to bite me? If those Mimics come back here, we'll need all the venom they can produce."

Nesso rose up and hissed to Jake. *"They will do it. But he mussst ssstrike them firssst or they won't bite."*

"They'll do it," Jake said. "But I should warn you, it really hurts, and I passed out. You'll also have to hit them to get them to bite you. But don't hurt them. They're very sweet; a tap will do."

"I wouldn't dream of harming them," Ben said. "Especially when they are so precious."

Tryn said to his mother, "Maybe you could analyze the venom and make more so we don't have to rely on the snakes."

"That's a very good idea," Tara said. "I will take some to Arious as well."

Ben rose and embraced Tryn. "Don't wait for me to wake up. You guys get moving. We'll take care of things here. Go save Zephyr and collect the Olympians from Earth. We'll meet you at the Temple of Arious. Please, be careful."

Tryn put his arms around his father. "We will. You be careful here, too. If the Mimics come back, dip anything you can in venom and use it. It will stop them."

"Understood," Ben said.

Jake was stunned when Tryn's mother and then sister hugged him as tightly as they did Tryn.

"Be careful and come back soon," Triana said. "I want to talk to you about Earth."

Jake blushed as Triana held him. "Um—er—sure. I'd really like that too."

Pegasus nickered impatiently.

"Yes, we're coming," Tryn said.

Ben reached over to tap the first snake, but Jake stopped him.

"Wait. Trust me, you'll want to sit down, or you'll fall down. That venom packs a punch and works fast."

Tryn's father took a seat and then tapped both snakes on the snout with a finger from each hand. The two snakes launched forward and bit him on the wrists. Ben's face contorted in pain and his breathing quickened as the venom shot up his arm. He looked up at his wife, gasped, and then passed out.

On the table, the two snakes were both unconscious. "Wow," Jake said, looking down at Nesso,
who was back around his neck. "You never said you
passed out too."

"I didn't know," Nesso responded.

Tryn's mother was checking his father's pulse.

"How is he?" Tryn asked nervously.

"His breathing and heart rate are up, but not danger-
ously so. He'll be fine. Go now and come back with
everyone as quickly as possible."

"We will," Tryn promised. He picked up his sack
of ambrosia and gave Fiisha a final pat on her hippo
head. He looked at Jake and Pegasus. "Grab your
ambrosia and nectar. Let's go."

20

ASTRAEA WANTED TO HELP CLEAR UP THE camp, but the pain in her leg was increasing. All she could do was rest on the bed of leaves that Darek set up for her and watch him and Zephyr work.

When they finished, Zephyr lay down beside Astraea and used her tail and wings to drive away the gathering of snakes that were encircling them. The largest snake, which had moved Cylus and Render into the cave, was right beside Astraea. She had named it Belis, and despite their lack of communication, the snake soon recognized and answered to the name. It continued to ask to be petted like an affectionate pet.

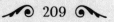

"I can't believe you actually named it," Zephyr complained.

"Why not?" Astraea said, stroking the snake. "Since I don't know it's real name, that seemed as good a one as any."

"Have you considered what we're going to do with all of them once this is over?"

Astraea shrugged. "We could bring them back here, or maybe some of them can stay with us on Titus. I think we should give them the choice. Nesso doesn't want to live here again. She wants to stay with Jake."

Zephyr snorted. "I don't think your kitten, Hiddles, will appreciate sharing your house with this enormous snake."

"She'll be fine." Astraea lay back in the leaves and shut her eyes. It had been a terrible night and she was exhausted and running out of energy. The lack of food was taking a heavy toll on all of them, leaving Cylus and Render unable to heal from their wounds.

As the long day passed slowly toward evening, Darek started to shout, "Cylus, Cylus!" He looked back to Astraea. "He's not breathing!"

"No!" Astraea cried as she dragged herself over to the centaurs. Render was so pale, he looked almost blue. But it was Cylus who had them all terrified.

She placed her head against his chest. "His heart is still beating—but it's so slow. Wait . . ." She looked up at Darek. "I think I heard him take a small breath."

Astraea sat up. "We're out of time. We can't wait for Tryn and Jake anymore." She reached for Cylus's hand and pulled off the Solar Stream ring he'd gotten from a dead Mimic and handed it to Darek.

"We have to use this to go back to Earth."

"But they don't have any ambrosia there," Zephyr said.

"No, but there was nectar. Even if we get a bit into him, it might save his life."

Darek had tears in his eyes as he nodded. "We have to try. Maybe someone there might know how to save him."

The centaur climbed to his feet. "What about the snakes? That was the whole point of coming here."

Astraea looked back at the large gathering of snakes. "They followed us here to the Mimic camp. Maybe they'll follow us into the Solar Stream."

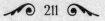 211

"You don't want to take all of them, do you?" Zephyr cried. "Please don't bring the big one."

"We don't have time to argue about this," Darek said. "Cylus and Render need help now. Let's just get the Shadow Titans moving and go!"

Astraea felt the pressure of time as she and Darek emptied several of the Mimics' food containers and started to put snakes inside. When the colorful snakes understood what was happening, they came forward to be loaded. After that, Astraea ordered the Shadow Titans to pick up the containers, while Darek ordered his own Shadows to lift Cylus. The centaur was limp in their arms, but for the moment, he was still alive.

Finally Darek helped Astraea onto Zephyr's back. She tried not to cry out when her leg was moved again, but she couldn't keep it in.

"That needs to be set soon," Zephyr warned. "You can't lose that leg. You must have nectar too."

"I'm all right," Astraea said through gritted teeth. "Cylus and Render are in more need than me." She held up the controller. "Shadow Titans, please follow us into the Solar Stream."

Darek was supporting Render, helping him stay

upright. He put on the ring and held it up. "Take us to Earth, Detroit, Michigan, Westward Junction, the Reynolds Steel plant at night."

The Solar Stream burst to life before them. Just as they were about to walk forward, a second Solar Stream opened, cutting across the first one with an explosive blast that sent sparks flying everywhere. The impact of the two Solar Streams' violent openings in the same place knocked everyone off their feet. Screams could be heard coming from within the blazing light.

Moments later, three Mimics crawled out of the sparking twin Solar Streams. Four Shadow Titans also managed to make it out, but the rest were sucked back into the swirling vortex and vanished from sight.

Astraea had been blasted off Zephyr's back and landed on the ground far from the opening. Darek and Render were thrown across the camp, and the Shadow Titans carrying Cylus were sprawled on the ground.

Moments later, both Solar Streams closed with loud snaps, leaving a strange, hushed silence after the ear-shattering roar.

The three Mimics climbed to their feet and looked around in bewilderment. When their eyes landed on the Titans, one of them raised a controller to its blubberous mouth. "Kill them all!"

The four Shadow Titans that had made it through the Solar Streams remained still. Seeing the failure, the remaining two Mimics raised their controllers and gave the same command. It worked, and the Shadow Titans charged forward.

Astraea reacted first. She pulled two controllers up to her mouth and pressed both buttons. "Shadows, stop the new Shadow Titans! Don't let them hurt us!"

Darek followed through with his controller. "Fight the newcomers!"

In just a few short hours, Astraea was witness to another terrifying Shadow Titan fight. This time, the Titan-controlled Shadows outnumbered the Mimic-controlled ones and were soon gaining the upper hand.

But despite their attempts to cut down the Mimics, the Shadow Titans' weapons were useless against them and cut through the creatures like a knife through butter, doing no damage at all.

But their attempts enraged the Mimics, and one of

them charged forward. "How dare you use our warriors!" He cast a tendril out to Darek.

The centaur was able to swat the first tendril away with his sword, but lack of food made his reactions slow and a second tendril made it through his defenses and caught hold of his back leg. Darek froze, and then collapsed.

"No!" Astraea cried.

Render, though badly wounded, tried to fight his way to Darek, but he was too weak to be effective and was soon downed by a Mimic's tendril.

With her leg broken, Astraea was unable to move, run, or fight. She could only watch in horror as the Mimics advanced on her.

Zephyr stood over Astraea and reared as the third Mimic came at them. It shot out a lethal tendril, which wrapped around Zephyr's front leg and knocked her down to the ground, unconscious.

"Zephyr!" Astraea howled. Instinctively, she caught hold of one of the snakes at her neck and threw it at the tendril holding on to Zephyr. When the snake struck, it bit into the tendril. The Mimic cried out and started to melt.

The two remaining Mimics saw their companion go down. "What have you done?" one of them howled. "You will suffer for that, Titan!"

It shot a tendril out at Astraea, but it never got close. Belis turned black and lunged forward, sinking its long fangs into the Mimic. Being a much larger snake, the venom must have been that much more potent, as the Mimic didn't so much melt as burst into a pool of goo.

There was only one Mimic left, when movement caught Astraea's attention. She looked up and saw Jake and Tryn flying over the trees and heading right to them. She gasped when she saw the most welcome sight in the world.

Pegasus was flying with them.

21

"JAKE, TRYN!" ASTRAEA CALLED, WAVING frantically at them.

Beside her, Belis slithered forward and attacked the remaining Mimic. With one bite, the hideous creature was defeated.

Astraea stared in stunned silence. Belis was as black as Lergo and somehow was immune to the Mimics and their residual goo. Lying in the puddle of dead Mimic, he was completely unaffected. Could it be true? Would Belis, Nesso, and all the snakes in the camp eventually grow into massive deadly snakes like Lergo?

The sounds of swords clashing broke Astraea

out of her thoughts as the Shadow Titans continued to fight. She gazed into the puddle of dead
Mimic closest to her and saw the small controller.
She reached for a stick to pull it free but had nothing to wipe it off.

"Jake or Tryn, get over here," she cried.

Jake was staring openmouthed at the fighting
Shadow Titans. He landed his skateboard on the
ground and ran up to her. "What's happening? Why
are they fighting each other?"

"Some of them are ours; the others just came from
the Solar Stream. Please, we must hurry. Do you see
that small metal cylinder in the dead Mimic? I really
need it."

Jake was too stunned to move, but Tryn arrived
and reached for some leaves. He picked up the controller and cleaned it off, then handed it to Astraea.
"What's it for?"

"It controls the Shadow Titans. I just hope this
is the one that works on them." Astraea pressed the
button and ordered the Shadow Titans to stop. The
four that came from the Solar Stream stopped, but
the Titan-controlled Shadows didn't. Astraea reached

for her own controllers and was able to call her original eight off. But that still left Darek's four Shadow Titans hacking at the stationary invaders.

"Darek has the other controller," she said, pointing at the unconscious centaur. "Find it, press the button, and order them to stop before they destroy them!"

"What do you mean stop them?" Jake cried. "Let them destroy each other!"

"No!" Astraea cried. "With these controllers, they become ours. We need them."

"She's right!" Tryn said. He dashed over to Darek and dragged the centaur away from the puddle of Mimic goo, then searched the area for the controller. When he found it, he picked it up, pressed the button, and commanded the Shadow Titans to stop.

The fight ended just as quickly as it started, and the Shadow Titans became still. In the aftermath, there were pieces of Shadow Titan armor scattered all over the place.

"Cylus is dying!" Astraea called. "He needs ambrosia and nectar—but it might be too late. Render's been badly hurt too!"

While Jake and Tryn checked on the centaurs, Pegasus examined Zephyr.

"How is she?" Astraea asked fearfully. "That Mimic got her good. She's so weak from Lergo's bite and lack of food. . . ."

"She is alive," Pegasus said. "Though I doubt she will be feeling very well when she wakes."

The stallion sniffed the puddle of Mimic goo.

"Be careful. Don't touch it!" Astraea warned. "That's what's left of the Mimics when they're melted by the snakes. That stuff is just as dangerous now as when they're alive."

Tryn and Jake were examining Cylus. "Oh, this is bad," Jake said.

Tryn pressed his head to Cylus's chest. "He's barely breathing." He reached into the bag he carried and pulled out a bottle of nectar. "We might be too late. He might not be able to drink it."

Pegasus trotted over. "Hold his head back and pour it slowly into his mouth. Even unconscious, we usually react to nectar and swallow. If he doesn't choke, we might still be able to save him."

Astraea dragged herself over and watched Tryn

struggle to hold Cylus up and his head back. "Now," he said to Jake. "Nice and slow, start to pour."

After almost half the bottle of nectar was gone, Pegasus said, "That should suffice. If he doesn't wake soon, I'm so sorry to say, he never will."

22

TRYN AND JAKE STOKED THE CAMPFIRE AS they all waited for the nectar to save Cylus's life. Each minute dragged on into an eternity, but still there was no change. Render responded quickly to the ambrosia and nectar treatment and was recovering.

Tryn and Jake set Astraea's leg again, and with the help of the ambrosia, she felt the bones knitting together. It wouldn't be long before she could walk again.

Tryn placed more logs on the fire and shook his head. "I never imagined two entrances to the Solar Stream could be opened in the same place at the same time. It must have been magnificent."

"Not the word I would use," Zephyr said.

"It was terrifying," Astraea added. Belis was still with her. He had returned to his normal colors and, after being cleaned off from the Mimic goo, wanted more attention.

"And noisy," Darek added. "Really, really noisy. Kind of like Jupiter's thunder bolts when he's really angry, but even louder."

"I just wonder what happened to the other Mimics and Shadow Titans that were sucked back into it," Darek mused aloud. "Were they destroyed when the two entrances collided, or were they sent back to where they came from?"

"There is one more option that I don't like to think about, but we must consider," Tryn said. "Since the two Solar Streams were open and you had already set your destination as Earth, it is not impossible to consider that they might have slipped into our Solar Stream and not theirs."

"You mean to Westward Junction?" Jake cried.

"That's exactly what I mean. But we won't know till we get back there," Tryn said. "We'll just get these snakes, Shadow Titans, and you guys to Xanadu and then Jake and I can check."

Zephyr looked at everyone. "What do you mean you and Jake can check? What about us?"

"Yes," Astraea agreed. "We're all going back to Earth."

"That is not a good idea," Tryn said. "First, you must take care of Cylus. So far he hasn't responded to the nectar. If anyone can save him, it will be Arious. And second, Earth is dangerous for you. It would be best for you all to go to Xanadu and let Jake and me collect Jupiter and the others from Earth and then meet you there."

"I don't like that idea one bit," Astraea said. "We've gone this far together. We should finish together."

Pegasus snorted. "I believe Trynulus has the right idea. It would not be wise for all of us to return to Earth to collect the others. We will be needed on Xanadu to work with the snakes and prepare for battle."

"But I wanted to see Earth again," Astraea said.

"And you will," Pegasus promised. "When this is over, I will ensure that Jupiter allows you all to visit there. Jake must return to his home, and I am sure you will want to go with him to make certain he gets there safely."

Jake leaned closer to Astraea. "What did he just say?"

Astraea crossed her arms over her chest. "He agrees with Tryn and you. We can't go back to Earth until we take you home."

"I'm sorry," Jake said. "But it really will be safer this time."

"That's easy for you to say—you live there," Astraea said. "I never get to go anywhere!"

Zephyr was eating a large slice of ambrosia and nearly choked. "Wh-what? What do you mean you never go anywhere? This horrible world is somewhere. Tartarus was somewhere, and you've already been to Earth. Now were going to Xanadu. How can you say you never go anywhere?"

"All right," Astraea said. "I've been a few places. I want to see more."

"And you will," Tryn said as he climbed to his feet. "Just not this time." He walked over to the Shadow Titans, which were now encircling the camp. The intact shadows had managed to repair the damage done to the others, so they were all intact again. He knocked on the chest of the nearest one. "They really do sound hollow." He tried to pull off a helmet, but it wouldn't move. "You're certain they won't come back to life?"

Astraea held up one of the controllers. "Not without this. But it seems that each controller works only four Shadows at a time."

Jake joined Tryn and inspected a large, dragon-like Shadow Titan. "I wonder if your mother will be able to figure them out. Maybe she can make some more for us to use."

"If we can control them, that would be good," said Tryn.

"No, it would not!" Pegasus snorted. "I have had more than my share of those monstrosities. The last thing we need is to create more. I am not overly comfortable having these ones here, let alone others."

"Pegasus doesn't like the idea," Tryn said to Jake as they returned to the fire.

Jake reached for another slice of ambrosia cake and handed a small piece up to Nesso, and they ate it together. "So," Jake started. "Nesso didn't have to bite me to be poisonous to the Mimics?"

Astraea nodded. "That's right. The snakes' venom is deadly without it."

Jake looked over to Tryn. "So your dad didn't have to be bitten."

"I guess not," Tryn said. "But at least he'll be able to talk to them the way you talk to Nesso."

"That issss the best part," Nesso hissed. *"Jussst like you and me, they have found a family with Tryn'sss father."*

"Very true," Jake agreed.

"Ugh . . . I think I ate too much," Zephyr moaned. "I feel sick."

"You can never have too much ambrosia," Pegasus said. "Especially after everything you have been through. You are all very lucky to be alive."

"Look who's talking," Zephyr shot back. "You were left for dead and buried on Xanadu!"

"I was buried by Brue, the Mother of the Jungle. She did it to protect me after those Mimics attacked us. Had she not pulled me away after I was touched, I am certain they would have killed me." He turned his white head to Jake and Tryn. "And if you had not found me, I might well have succumbed to my injuries."

"It was Brue who led us to you," Tryn said.

"Then I owe her much gratitude," Pegasus said.

Astraea listened to what happened on Xanadu in complete shock. She couldn't believe that the Mimics would have ever attacked there first and been able to defeat Emily and Riza.

"This is so much bigger than I ever imagined," she finally said. "The Mimics attacking Titus was bad enough. But to hear that they've taken Emily and Riza too . . ."

"We will get them back," Pegasus insisted. "They will not keep Emily or the others for long." The stallion rose to his hooves. "I appreciate that you are all tired and recovering, as am I, but time is not a friend to us. Cylus needs Arious. We can't wait for him to recover. Without her, he may not recover at all."

Jake and Tryn burst to their feet. Darek and Render were much slower, and Zephyr didn't move at all.

Pegasus stepped up to her. "If you are still feeling unwell, perhaps you should stay here a bit longer and rest. We can come back for you."

"Stay here!" Zephyr jumped to her hooves. "No way. I want to be the first to leave."

Pegasus winked at Astraea but said to Zephyr, "If you are certain. I would not want you to stress yourself."

"Stress? What stress? I'm feeling fine. Perfect, in fact. I could fly around this world!"

Astraea had never spent any time with Pegasus and didn't really know him. But when he winked at her, she realized he was teasing Zephyr. "He's right, Zeph. You could stay for a bit longer. I know how much you love it here."

"Don't you start!" Zephyr cried. She said to Darek, "Put Astraea on my back and let's get out of here."

When Darek reached for Astraea, she took his hand but started to rise on her own. "I never realized how powerful ambrosia and nectar are. I feel a lot better, and my leg is almost healed."

"Maybe," Zephyr said. "But you're not back to normal yet. Let me carry you for a bit longer."

Pegasus raised his brows as Astraea was settled on Zephyr's back. He walked up to Zephyr. "I thought you believed it was demoralizing to be ridden—that it lowered us to the level of horses. I know that's how you feel when Emily is with me."

Zephyr pawed the ground and looked down. "This is different."

"Is it?" Pegasus teased. "Please, do tell me how."

"It just is," Zephyr snapped. She looked at Tryn. "Can we go now, please!"

Tryn nodded, trying to suppress a smile. "Sure. We'll just get Cylus organized. . . ." Once the Shadow Titans lifted the fallen centaur, Tryn held up the ring Arious had given to him on Xanadu.

"Trynulus, wait," Pegasus called. "May I suggest that you have it deliver us to the glass lake on Xanadu? I am sure we will terrify the Rheans at the Temple of Arious if we appear there with all these Shadow Titans."

"You want us to land in a lake?" Darek said.

"It is not a real lake," Pegasus said. "It is not made of water. It is a very large piece of black glass that looks like a lake. It is, in fact, the remnants of the ancient Xan when they released themselves to the universe. The glass lake is large, so it will be good for an easy landing."

"What did he say?" Jake asked Astraea. When she told him, he went, "Yeesh, we're landing on bodies?"

Pegasus looked back at him and nodded.

"That I understood," Jake said. "I'm freaked out, but I understood."

Tryn held up the ring and called back, "Get your warriors ready to move."

Astraea, Darek, and Jake had their controllers ready. Darek was responsible for the Shadow Titans carrying Cylus, while Astraea and Jake carried containers of snakes. They all commanded their Shadows to follow them.

Tryn called out to the ring, "Take us to the black glass lake on Xanadu."

The Solar Stream opened before them. Pegasus was the first to walk through, followed by everyone else. Just as she entered, Astraea looked back and gasped. All the other snakes that were to be left behind were following them into the Solar Stream, including Belis.

23

IT SEEMED AN ETERNITY AS THEY JOURNEYED to Xanadu. As the time passed, Astraea grew weary. Leaning forward on Zephyr's neck, she closed her eyes and drifted off to sleep.

She awoke with a jolt and felt the ground beneath her moving. When she opened her eyes, Astraea discovered that it wasn't the ground that was moving; it was Zephyr. She was slipping and sliding as she flapped her wings to keep her balance.

"Whoa, whoa!" Zephyr cried, trying to stay upright. "What's happening here?"

Jake fell to the ground and was trying to stand up while Tryn was sliding across the black surface on his backside. The two centaurs were also struggling to stay on their hooves. Render finally fell and slid into Darek, knocking him to the ground beside him.

Pegasus was standing still and watching them with a mirthful twinkle in his eye. "Everyone, be careful; the glass lake can be a bit slippery. . . ."

"A bit slippery!" Darek cried. "I've never felt anything like it!"

"Just stand still and do not fight it. If you must fall, then let yourself fall," Pegasus called.

Zephyr finally regained her balance and stood still with her four legs splayed. Her wings quivered as she tried to keep her balance. "What is this?"

"I told you, it is the remnants of the Xan when they released themselves to the universe. This is very fine glass, but it can be as slippery as ice."

"What's ice?" Astraea asked.

"It's frozen water," Tryn called as he carefully climbed to his feet. "My dad told me about it, but I've never seen it before."

"Yeah," Jake called, still trying to stand up. "This is exactly like ice. I'd be better if I had my skates. Ice and shoes never mix."

Behind them the Shadow Titans were also sprawled on the ground. Cylus was down among them. When he hit the black glass, they all heard him grunt. As Darek made his way over, Cylus opened his eyes. "What's happening?"

"He's awake!" Darek cheered. "Everyone, Cylus is awake!"

There were loud cheers from everyone on the slippery glass. Cylus raised his head. "Where are we?"

"We're on Xanadu," Tryn said as he slid over to Cylus. He knelt down beside him. "You've been badly wounded. I have some ambrosia. I need you to eat it."

"I—I don't remember . . ." When his eyes landed on the Shadow Titans, he screamed and flailed his hooves, trying to get away.

"Cylus, calm yourself," Pegasus called as he treaded over. "I do not care for the Shadow Titans, either, but these are under our control. Calm yourself or you will reopen your wounds."

Cylus looked from Pegasus over to Zephyr and back to Pegasus again. "Wow, you two really do look alike!"

Astraea felt Zephyr tense at the comment. She leaned forward and stroked her neck. "It's all right."

Pegasus turned and looked at them. There was a twinkle of mirth in his eyes, but he said nothing about it. Instead, he said to Cylus, "We are taking you to Arious to be cared for."

"I'm fine," Cylus said, though there was no strength in it. "We have to go to Earth to get my mother and the others."

"We will," Tryn said. "But you're staying here. You're too weak to travel."

"Who are you calling weak?" Cylus challenged.

"He'll live," Astraea said to Zephyr. "The old Cylus is back."

"What's that supposed to mean?" Cylus demanded. Then he softened. "I'm sorry. I'm just not feeling very well."

"You will recover faster if you keep eating ambrosia," Pegasus offered.

The containers of snakes were scattered around them, and the loose snakes were trying to move on the black glass. Belis was also struggling to slide on the unfamiliar surface.

"What's that thing doing here?" Zephyr cried when she spied the large snake.

"I couldn't tell you in the Solar Stream," Astraea said. "But all the snakes that didn't get into the containers followed us."

"They're all here?" Zephyr cried.

"Not all," Nesso said to Jake. *"Jussst the oness that had gathered together in the camp."*

"Nesso says it's not all the snakes from Zomos. Just the ones you all gathered together." Jake looked warily at Belis. "That really is one big snake!"

"We've seen bigger," Cylus said softly. "In fact . . ."

"Cylus, don't," Astraea warned. This wasn't the time to tell Jake there was a chance that Nesso was the same kind of snake as Lergo and that one day she could be as big. "Yes, Belis is big, but he seems very sweet. And I still don't understand how, but he's immune to Mimic goo. It was all over him, but he was fine."

"It could be his age," Tryn suggested. "Whatever it is, it's a real advantage."

Nesso hissed a bit, and Belis slid closer and rose up to Jake's face height to hiss back at her. "Um, Nesso," Jake said nervously "He's a bit close. He's not dangerous, is he?"

"No, he'sss not dangerousss. He wantsss usss to tell Assstraea that he likesss the name she gave him and that he likesss her very much."

When Jake repeated the message, Astraea patted Zephyr's neck. "See? I told you he was sweet."

"Oh yes, he's a real darling," Zephyr said.

"Tryn . . . !"

Everyone turned and saw a figure trying to run on the slippery glass surface. Tryn frowned and called, "Triana, is that you?"

"Tryn!" Triana called again.

"Who's that?" Astraea asked Jake.

"That's Tryn's little sister, Triana," Jake said.

Triana was half running and half sliding as she approached them and moved fearfully around the line of fallen Shadow Titans. When she made it to them, her face showed several black bruises and a cut on her arm that bled deep silver blood. Her clothes were torn, and she looked terrified.

"Triana, what's happened to you?" Tryn cried as he embraced her.

"They're back!" Triana gasped. "The Mimics came back. There are so many of them here. Not long after you left, we went to the Temple of Arious to prepare for your return and they attacked us. There were Shadow Titans with them. Mom and Dad were in with Arious, but everyone else was outside. We couldn't fight them. Everyone who tried was touched and they collapsed."

"Did they do this to you?" Jake asked, inspecting the cut on her arm.

She shook her head. "No, a Shadow Titan did. It tried to grab me, but Brue attacked it. Then they tried to attack her. She brought me here to the glass lake and then went back for the others, but I haven't seen her since. I'm so scared they've killed her."

"She just left you here?" Tryn cried.

Triana nodded. "The Shadow Titans can't walk on the glass and the Mimics kept falling, so they won't try anymore. They just stayed on the edge and tried to catch me with their tendrils, but I ran and they couldn't reach me. I've been staying on here ever since." She was still panting as she pointed to the opposite shore of the glass lake. "They've surrounded the lake and are waiting for me to leave it."

Everyone looked back and gasped at the sight of

the Shadow Titans standing on the distant shore. Beside them was a Mimic. The gray creature was pointing at the new arrivals.

"Looks like they know we're here," Jake said.

Astraea looked over to Pegasus. "If you hadn't told us to land here, we'd have been captured."

Cylus sat up weakly. "Jake, would you tell the snakes to give us more venom? We are going to have to fight."

"You can't!" Triana cried. "There are too many. There were hundreds at the temple, and more were coming. Mom thinks they're going to the Rhean continent as well. Maybe even all of Xanadu."

"Why?" Tryn asked. "Why would they come back here when they already took everyone from the temple area away?"

"It makes perfect sense," Pegasus said. "They know a large group of Olympians and Titans escaped from Tartarus. This would have been the logical place for them to come—which is what we *were* planning to do."

"Plus, Arious is here," Tryn said. "I wouldn't be surprised if they're trying to get to her as well. She knows the universe and all the places the Xan have been. If the Mimics are going to expand on a large scale, it would be helpful to know about compatible worlds."

"Indeed, it would," Pegasus agreed. The stallion turned and looked at the Mimics on the shore. "I doubt they will have suspected Earth as our hiding place, as it was quarantined. So we have that advantage over them."

"That's not much of an advantage," Zephyr said. "Not if there are hundreds of them here."

While Pegasus spoke, Astraea worked as a translator for Jake. But when movement on the shore caught her eyes, she pointed and said, "It looks like they're coming to get us."

More Mimics and Shadow Titans arrived on the shore. The Shadows tried walking out on the glass, but each time they did, they slipped and fell. The Mimics made no attempt to step onto the glass at all.

Jake looked at everyone in the group. "What do we do now? We can't go back to Earth with all these snakes and Shadow Titans. Do we go back to Nesso's world?"

Astraea shook her head. "Going back there won't help anyone but us. We must go back to Earth. Jupiter is counting on us to bring the snakes. Before we left there, Vulcan was making weapons. They're our only defense against the Mimics."

"Astraea is correct," Pegasus said. "We must go to Earth. And although I do not like Shadow Titans, we are taking these ones with us. We have their controllers. If we leave them here, they may fall back into the hands of the Mimics to be used against us again."

When Astraea finished translating for Jake, he gasped. "You want to take Shadow Titans to Earth?"

Pegasus nodded. "This will not be the first time they have been there. But I hope it is the last."

Astraea repeated the message, and Jake shook his head. "This is too much! I just hope they don't get loose in Detroit."

"I hope we make it to Detroit," Tryn said, looking back to shore. "Because if we don't leave now, we won't be going anywhere at all."

There were increasing numbers of Mimics and Shadow Titans gathering on the shore of the glass lake. Before long, they were completely encircled. In one area,

Shadow Titans were moving onto the glass. When they fell, others climbed on top and used them as the bridge. Seeing that it was working, the Mimics ordered all the Shadow Titans to join in the strange bridge across the glass. Soon a Mimic climbed on top of the fallen Shadow Titans and started to move toward them.

"They're coming for us!" Triana cried.

Tryn looked over to Jake. "Tell Nesso to get the snakes into the containers and we can go!"

Nesso started to hiss, and soon the snakes were crawling into the containers. Those that couldn't fit were told to follow directly behind. Darek, Tryn, and Jake each picked up a container and prepared to go.

Astraea held up her controllers. "Shadow Titans, get on your hands and knees. When the Solar Stream opens, crawl into it behind us."

Darek and Jake gave the same command to their Shadow Titans. Darek offered his hand to Cylus. "Are you strong enough to stand, or do you want me to carry you?"

Cylus swatted it away, but then softened and accepted the offered hand. He rose painfully to his hooves. "I should be fine if I can lean on you."

Tryn held up the ring to his mouth and whispered, "Earth, Detroit Michigan, Westward Junction inside the Reynolds Specialty Steel plant."

The Solar Stream burst to life on the glass lake.

Zephyr looked up at Astraea on her back. "What were you saying about never going anywhere?"

"This is different. We don't have any choice." Astraea looked back and called to Belis and the other snakes. "Come on, everyone. You can do it. Follow us."

Moments later, everyone was in the Solar Stream again. Astraea kept looking back to see if any of the Mimics or their Shadow Titans had managed to follow them. Luckily, they hadn't. All she saw behind Zephyr were a lot of snakes and their own Shadow Titans on their hands and knees. The sight of the terrifying warriors crawling was almost comical.

But the reason for their rushed journey wasn't. The Mimics were becoming more dangerous. Astraea just hoped when they arrived on Earth, Jupiter and the others would be ready.

24

ONCE AGAIN, THE JOURNEY FROM XANADU to Earth seemed almost as if it was from Zomos to Xanadu. But eventually it ended in the now familiar brilliant flash.

When they arrived in the steel plant, there were loud cheers from the Olympians and Titans working inside.

It was warmer than Astraea remembered it to be, but then she saw the intense glow from the forge and Vulcan's crew stoking the flames. Vulcan's face was black with soot and covered in a film of sweat, but he was in his element.

Astraea's parents rushed forward, and Astraea slid

off Zephyr's back and embraced her mother tightly. "We have so much to tell you! The Mimics have taken Xanadu! They've abducted Emily and Riza and nearly killed Pegasus."

"What?" Jupiter called as he limped over. He was being supported by Juno.

"What happened to you, Uncle?" Pegasus asked.

"It is nothing. A small accident," Jupiter said. "A pile of steel fell on me. Without ambrosia, the wounds will not heal."

"We brought ambrosia and nectar from Xanadu," Tryn said. "We collected it before the wave of Mimics arrived. It won't sustain everyone for very long, but it will help."

"Do not worry about me," Jupiter said. "Tell me, what has happened?"

While Jake and Tryn distributed the food, Astraea and Zephyr explained what happened on Zomos and what they'd learned about the Mimics and how they were linked. "We've also discovered they don't see very well in the dark."

Finally Pegasus came forward and explained what happened on Xanadu. "The situation is dire," he started. "The Mimics have cleared the Olympian settlement and moved against Arious. Everyone was taken, and I was gravely wounded. Thankfully Brue hid me until Tryn and Jake arrived and saved me. After we journeyed to Zomos to collect the others, we returned to Xanadu only to discover that the Mimics had returned in greater numbers. We cannot go back unless we are prepared to fight."

Cylus's mother was clinging to her son. "It must have been dreadful for you."

"It was," Cylus admitted. "I thought I knew how to fight, but Shadow Titans are impossible."

"Cylus fought bravely," Darek said. "So did Render. They weren't defeated by the Shadow Titans; they were simply overwhelmed by their numbers."

Everyone turned back to gaze warily at the line of Shadow Titans. Jupiter held one of the controllers in his hand. "And this tiny piece of metal controls them?"

Astraea nodded. "Try it. Press the button and tell them to do something. They won't move otherwise."

Jupiter did as Astraea instructed and ordered the Shadow Titans to raise their hands. Four of them did. "This is very disturbing. They are simply moving statues."

"But they can also be very useful," Vulcan said.

"I hope so," Jupiter said.

As everyone ate ambrosia, Jupiter gazed over the group. "We are many here, but most are not warriors. We now must clear two worlds of Mimics. Xanadu must not be lost. We need help."

"From where?" Jake said. "Here on Earth?"

Jupiter shook his head. "No. I do not wish to involve humans if we do not have to. I am thinking of Titus. I believe one or two of us must go back there and seek help."

"How?" Pluto said quietly. "The Mimics attacked there first. There is no telling how much damage they have done since we left. Or who is one of us and who is a Mimic."

"I don't think they have achieved much," Astraea put in. "The Mimic that had Zephyr and me said we'd disrupted their plans. Maybe it means they have slowed down their attack on Titus."

"We cannot know what it means," Vulcan said.

"Indeed," Jupiter agreed. "Which is why we need a

volunteer to go back there on the sly and see what is happening. Perhaps they can reach Hyperion, and if he is still free, he can get a group of warriors together and come here to join us as we prepare to engage the Mimics."

"I'll go," Tryn volunteered.

"And me," Darek added. "My family is still there. I need to check on them."

Several other Titans raised their hands and offered to go, but Jupiter shook his head. "Thank you all for your offer; that is very brave of you. But I have someone in mind for this very special mission. Someone who has fought the Mimics firsthand. Someone who knows what we are up against." He turned and looked at Astraea. "It grieves me to ask you this, but would you do this for me . . . ?"

"What are you saying, Jupiter?" Astraea's mother demanded.

"I am asking Astraea if she and Zephyr would head back to Titus to find Hyperion and my father. Saturn was a powerful warrior before he retired. If he hasn't been taken, he will be a great asset to us. With more numbers here, we stand a chance of saving both Xanadu and Titus."

Astraios charged forward. "You want to send my daughter back to Titus with all those Mimics there?"

Jupiter nodded. "I know it is not ideal, but she and Zephyr have the most experience with these creatures. Now that we have seen how they are spreading, we need more warriors. I am certain that with our prolonged absence, Saturn, Hyperion, and his brothers must know something is very wrong. But they do not have the weapons to fight the Mimics. We have the snakes. We must pool our resources and prepare for war."

Aurora shook her head. "Astraea and Zephyr have only just returned to us after a terrible ordeal on Zomos and Xanadu. They need to rest, not go to Titus."

Jupiter sighed. "I would go myself, but to be honest, I am too weak."

"We wouldn't let you go," Astraea said. "The Mimics are looking for you." She looked at everyone in the plant. "They're looking for all of you. You are the Titus council and hold positions of power. The Mimics that had us on the beach on Zomos were going to torture me to find out where you were. That means you are still valuable to them and that maybe Titus hasn't fallen completely yet."

"See?" Jupiter said to Aurora. "Astraea has the most experience with these creatures. Plus, Hyperion is her grandfather. He will listen to her."

"Let me go too," Tryn offered. "I have my skateboard. I can fly with them."

"Or we could go with her," Cylus said. He was still leaning heavily on his mother, but he had a fierce, determined expression on his face.

"You are not going anywhere but to bed," his mother said. "You are still recovering. That wasn't a small wound you suffered. You nearly died."

"But I didn't die and we're a team," Cylus said.

"Yes, we are," Render agreed. "We should all go."

"No," Astraea said to the centaurs. "Not this time. Thank you for offering, but Jupiter is right. Grandfather knows me. He'll believe what I tell him. Zephyr and I will fly in quickly and be gone before the Mimics know we're there."

"Besides," Zephyr added. "There is still the question of Mimics making it to Earth because of the two

Solar Streams colliding. You have to look for them."

Tryn considered a moment and nodded.

"What did Zephyr say?" Jake asked. When Tryn told him, he nodded too. "She's right. We can't let those creatures loose on Earth. If they're here, we have to find them."

Astraea's father was fuming as he turned on Jupiter. "I am sorry, Jupiter, but I will not allow my daughter to return to Titus. You wanted her to go to Zomos, and despite my protests she went—and she and her team were nearly killed."

"Dad, I want to go," Astraea said. "We'll have snakes and weapons with us, and we'll only move around at night." She looked at Zephyr. "You like to stomp people. How about we spread some venom on your hooves? Then you can stomp all the Mimics you like."

"Yes, and then I'll die when I get my hoof stuck inside one."

"All right, then don't stomp them," Astraea said. "You don't even have to come if you don't want to."

"Hey, I never said I wasn't going to go. I just said stomping Mimics isn't a good idea. This whole thing is a bad idea. But we don't have much choice. Jupiter is right. We need more fighters."

Jupiter nodded. "It is not ideal, but it is decided." He looked at Aurora. "Would you take Astraea and Zephyr upstairs? They need to rest before they head out."

"I'm fine. I can go now," Astraea said.

Jupiter smiled, but it held great sadness. "Be truthful. How much rest have you had? After the story you just told us, it doesn't sound like a lot."

"Well . . ."

"Do as I ask and rest. In a while, you can leave." Jupiter looked at Tryn and Jake. "That includes you two. There are jobs that need doing here. But you must be fresh. Take some time to recover."

"We have to look for Mimics," Jake said.

Pluto nodded. "We already have sentries on the roof. They will alert us to anyone coming. Get some rest. We have a big fight ahead of us."

Astraea hated to admit it, but she was exhausted. With her arm still around her mother, she started walking through the plant. The changes that had been made while they were away were remarkable.

When they moved, Belis started to follow.

"Astraea, can you please tell your pet to stay here?" Zephyr asked.

Astraea turned to the snake and held up her hand. "Stay, Belis. I'll be back later."

Nesso started hissing at Jake's neck. *"Belisss likesss Assstraea and wantsss to ssstay with her. He saysss he mussst protect her."*

When Jake repeated the message, Zephyr moaned. "Maybe you should kick him or something, so he won't feel so protective."

Astraea gasped. "I would never kick him! He's too sweet."

Zephyr snorted. "Snakes are not sweet. Especially big ones that look like Lergo."

Astraea hadn't told Zephyr that Belis was exactly like Lergo and even turned black like him. "Just relax," she finally said. "If you don't bother him, he won't bother you."

Zephyr muttered under her breath and kept staring angrily at Belis. But the snake stayed with them.

As they moved toward the stairs, they saw fresh piles of junk steel that hadn't been there before.

"Where did all of this come from?" Jake asked. "There's way more here now than there was."

Aurora nodded. "I lead a team of scavengers that go out each night searching for bits and pieces of steel to bring back for Vulcan. We have discovered something called a junkyard, which is filled with all kinds of treasures that we can use."

They climbed the stairs to the top level. Astraea was surprised when she left the stairwell and saw that the entire top floor had been turned into living quarters. There were beds and chairs set up, as well as an area for the centaurs.

"Did you find all these beds at the junkyard?" Astraea asked.

"No. These we bought when Jupiter and Juno sold some of their rings and jewelry. I've been finding extras at the junkyard to try to make it comfortable. It is not Titus, but it is functional. We have a large dining area on the floor beneath us. There is a grocery store not too far from here that carries a lot of sugary foods. We are growing weaker, but at least it sustains us." She looked back at Tryn and Jake. "I am so grateful you were able to bring back ambrosia.

Despite Jupiter saying his injury wasn't bad, it is. Very bad. A few of us have been hurt since we arrived."

"I hope it's enough," Jake said.

"Me too," Aurora agreed. She led them between a large setup of cots. "Astraea, this is yours." There were several blankets laid out on the floor beside it. "I hope that is all right for you, Zephyr."

"It's perfect. Thank you, Aurora."

Astraea's mother smiled, but it held great sadness. "Try to get some rest. You are facing another terrible ordeal. I just wish Jupiter would let me go instead."

Astraea hugged her mother tightly. "I understand why he's asked us. Don't worry. We'll be fine."

"I can't help but be worried. You may be almost grown, but you're still my baby girl. All my children will always be my babies. I'm so frightened for your brothers. . . ."

"Me too," Astraea said. "If I can find them, I'm bringing them here too."

Tears welled in her mother's eyes. "Thank you, my darling girl."

When they parted, Astraea lay down in the bed. Zephyr settled on her left, and Belis slithered up to her right side and coiled beside the bed. Jake and Tryn took beds opposite her.

Astraea knew she was tired; she just didn't realize how tired until she tried to say good night to Zephyr, but the words never left her mouth as she drifted away.

When Astraea awoke, she yawned, stretched, and raised her head to look around. Tryn and Jake were already up and away. Beside her Zephyr was sleeping soundly. When she moved, Belis raised his head and laid it on the cot beside her.

"Good morning, Belis." Astraea stroked the snake's cool scaled head. "Did you rest well?"

The snake's red tongue darted in and out of its mouth, and it tilted its head to the side.

"I sure did," she said, stretching again. She flapped her tiny wings and settled them down on her back.

Just a few feet away were Cylus and Render, both sound asleep in a pile of blankets on the floor. Cylus's mother was lying on her haunches, keeping watch over them. When she saw Astraea, she nodded in greeting.

Astraea nodded back and rose from her bed. She

treaded over to one of the boarded-up windows and found a spy hole that had been cut into one of the boards.

The day was gray and dull as heavy dark clouds filled the sky. She had no idea if it was morning, afternoon, or early evening. The road near the plant was quiet and there was an icy cold wind blowing in from the broken window behind the board. She realized that because the forge on the main floor was being constantly stoked, it was keeping the whole building warm.

Leaving Zephyr still sleeping, Astraea and Belis returned to the main floor. Weapons production was in full swing, with Vulcan and his helpers working at the forge while others sharpened the newly made swords.

In another part of the plant, Astraea spied a large centaur teaching both Titans and Olympians how to wield the new swords. Another was teaching them how to accurately use a bow to shoot arrows. Looking at the students, Astraea noted that most were from Jupiter's upper council. She was surprised to discover that they would need teaching. Then she realized it had been a very long time since they'd had to fight. If the council members ever did fight.

Astraea was also stunned to discover that some of the Shadow Titans had been put to work and were commanded to carry large chunks of metal over to the forge, while others were sparring with wooden swords against the training Titans.

"Astraea!" Jupiter called. He walked over to her. Since eating ambrosia, he'd lost his limp. "I am so glad you are up. We must not waste a moment." He looked behind her. "Where is Zephyr?"

"She's still asleep," Astraea said. "She's been through so much on Zomos; she needs to rest."

"I appreciate that," Jupiter said. "But, unfortunately, we must not waste a moment. It is time for the two of you to get moving. Please go wake her and bring her to me. Juno, Pluto, and I have a plan that we want to share with you."

Astraea nodded. "Of course, Jupiter. I'll go get her." She started to run back through the plant to the stairs and was surprised to find Belis keeping up with her. She never imagined the huge snake could move so fast.

When she reached the top floor, she went to Zephyr, who was still down and asleep. It took her several tries to wake her friend.

"I'm awake," Zephyr moaned.

"Then open your eyes," Astraea said softly.

"They are open."

"No, they're not. Because if they were, you'd see that Belis was right in front of you and ready to lick your face."

Zephyr's head sprang up and she looked wildly around. Then her eyes landed on Belis several feet away. "Hey, that was not nice!"

"Maybe, but it worked," Astraea said. "Jupiter told me to get you. He, Juno, and Pluto want to talk to us before we go."

As Zephyr climbed to her hooves, she looked at Astraea. "Are you ready for this?"

Astraea shrugged. "Honestly? I'm scared out of my mind. But I just saw what's happening downstairs. Some centaurs are trying to teach the council members how to fight. They're not very good."

"They don't have to be," Zephyr said. "If they have venom on their blades."

"That's fine against Mimics, but what about Shadow Titans? They're down there too and have been ordered to help teach people to fight. But from what I saw, they win every time."

"You're right," Zephyr said. "We do need better fighters."

"I just hope there are some left."

"Well, there's only one way to find out."

Astraea nodded. "We go see for ourselves."

They made their way downstairs just as Jake, Tryn, and Triana were coming up. There was a long line of snakes following behind them.

"Morning," Jake said. "We're starting to gather venom. Wanna help?"

"We can't," Astraea said. "Jupiter wants to see Zeph and me before we go."

Tryn had an unreadable expression on his face. "When do you leave?"

"Soon, I think," Astraea answered.

"Don't leave without saying good-bye," Tryn said coldly as he stormed past them and out of the stairwell.

Astraea watched him go. "What's his problem?"

"He's Tryn," Triana said. "Sometimes he gets in these moods when he's upset. It's best to just ignore him when he's like that."

"Is he mad that Zephyr and I are going back to Titus?"

Triana shook her head. "Not mad. If I know Tryn, and I do because he's my brother, he's frightened for you. He doesn't always like to show his emotions, but when he's really worried about someone he cares for, he becomes impossible to be around. He's going to be a nightmare once you're gone."

"I wish he were coming with us," Astraea said. She looked at Jake. "I wish you both were."

"Me too," Jake agreed.

Darek entered the stairwell. "There you are! Jupiter sent me to find you both. He's waiting for you."

Astraea nodded. "We're coming." She looked at Jake and Triana. "We'll see you before we go."

"You'd better," Jake said.

Astraea and Zephyr followed Darek out of the stairwell. "Wow, this place is jumping!" Zephyr commented.

"It sure is," Astraea agreed as they wove through

the plant, around machines and people. They paused to watch a single Shadow Titan use its wooden swords against two Titans also holding swords. With very little effort, the Shadow struck the Titans down.

"If I ever doubted that we needed fighters, that just proved it," Zephyr said.

"I know," Astraea agreed.

They reached an area that in the past had been used as an office. There was an old desk and a couple of filing cabinets. Jupiter, Juno, and Pluto stood at the desk looking at a drawing.

"Ah, there you are," Jupiter said. "Come in, come in. We've been drawing up some plans that we want you to study."

Astraea looked at the complicated map showing the layout of several buildings from Titus.

"You may recognize these. Here is Hyperion's home." Jupiter pointed to a building on the plan. His finger moved across it. "And this is my father's palace. It used to be the seat of power in Titus before Olympus was destroyed. Since we moved there, a new palace was built. Now this old one is just our father's private home."

"That's some home!" Zephyr said. "Mind you, after what Brutus did to your palace to help us reach the arch, you may need to move in there again."

"I do not care where we live as long as it is on a Titus free of Mimics," Juno said.

"Indeed," Jupiter agreed. He looked over to Astraea and Zephyr. "If Saturn is still himself, this is where you will find him. However, if the Mimics have taken him . . ." Jupiter's voice trailed off. It was obvious he still cared for his father despite their warring past.

"What Jupiter is trying to tell you," Juno said, taking over, "is that to be sure, you will need to sneak into the palace to rescue him."

Astraea nodded, feeling a stone settle in the pit of her stomach. Jupiter and Juno were expecting them to go against the Mimics to rescue the Titans? She just hoped she and Zephyr were up to it.

Zephyr neighed. "If that is a palace, even an old one, it will be hard to sneak into it without being seen. Especially for me."

"Well, if you weren't so big . . . ," Darek teased. He walked into the office and was unrecognizable. All his long, shaggy hair was gone, cut short to his scalp.

He was wearing two big bracelets, which reached from elbow to wrist.

"What happened to you?" Zephyr cried.

"I'm in disguise," Darek said. "So the Mimics won't recognize me. At least from a distance."

"What Mimics?" Astraea said.

"The ones on Titus," Darek said. "I told Jupiter I'm coming with you."

"But—but you can't fly!" Astraea said. "What if we get into trouble? How will you get away?"

"I'll use the ring to escape." Darek held up one of the Solar Stream rings taken from the Mimics. He then handed another one to Astraea. "Look, we need to move fast. While you two are going into the palace to find Saturn and Hyperion, I'm going to Arcadia to get some of my friends together. We need fighters, and centaurs are the best. Even young centaurs. Since the Mimics don't value us, I'm hoping the students are still there."

"That is the Mimics' biggest mistake. You are the saviors of our world." Jupiter looked at Astraea. "I hope you understand that I have asked Darek to join you on this mission."

"I don't mind at all," Astraea said. She was relieved that he was coming. Darek had proven to be a brave fighter and was now a good friend. She looked at the bracelets on his wrists. "Those are new."

Darek help up his arms. "Do you like them? Vulcan built them for me. Look . . ."

Astraea and Zephyr looked closely and saw that the bracelets had hidden compartments. When the centaur opened the latches, they saw two snakes curled up inside each compartment. "Nesso asked them if they would help, and they agreed. Vulcan is making bracelets for you as well. You can put your two friends inside, so the Mimics don't see them."

Astraea had grown so used to the two snakes around her neck, she forgot they were there. "These two are fine where they are."

"No, they are not," Juno said. "Should you be captured, they will likely be taken from you and killed. If we hide them, they can help you against the Mimics."

Astraea looked at Darek's bracelets again and realized that no one would ever suspect that snakes were hidden inside. "All right," she finally agreed. "But only if these two agree to do it."

Zephyr neighed and nodded to Belis. "I don't think there's a bracelet big enough to hide him!"

Astraea looked at Belis, who was beside her. "I know. Part of me wants him to come with us, but it will be too dangerous. Especially since the Mimics know about the snakes."

"Yeah, like he'd let you go without him," Zephyr teased. "That snake is stuck to you like glue."

"I'll ask Nesso to tell him to stay here."

"It won't work," Zephyr said.

"All right," Jupiter said, drawing their attention back to the plan on the desk. "These homes, here, here, and here"—he pointed to different locations—"are where you will find Hyperion's top security people. If you can't find him, try them next."

Astraea looked at the plan and committed it to memory. "Will you remember it?" she asked Zephyr.

Zephyr nodded. "I hope so."

"You must," Darek added. "I'll remember it too."

"Good," Jupiter said. "It is time for you to move." He walked around the desk and up to Astraea. He put his arms around her and held her tight. "It grieves me to ask you to do this, but we have no choice."

"We understand," Astraea said. "We'll be back soon with more help."

Juno came forward and hugged Darek, Zephyr, and finally Astraea. She whispered in Astraea's ear, "Thank you, child. All our hopes go with you. Stay safe."

"I'll try," Astraea whispered back.

When they left the office, Vulcan was waiting outside with two beautifully ornate bracelets. Astraea was amazed that he could create something so beautiful from the scrap lying around the plant. "These are for you," he said gruffly as he handed them over. His hands were burned and blistered from working the hot steel at the forge. It must have been agony for him, but still he kept working. He showed Astraea how to move the secret panel. Inside was a place for the snakes.

"Thank you, Vulcan," Astraea said. "I will treasure them."

Vulcan smiled and his teeth showed bright white against the grime and soot on his face. "Just come back safe."

"We will."

He turned and walked back to the forge.

"Come on," Darek said. "Let's go tell Nesso to talk to your snakes. Then we can get going."

Darek looked so different without his shaggy hair obscuring most of his face. She'd never realized he had dimples in his cheeks and sparkling green eyes. Short hair suited him much better than his long, tangled mane.

They walked back into the stairwell and up to the next floor. This level was as much a shock to Astraea as the main and top floors were. A whole large dining area had been built. Several Titans were eating at trestle tables, while others were in the makeshift kitchen preparing meals.

At the back of the large floor were several Olympians being taught how to milk the venom out of the snakes. Jake was at the head of a table, working with Nesso.

"See?" he was saying. "The snakes know what to do. You just hold the glass up to them and they do the rest."

There were snakes scattered all around the floor, awaiting their turn.

Zephyr walked carefully forward. "Have I ever told you I really don't like all these snakes? One or two are fine, but look—the floor's covered in them."

"You might have mentioned it once or twice," Astraea teased. "Jake," she called. "We need to speak with Nesso."

Jake left the table and walked carefully through the carpet of snakes. His eyes landed on Darek and he gasped. "Dude, what happened to you?"

"I'm in disguise," Darek said. "I'm going with Astraea and Zephyr to Titus."

"What?" Tryn called as he stormed over. "Why do you get to go when Jake and I can't?"

"Because I'm going to Arcadia to gather more centaurs and students to bring here for the fight. You are still new to the school and they don't know you." His eyes settled on Jake. "And being human, well, you remember how it was when we first saw you."

"Oh, I'll never forget!" Jake said. "Cylus nearly killed me."

Tryn looked back at Jake. "We should go with them."

Astraea felt trapped. "Tryn, please. I want you to

come, but Darek is right. You don't have friends at Arcadia, and with Jake being human, you know what will happen to him. Besides, you are needed here."

"But, Astraea, you need us," Tryn insisted. "You know how strong I am."

"Yes, I do know, but Jupiter needs you more. We all know there were Mimics sent through the Solar Stream when they collided on Zomos. What if they came here? If they find Jupiter and the council, they will communicate with the others and then Earth will be overrun with Mimics. You know they need Jupiter and the others in their plan against Titus. They must be protected by the strongest among us."

"Tryn, she's right," Jake said. "I feel rotten for saying it, but if the Mimics make it to Earth, we have no defenses against them. The authorities don't know about the snakes."

"It's still not right," Tryn insisted. He crossed his arms over his chest and turned his back on Astraea.

"Please, don't make this any harder for me," Astraea said softly. "You know I want you to come. We're a team. But this time it's not possible. Just wish us luck and we can go."

Tryn turned around slowly. He suddenly leaned down and kissed Astraea on the cheek. "Good luck and stay safe!" He ran from the room and disappeared in the stairwell.

"Wow!" Zephyr said. "I did not see that coming."

Astraea's cheek was tingling from Tryn's kiss. She caught her breath and couldn't speak.

"I think he's got it bad," Jake said as he watched Tryn go. "And by the color of your cheeks, I'd say you've got it bad too."

Astraea felt flushed. She turned toward the stairs.

"Got what?" Darek asked.

"Never mind," Jake said. He pulled Nesso from his neck. "What do you need her for?"

Astraea was still watching the stairway where Tryn had disappeared. "I—uh—I . . ."

"Astraea, focus!" Zephyr said.

"Yes," Astraea said, shaking her head. "I need Nesso to ask my two snakes if they want to come with us. If they do, they'll have to hide in my bracelets like the others are doing with Darek."

Darek opened the compartment and showed his snakes. "Just like you did for these guys."

"And," Zephyr said, "don't forget to tell Belis to stay here."

Astraea nodded. "Nesso, would you please ask Belis to stay here. It's very dangerous for him to come."

Nesso hissed and the two snakes in Astraea's hands crawled into the compartment on one of the bracelets. Then two more snakes arrived at her feet. Astraea picked them up, and they crawled into the compartment of the second bracelet.

"They will do what you need them to," Nesso said.

When Jake repeated her message, Zephyr asked, "What about Belis?"

Astraea repeated, "What about Belis?"

Nesso hissed, *"I told him what you wanted, but he refusssesss to ssstay. He will not do asss I tell him to becausse he isss much older than me and hasss ssseniority. He doesss asss he wantsss, and he wantsss to ssstay with Assstraea."*

Jake repeated the message and said, "But it's dangerous for him on Titus."

Nesso hissed, *"He sssaysss he musst protect Assstraea and Zephyr. Pleassse tell them that he isss loyal and will help them on their misssion. He isss ssslowly learning their language and will mosstly undersssstand them."*

"Belis can understand us?" Jake said.

"Yesss. They are all learning. It isss not asss fassst asss I did, but that isss becaussse of our connection. But they are learning."

"Well, Zephyr," Jake started. "You might not like him, but it appears Belis likes you. He's refusing to stay and says he'll protect you both. Oh, and Nesso says the snakes are learning to understand us."

"That's just great," Zephyr said. "Now Belis will understand me when I insult him."

"So don't insult him," Astraea said.

"He's a snake, Astraea. What else am I supposed to do?" Zephyr said.

Astraea's parents arrived on the second floor to say their good-byes. As Astraea held them, she felt a lump form in her throat. This would be her most dangerous mission yet.

"Please be careful," Aurora said.

"Yes, no foolish risks," Astraios added.

"We will." Astraea sniffed. She walked over to the wall with Zephyr and Darek, and Darek held up his ring. "Take us to Titus, at the back of Arcadia One, at night."

The Solar Stream burst open before them. Astraea looked back at her family and friends and wondered if it would be the last time she ever saw them. Taking a deep breath, she walked forward into the light.

25

THEY BURST THROUGH THE SOLAR STREAM not far from the bush where Jake had first hidden. It felt like a lifetime ago that they'd met him. That one night had changed everything.

Astraea took a deep breath, savoring the sweet fragrance of her home world as she gazed around. Everything was quiet. Everything appeared normal. The torches around Arcadia One were lit, and there were a couple of people walking on the path around the large school. Not far away, the night dwellers were out and working silently tending the grounds of the school.

Looking at it, one would never suspect that there

was a terrible invasion going on. Unless, Astraea thought darkly, the Mimics had already taken over everything and it was them she was seeing around.

Astraea heard movement behind her and saw that despite their request, Belis had indeed followed them.

"How are we supposed to hide him?" Zephyr complained. "He's massive!"

"I don't know," Astraea said. "We'll have to figure something out."

"While you do, I'm going to head out to find some of my friends," Darek said. "Maybe if they haven't all been taken, we can warn some of the teachers. Especially Minerva. She was a great warrior."

"So how will we find each other?" Zephyr asked.

"When I've gathered everyone I can, we'll come back here and wait for you. Just be back before dawn," Darek said. "If I'm not here, you'll know something is wrong. Go back to Earth without me. If you're not here, I will do the same."

"That's a good plan," Astraea said. "Please be careful."

"You too," Darek said as he started to walk away. "You've got Belis and your snakes. And you've got your dagger. Don't be afraid to use them if you have to."

"I won't," Astraea said.

She and Zephyr watched the brave centaur trot off into the darkness. There was such confidence in his stride. She wished she felt the same. "I hope he'll be all right."

"Me too," Zephyr agreed. She looked resentfully at Belis. "So, now what? How are we supposed to sneak around with him here? I had hoped to fly, but now we're grounded."

"Maybe that's a good thing," Astraea said. "The Mimics know you fly, and there aren't that many flying Titans or Olympians. It might be safer to stay on the ground. Besides, we have another problem."

"What's that?"

"You," Astraea said. "Zeph, you are really glowing brightly tonight."

Zephyr looked down at herself. "You know it gets worse when I'm nervous. I'm not just nervous—I'm terrified."

"It shows," Astraea said. "I just hope there aren't that many Mimics out at night. Since they don't see well in the dark, maybe they're all inside."

"That's not very reassuring," Zephyr said.

"I know, but it's the best I've got," Astraea said. "Let's head over to Hyperion's first. It's closer."

Walking together, with Belis slithering beside them, they made their way across the Arcadia One field. Looking at the school, Astraea had the eeriest sensation. Everything looked the same. There had been no damage done. There were no signs of war. But it was a war they were fighting. A war they were losing.

Moving away from the school, they noticed just how empty the streets were.

"This isn't good," Zephyr said. "It's never this quiet here."

"I know," Astraea agreed. They entered an area where there were no lit street torches at all. "No one's lighting them. Are you thinking what I'm thinking?"

"If you mean, am I thinking that the Mimics have already completed the takeover and everyone is gone, then yes, I'm thinking what you're thinking."

Astraea stopped. "We're not far from my grandfather's and no one is around. But this is a busy area, and Hyperion would never allow it to go dark. What if he's been taken?"

"If he has, we go to Saturn's palace," Zephyr said.

"And if he's been taken too?" Astraea asked.

"Then we try to find them," Zephyr said. "We'll meet up with Darek and his friends and maybe head to Tartarus again."

They kept walking past lovely marble houses with bright lights shining out of the windows. In some houses they could see inside and saw people. But whether they were real Titans or Mimics, it was impossible to tell.

"In all my life, I never thought I'd says this about Titus," Zephyr said. "But this place gives me the creeps."

Astraea nodded. "I'm getting really scared that everyone's gone. Would they take them to Tartarus, or do what they did with Emily Jacobs and the others from Xanadu and take them to their home world?"

"Good question," Zephyr said.

As they approached Hyperion's house, Belis rose up and his tongue flicked in and out of his mouth much faster than normal. Hissing loudly, he cut in front of Astraea and Zephyr and started to herd them away from the pavement.

"What's that crazy snake doing now?" Zephyr demanded. "Look—he's turned black!"

Belis's scales were jet-black, his eyes were dilated, and he was pressing against Astraea to get her to move. She saw a dense line of flowering bushes not far from the start of another park beside Hyperion's house. That seemed to be where he was directing them.

"Zephyr, quiet," Astraea said. She looked around but didn't see anyone. But that didn't mean they weren't there. "Follow me." She stopped resisting Belis and ran to the bushes.

"Why are we hiding?" Zephyr whispered.

Astraea was standing beside Zephyr and whispered, "I don't know. But I think Belis turns black when there's danger. He did it on Zomos right before he attacked the Mimics threatening me."

Hidden behind the bushes, Belis rose and draped himself over Zephyr's back.

"What's he doing now?" Zephyr cried. "He's really heavy. Is he trying to squish me?"

"I think he's trying to get you to sit or lie down. He's covering your glow."

"I don't want to lie down. I'll get dirty."

Astraea slapped her hand over Zephyr's mouth. "Be quiet and lie down. I hear something."

Zephyr lowered herself to the ground. When she did, Belis encircled both of them and lay across Zephyr's back again. Her eyes were huge, as Belis's face was right next to hers.

Astraea peered through the bushes and saw Hyperion and another person walking together. She was about to call out to her grandfather, but then stopped. Hyperion was holding a torch. Despite the light, his eyes were squinting as though he was having a difficult time seeing.

Astraea's hand went to her mouth to keep from gasping when she realized the terrible truth. Her grandfather could see perfectly well in the dark. Why would he need a torch and still squint? The answer was simple in its horror.

Hyperion was a Mimic.

26

THREE DAYS PASSED AND THERE WAS STILL no word from Astraea and her team. Jake kept busy working with the snakes and doing whatever he could. But there wasn't a lot else he could do. He wasn't strong enough to move the heavy pieces of metal, and Vulcan had organized a crew to work on the weapons, so he wasn't needed there, either.

The main thing Jake was doing was keeping Tryn from using his Solar Stream ring to go to Titus to check on Astraea.

"Something is wrong," Tryn insisted as he started to pace. "I can feel it. I told you we should have gone with them!"

"I don't like staying here either," Jake agreed. "But Jupiter was right to keep us here. We're both foreigners on Titus and they don't trust us yet. Me especially because I'm human. Astraea is smart. I'm sure she won't do anything stupid."

"But Zephyr is hotheaded. What if she loses her temper and really stomps someone? And Darek is a centaur. They love to fight."

"They won't."

Tryn turned to Jake. "You can't be certain."

Could he? Tryn was right, Zephyr was hotheaded, and what he knew of centaurs was that they had a hair trigger. But in all the times Zephyr had threatened to stomp someone, she hadn't actually done it. And only Cylus seemed to fight.

"They're going to be fine," Jake said. "We're just going to have to stay here and make the best of it. Look at me. I've been back all this time and really want to call home to let my mom know I'm okay. But I can't. None of us get to do what we want until this is over. Tryn, you've just got to calm down and trust in Astraea and her small team."

Jake was surprised at Tryn's behavior. He was always

the calmest of them. At first Jake had thought Tryn didn't have any feelings at all. He realized now it was the exact opposite. He felt more than Jake imagined and he was terrified for Astraea, Zephyr, and Darek.

Finally Tryn nodded. "You're right. It's just that— it's just . . ."

"It'sss becausse he caress deeply about them," Nesso said.

"I know. Me too," Jake agreed.

Tryn spent the rest of day helping Jake draw venom from the snakes. It was dark out by the time they finished. They left the second floor and headed downstairs to see what was happening. Vulcan and his team were still at the forge. If anything, they seemed to be working even faster, producing weapons out of junk metal at astounding speed. Across the floor were the classes on swordplay and fighting. Triana was standing opposite a Titan. They were both holding wooden swords and being coached by a senior centaur on how to use them.

"Want to join the class?" Jake asked.

Tryn shook his head. "My mother would be horrified to see Triana with a weapon."

"I think she'd be happy, considering what the

Mimics nearly did to her on Xanadu. As least now she'll be able to defend herself."

Tryn nodded, but he wasn't convinced.

Across the floor, the loading dock doors were being opened. Aurora and her group of scavengers were returning with a load of scrap metal from the junkyard. Aurora's beautiful face was smudged with dirt, and her once-white tunic was torn and filthy. The feathers on her wings were covered in dirty oil and rust. But there was the glow of satisfaction on her face and the faces of those with her.

Walking past Tryn and Jake, Aurora smiled, but there were worry lines on her face. She was feeling the same as they were. They were frightened for Astraea and the others.

They dropped their load near the sorting area where the various metals were categorized in order of their usefulness. When she put down the car fender she was carrying, Aurora came back to Jake and Tryn and asked the same question she had asked many times before.

"Have they returned yet?"

"Not yet," Jake said. "I guess it hasn't been that long the way time works on Titus."

"Perhaps," Aurora agreed. "But every moment is a worry."

Triana ran over to them. Her face was flushed, and she was still carrying her wooden sword. "Aurora, what is happening outside? What is that white stuff falling from the sky?"

They turned to the doors as they were being closed.

"It is called snow," Aurora said. "Have you never seen snow before?"

Triana shook her head. "Our father told us all about it, but we've never seen it. It looks so pretty. Maybe we can make a snowman?"

Aurora chuckled. "It is just starting, so perhaps not yet. But based on the look of the sky, it could be a big storm."

Jake hadn't been out since they'd arrived back as they didn't want to alert anyone to their presence in the building. Only a few Titans were allowed out to buy food or gather items. Even then, it was only at night. With the blazing heat from the forge warming the whole building, he hadn't been aware of the temperature change. "Snowstorm?" he cried. "How? It can't be winter yet."

"It is," Aurora said.

Jake shook his head. "See what I mean about the time thing? It feels like only a couple of weeks since everything started. I was taken in the summer, and now it's snowing out. I must have been gone from Earth for months. My family is going to be thinking I'm dead."

Aurora put her hand on Jake's shoulder and shook her head. "No, Jake, your mother will not be thinking that at all. No mother would. We hold on to hope much longer than you can imagine—perhaps even longer than we should. She knows you are out there somewhere. She can feel you. I am so sorry that you must put your family through this. They do not deserve it. But it is for the best that you not contact them."

"I know," Jake said softly. "But it's hard, especially as I'm here on Earth and just a phone call away."

Aurora nodded. "When this is over, you will have the gratitude of everyone. Perhaps Jupiter will allow you to bring your family to Titus to show them what you have helped to save."

"Really?" Jake cried. "That would be awesome."

Aurora smiled. "I will talk to Jupiter about it. I am certain we can work this out. In the meantime, if you would like to see the snow for yourselves, I am sure you could go up on the roof. There are sentries posted there, but they should let you up."

"That would be cool," Jake said. He looked at Tryn. "Do you want to?"

Tryn shrugged, but Triana jumped up and down with excitement. "Can we?"

"Of course you may," Aurora said. "But you are going to need more to wear than that. Being from a warm world, you will feel the cold. All the clothing we have been scrounging is on the third floor. I am sure there is plenty that will fit you."

Triana squealed with joy. "Come on, Tryn, let's go!"

Triana was talking a mile a minute as she walked with Jake and Tryn to the stairwell. On the top floor, they found the stash of extra clothing.

"Snow is really cold," Jake said. "You'll have to wrap up warmly." He petted Nesso. "You too. I don't want you getting cold."

"I won't get cold if I am with you," Nesso said.

"Thanks, but this time you will."

Tryn said very little as they went through the clothing and pulled out several choices. As they put on the layers, Jake was surprised by the differences between Tryn and Triana. They were brother and sister but couldn't be more different. Then he thought of his own moody sister, Molly, and realized they were just as different.

Jake was wearing three tattered sweaters, including a black turtleneck that completely covered Nesso until she poked her head out one of the holes in the neck of the old garment. When they were dressed, they made their way to the stairs leading up to the roof. The door was unlocked. They walked out onto the roof and were hit with a blast of cold wind. The snow was coming down hard and starting to collect.

As Aurora said, there were several Titans already up there, posted at each corner of the large roof, keeping watch. One Jake recognized was Themis, who was the principal of Arcadia One. The first time he met her was in Tartarus when they freed her from a cell. She waved and called a greeting to them, then returned to her duty. All the guards were wearing heavy, dark coats and looked like ordinary humans.

"Wow!" Triana squealed. "It's so beautiful up here!" Like a child, she tried collecting snowflakes in her hand, but they melted on contact.

Even Tryn was impressed by the sight of snow. "I know it's just frozen water, but I never imagined it would look like this."

"It's awesome," Jake said. "When I was younger, we went skiing. That was the best."

"Skiing?" Triana repeated. Her head was back, and she was catching snowflakes on her tongue.

"Yes. A ski is like a thin, polished board. You clip them on to your boots. Then you slide down a hill on them. You can go really fast and it's really exciting."

"I want to go skiing!" Triana said. "I have to ask Dad to take us."

"I don't know if it snows anywhere on Xanadu," Tryn said softly.

"Then I'll ask Riza if she can make us some."

Jake shook his head. "I've really got to meet Riza. She sounds amazing."

"She is," Tryn agreed.

They walked up to the edge. A brick ledge ran around the entire roof to protect visitors from falling off. Peering over, they saw that the road down below was empty. The lack of tracks meant no one had driven down the road since the storm started. The falling snow hushed the sounds of the distant traffic—filling the area with a quiet calm.

"It's very peaceful up here," Tryn commented.

"It's the snow. It always deadens sounds. That's what I really like about it."

"Tryn, look how bright the sky is even though it's nighttime," Triana said.

"Snowstorms do that too," Jake said. "It can be the middle of the night, but the clouds seem to reflect light."

They stood in silence, watching the large flakes collecting all around them. In just a few minutes, there was almost half an inch lying on the railing.

"Jake and Tryn, would you come here, please," Themis called. She was standing on the corner that was closest to the main road. There was a look of deep concern on her face.

"What is it, Themis?" Tryn asked.

"Please go back downstairs and find Jupiter. Tell him that I feel something is wrong. Trouble is coming. I cannot say what it is yet, but we are in danger. Tell him to move the non-human-looking Titans off the main floor and hide all the snakes if you can. Hurry. We do not have long."

Jake frowned, but Tryn was already running.

Jake and Triana caught up with him in the stairwell. "What was that all about? I don't understand."

Tryn paused for a moment on the stair. "Themis is a seer. She sees the future and is never wrong. If she says trouble is coming, then it's coming."

They started to run again. When they made it down to the main floor, they ran through the workers to the office. Jupiter, Juno, Pegasus, and the senior council were inside. Without knocking, Tryn burst in.

"Forgive me, Jupiter, but Themis is on the roof. She says danger is coming. We have to hide the snakes and move the non-human-looking Titans off this floor."

Jake wasn't sure if he believed that Themis could see the future. But by the reaction from Jupiter and everyone else in the office, they did.

"Thank you, Tryn," Jupiter said. "I want you, Jake, and Triana to go upstairs. Gather the snakes together and hide them if you can." He looked over to Pegasus. "Please go with them. You must not be seen."

Pegasus whinnied and started to move.

"And take the Shadow Titans with you!" Jupiter called.

Within minutes of Themis's warning, the entire plant was on alert. Soon all the snakes were gathered together in one area on the top floor and covered with blankets. Nesso warned them all not to move or make a sound.

The Shadow Titans were also on the top floor, with their Titan handlers holding on to their controllers. The nymphs, fawns, and centaurs were all gathered together. Aurora remained below with her wings covered with rags and bulky clothing.

In addition to the Titans, a large supply of swords and weapons were carried to the top floor and hidden as well as possible. But not before everyone was given at least one weapon to use if necessary.

Once everyone was in place, all the torches were extinguished, casting the entire plant into darkness.

Jake, Tryn, and Triana stood at the boarded-up

windows, peering out. So far, despite Themis's warning, nothing was moving out there. The snow continued to fall and had reached over an inch before there was a warning cry from the opposite side of the large room.

"Jake, please come," called an Olympian standing at the windows. "There are red and blue flashing lights heading this way. What does it mean?"

Jake and the others ran across the room to the windows and peered out. Jake gasped, and Pegasus whinnied in warning. This was the worst news possible.

"What is it?" Tryn demanded.

Jake looked at the long line of cars turning onto the road that led straight to the plant. He lost count after twenty. "I don't understand how they found us. I didn't call home, but those are the police, and they're heading this way!"

27

ASTRAEA HAD TO FOCUS ON REMAINING silent as she watched the Mimic that looked like her grandfather walking down the street. There was someone beside him, but she couldn't clearly see who it was. Whoever they were, they didn't seem to need the light. Did that mean that he was still a Titan? If so, how could he not know about Hyperion?

After they passed from view, Astraea looked over to Zephyr. "My grandfather is a Mimic."

"This is worse than we expected," Zephyr said. She struggled beneath the weight of Belis. "Can you ask him to get off me now?"

Before Astraea could speak, Belis moved off Zephyr

and she could climb to her feet again. "I knew he was big, but I didn't expect him to be so heavy!"

Belis returned to his normal colors and his head slid up to Astraea.

"Thank you, Belis," she said, stroking him.

"Yes." Zephyr finally surrendered. "Thank you, Belis. I think you just saved our lives."

Belis tilted his head to the side. "Yes, I said thank you!" Zephyr finished. She looked back at Astraea. "So now what?"

"Now we go see if they've grabbed Saturn."

"Of course they have," Zephyr said. "There's no way they wouldn't have taken him if they've taken Hyperion. The question is, are they holding them at the palace?"

Astraea shook her head. "I don't think so. I know Jupiter told us to check there, but I think it's a waste of time. Saturn and my grandfather are equally as strong as Jupiter. I doubt there is anywhere in the palace strong enough to contain them. It must be a prison. Probably Tartarus."

"Oh great," Zephyr said. "My favorite place in the universe."

"I don't like it either, but if they're holding every-one there . . ."

"I know. We have to go. So do you want to go now, or let Darek know what we're planning?"

"I think we should let him know." Astraea paused. "I've been thinking. . . ."

"Everyone stand back!" Zephyr teased. "Astraea's been thinking again."

"Ha-ha, very funny," Astraea said. "No, listen to me. Before we go to find Darek, how about we check out Crius's house? It's not far from here."

"Astraea, if they've taken Hyperion, it's only logi-cal for them to take his brothers. They're probably gone too."

"But we have to try."

"How did I know you were going to say that?"

Astraea looked around, then pointed to the oppo-site side of the park. "Crius's house is over there. We can just go look. We don't have to go in."

"Good, because I'm not going in," Zephyr said.

"I didn't ask you to."

"Good."

"Good," Astraea repeated. "Now can we go?"

"Lead on."

They started out across the park. Astraea kept her eye on the snake for any changes. Zephyr did too.

"You know something," Zephyr said. "Belis reminds me of Pluto's three-headed dog, Cerberus. He'll warn us of any trouble."

"And he seems to be just as vicious toward the Mimics." Astraea reached out and stroked the smooth scales of the snake slithering right beside her.

After a short walk, they approached a line of the same kind of flowering shrubs they had hidden behind. Astraea stopped. "So, on the other side of these bushes is the path to Crius's house. His is the middle house between those three homes."

"We're not going anywhere," Zephyr said.

Astraea frowned and looked at her friend: "If you're frightened, you can stay here."

"That's not what I mean. Look at Belis." The large snake had turned black again. "He changes color faster than you change your tunics."

Belis was starting to hiss.

"Belis, please stay here," Astraea said, holding her hand up to the snake. "I'm going to slip through the bushes to see who's around. I'll keep hidden and won't talk to anyone, I promise."

"Be careful," Zephyr called as Astraea pushed through the flowering bushes.

Astraea stopped before the greenery opened on the pavement, across from Crius's home. She peered out and had to cover her mouth to keep from making a sound. There was a full, undisguised Mimic standing with her great-uncle Crius and Saturn. They were all holding torches.

A moment later, the Saturn Mimic lowered his head and handed its torch to Crius. The undisguised Mimic and Crius took a step back and nodded to Saturn just as he started to melt.

The two remaining Mimics watched until Saturn was just a puddle. Then they resumed their conversation as though nothing had happened. Finally, they started to walk away, moving down to the end of the street and then crossing over.

Astraea darted back through the bushes. "We're too late coming back to Titus. I just saw three Mimics. One looked like Saturn, another looked like Crius, and the third was just a Mimic. Then Saturn melted and it looked like the others just didn't care. They've gone down the street. I want to follow them."

"You can't!" Zephyr cried. "If you try that, Belis will attack them and everyone will find out we're here."

"But we must. We know that the Saturn Mimic just melted. They are going to need a replacement. Maybe that's where Crius and the undisguised one went—to find Saturn to make another."

"Good point," Zephyr said. "Which way did they go?"

Astraea pointed. "Down there. Then they turned left."

Zephyr nodded. "Stay here with Belis. I'm going to follow them from the sky. Even if I am glowing, with their eyes, they probably won't notice."

"But we should stick together."

"Do you see wings on Belis? Because I sure don't. If we go flying, he's going to try to follow us. Then he'll be discovered and our mission will fail. Trust me, Astraea. Staying here right now is the best thing you could do. Just keep hidden."

Astraea hated being left behind. She loved riding Zephyr, especially when she was flying. But her friend was right. Belis did have to be considered. "All right, we'll stay. Just be careful."

"I will," Zephyr promised as she backed away and opened her wings. "Don't go anywhere. I'll be right back."

Zephyr took off and Astraea followed her progress in the sky. At first Zephyr looked around, but then she saw her target and changed direction. She finally vanished in the distance.

"I guess all we can do is wait," Astraea said to Belis. She hadn't really been aware of it as she'd been watching Zephyr. But when she looked at the snake again, she realized he had been coiling around her. Not touching her, but completely enclosing her in the circle he formed. He was even lying over himself to form a wall that came up to her chest level. He was also turning black again.

Astraea looked around but couldn't see anything. She could hear soft voices coming from the opposite side of the bushes beside them. Then she saw the light of torches peppering through the leaves. As the voices drew nearer, she heard they were speaking the Mimic language.

Part of her wanted to see who was there, but with Belis completely encircling her, there was no way she could get out. His scales were too smooth and slippery for her to climb. There was nothing she could do but wait.

After the voices faded into the distance, Belis returned to his striped colors. But he didn't uncoil. Astraea realized that if the snake wanted to, he could easily constrict around her and there would be nothing she could do to save herself.

But Belis wasn't like that. He may one day grow to the size of Lergo, but he was nothing like the serpent that attacked Zephyr.

With nothing to do but wait, Astraea sat down and gazed up at the stars. The stars she had known all her life and watched so many evenings sitting out with Zephyr. But now those stars weren't the same. They shone down on a world completely transformed, and if they didn't stop them soon, it would be a world completely occupied by the Mimics.

Time seemed to stop as she waited. But eventually she heard Zephyr land and call out to her softly, "Astraea, are you all right?"

Astraea stood and peered over Belis. "I'm fine. We heard more Mimics and Belis just encircled me." She tapped the snake's side. "Thank you, Belis. Would you let me out now?"

As Belis started to uncoil, Astraea reached out and touched his smooth scales. She felt the powerful muscles beneath them moving in waves as the snake went.

"What did you find?"

"Well," Zephyr started. "There's good news and bad news."

"Please don't start that again. Just tell me."

"You know, you're no fun anymore," Zephyr teased.

"Zephyr!" Astraea cried in frustration. "Please . . ."

"All right, all right," Zephyr said. "I followed Crius and the Mimic to the Titus prison. They both went in, and a few minutes later, Crius and Saturn came out again."

"The prison!" Astraea cried. "Of course. Why didn't I think of it! It makes perfect sense. They needed someplace strong to hold everyone. Why not put them in a prison built by Titans to hold Titans!

It's much easier to get to than Tartarus and it's already here."

"And smells better!" Zephyr said.

Astraea nodded. "All right, so what's the bad news?"

"There were a lot of guards posted outside it. So we won't be going in the normal way."

"What about the secret—"

"Let me finish," Zephyr snorted. "The secret passage. So I flew over that, too. The Mimics must have either sealed it or didn't realize it was there. Because no one was posted there."

Astraea nodded slowly.

"I don't like that look on your face," Zephyr said. "That's the look that says, 'Come on, Zeph, let's go see if we can get in.' Well, you can just forget it! There are a lot of Mimics outside the prison, meaning there will be a lot inside it too. We are on a mission. Not a suicide mission."

Astraea approached her best friend and stood before her. "Zephyr, Jupiter is counting on us to bring back help. Inside that prison could be all the help we need in just the one place. We have to go inside to check."

Zephyr narrowed his eyes. "I knew you were going to say that. So just for you, I checked the best route for us to get there without being seen." She made a sound like a sigh. "Come on, it's this way."

Astraea put her arm over Zephyr's neck and walked beside her. "You know something, Zeph? You're the best."

28

ASTRAEA, ZEPHYR, AND BELIS HEADED toward the secret entrance. Zephyr was right. There was no one around as they made their way to the large park with the monument building in the center of it.

"There it is," Astraea said as she gazed around. "It all looks the same."

"Except there are no night dwellers around. I don't get it," Zephyr continued. "Titus is a big world with a large population—where is everyone? They couldn't fit everyone in the prison."

"Maybe those who aren't in this prison have been sent to Tartarus."

"Maybe," Zephyr agreed. "My question is, is there anyone left? What about Darek? He's out here alone. If everyone is gone, has he been discovered?"

"I guess we'll find out later if he's not at the meeting place."

As they started across the park, Astraea kept her eyes on Belis. So far the snake hadn't changed color. They reached the small white building with the marble pillars out front. Astraea tried the door and found it open. She looked back at Zephyr. "So far, so good."

They entered the building and discovered the center plinth with the eternal flame still there and still burning. They moved past the bronze plaque dedicating the monument to the fallen from the War to End All Wars.

At the back wall, Astraea reached for the small handle on the tiny door. When she tried it and it opened, she looked back at Zephyr. "I'll just go in and see who's inside. Then I'll come out again."

"And as always, I'll just stand here and wait," Zephyr said. "What about Belis?"

Astraea looked back at the large snake that had squeezed past the plinth on the other side. Half of his

body was still outside the monument. "Belis, please stay here with Zephyr and keep her safe."

Belis's tongue flashed in and out. When Astraea entered the secret tunnel, despite her request, the snake squeezed in right behind her. "Please, Belis, I'll just go in and be right back." But no matter what Astraea said, the snake refused to obey.

"Forget it, Astraea. He's going to follow you whether you want him to or not. Just go and hurry back. And don't worry about me. I'll be fine out here, all by myself. . . ."

Astraea grinned at her friend. "Try not to miss me too much." She turned and darted down the dark tunnel.

One of the first things she noticed was all the torches had burned out. Meaning no one was tending to them. Meaning if the Mimics knew about the tunnel, they didn't care. She could see relatively well, but in the complete darkness, the world turned black, white, and shades of gray to her eyes.

Belis made no sound behind her as they moved forward. But when they reached the door that led into the prison corridor, the snake's tongue flicked in and out, and he blocked Astraea's path. Moments later, he turned black.

Astraea stopped and whispered, "I understand. Please let me closer. I won't open the door."

This time the snake obeyed and backed off to allow Astraea up to the door. She pressed her ear to it and heard voices speaking and, behind them, the sound of soft weeping.

Astraea kept her ear to the door and her eyes on Belis. After a time, the voices moved away. Not long after that, Belis's stripes returned. Astraea reached for the handle and pulled the door open.

She was immediately struck by the stale, muggy air and the stench of unwashed people. It was almost as bad as Tartarus had been. The cell directly across from the door was filled to bursting the Titans and Olympians. There was no room for anyone to lie down or even move.

The next cell was the same. As was the one after it and then after that. Astraea could hardly believe the horrors the Mimics had done to her people.

When the cell occupants saw her, they didn't say a word. One pointed through the cell bars and

mouthed, *Be careful—they are just through there. . . .*

Astraea looked back to the large doors that separated the cell blocks. It was behind those doors that she'd nearly been killed by the living rock. She then approached the cell and whispered, "Is my grandfather Hyperion here?"

"Yes," responded a Titan that Astraea didn't recognize. "He and the other new leaders are down at the end."

"Thank you," Astraea said. "Don't worry. You'll be out of here very soon."

"I hope so," said an Olympian softly. "They are killing us slowly in here."

Word of Astraea's arrival spread through the corridor in hushed whispers and soft murmurs. As she walked down the corridor, the cell occupants waved and stared openmouthed at the huge snake slithering beside her.

"Astraea!" her grandfather called in a hushed voice as he pressed against his cell door. "Where have you been? I have been frantic."

Astraea clutched her grandfather's hand and kissed his cheek. "We have so much to tell you. Jupiter and the council are safe. We're getting you out and taking you to him. We're preparing for war against the Mimics—that's what we're calling those creatures that can make copies of us." She looked around the cell. "Where is Grandmother?"

"I am here." Her grandmother's voice sounded softly from the back of the cell. "I am with Saturn."

Hyperion nodded. "Those creatures, the Mimics, have just attacked him to create another duplicate. He has grown so weak. The artificial Saturn has taken over. He told our people that Jupiter and Juno and the council have gone to Xanadu and that Saturn is in command until they return."

Astraea shook her head. "They aren't on Xanadu. It has been invaded by the Mimics too. They've taken everyone from there, including Emily Jacobs and Riza. They tried to kill Pegasus, but he's with us now."

Crius approached the bars. It was then that Astraea noticed there were still humans in some of the cells, as two were pressed close to him. "We tried to fight them, but they defeated us. How can we stand against an enemy that we can't touch?"

"We have a secret weapon. You don't have to touch them to destroy them," Astraea said.

"What weapon could defeat those monsters? I doubt even Medusa could have stopped them," Hyperion said.

Astraea looked at Belis and patted his large head. "He and his kind can."

Hyperion eyed the snake questioningly. "I do not understand."

"It's these snakes. Their venom is lethal to Mimics." She reached for one of her bracelets and opened it to reveal the two snakes inside. They popped their heads out, but stayed in their compartment. "These are very intelligent and kind. They have agreed to help us. We have thousands of them donating their venom. All we have to do is coat arrows, swords, and daggers with it and even a graze causes the Mimics to melt." She looked at the huge snake at her side. "This is Belis. When he bites the Mimics, they don't just melt; they burst into goo. And he's big enough not to be affected by their residue. Unfortunately, the little ones are like us and they pass out when touched."

There were shocked expressions from everyone in the

cells around them. "How did you find these snakes?" Hyperion asked. "Where do they come from?"

"That's too long a story to tell," Astraea said. "I don't know how long we have before they come back. Grandfather, we need to get all of you out of here. Where are the keys to the cells?"

"The Mimics have them," Hyperion said.

"Then we'll use these." She held up her hand to reveal the Solar Stream ring.

Hyperion shook his head. "The Solar Stream does not work in here. I supervised the building of this prison. It is stronger than Tartarus. Your ring will not work; nor can the walls be knocked down. Not even Brutus and his giant friends could break us out. The keys are the only way."

"Then we will get them. Do you know which Mimic has them?"

Hyperion nodded. "I have them. Or rather, the Mimic that looks like me. The keys are always with him. And when they make another duplicate of me, that new one is given the keys."

Astraea nodded. "All right, we'll have to get them from Mimic Hyperion."

Crius spoke again. "Who is with you?"

"Well, there's Belis," Again Astraea patted the snake. "You know Zephyr; she's here too. And we have another friend, Darek, with us. He's a centaur."

"Is that all?" Crius said. "You're just children."

Astraea nodded. "Yes, we're young, but we're effective. The Mimics don't consider young Titans or Olympians a threat. They just call us spawn. But so far we've done a lot against them. Right now Darek is gathering more students together. We're meeting up later. Then we'll plan how to get the keys from the Mimic."

"I am so proud of you," Hyperion said. "But you must be careful. These monsters are unlike anything we have ever encountered before."

"I know," Astraea said. "But we'll get you out of here and show those Mimics they made a mistake coming here."

Hyperion squeezed Astraea's hands. "There is so much I want to say and ask you. But you must go. It's too dangerous for you to linger here. I assume you used the emergency escape tunnel to get here. Use it again. Go now and get the keys. Free us from here."

He reached through the bars and gave Astraea an awkward embrace. "Go now and be careful."

Astraea released her grandfather. "I will." She looked around the cells. "I'll be back and then we'll free all of you very soon."

"Good luck, kid."

Astraea turned around and saw the human prisoner she'd seen last time, the clown who had brutally grabbed her wing. His face was no longer painted white, and he looked thin and gaunt. "We're counting on you."

"We won't fail," Astraea said. "We can't if we want to save Titus."

29

"LET ME GET THIS STRAIGHT. SO NOW WE have to steal the prison keys from a Mimic?" Zephyr cried. "That's insane!"

Astraea nodded. "It's the only way. Zeph, you should have seen it in there. It was horrible. The cells are so full that no one can sit down. That clown guy was still there, but he was so thin, I don't think the Mimics are feeding anyone now."

They were walking away from the monument and heading back to Arcadia One to meet up with Darek. It was still dark out, but it wasn't long before the dawn.

"I just hope Darek found some kids. We're going

to need all the help we can get to free everyone from prison," Astraea said.

Along the way to the prison, they had to stop and hide several times when Belis warned them of Mimics. Each time he did, he turned black and surrounded them.

"It bothers me every time he does that," Zephyr admitted. "It shouldn't because I know he's protecting us. But it does."

"I don't mind it now," Astraea said, patting the snake's head. "It was a bit scary at first, but now I know why he's doing it. What does bother me is how many Mimics there are out here. For being half blind at night, they are spending a lot of time outdoors."

"I know," Zephyr agreed. "I wonder why that is."

Astraea stopped walking. "Zeph, I'm frightened. What if we're too late and they've taken over completely? That's why there are so many out tonight. Think about it. The prison was full to bursting. What if there are no real Titans left?"

"If that were true, the Mimics would be in their own shape, wouldn't they? I mean, why would they need to keep duplicating Saturn and Hyperion and the others to keep pretending to be Titans? To me it means we're not too late."

That comment gave Astraea a bit of hope that there was still a chance to save Titus and maybe even Xanadu. But it was a monumental task and one they needed a lot of help to accomplish.

They made it to the Arcadia One field. When they started to cross it, Astraea's eyes went wide at the sight of Darek standing at their meeting place with a large group of kids. There were both Titans and Olympians of all shapes and sizes, talking together.

"Astraea!" Darek cried as he trotted over and gave her a huge hug. "I've been so worried. This place is crawling with Mimics."

"I know!" Astraea said. "But Belis alerts us to any Mimics around us. He turns black and then circles around us. He's done it a lot tonight."

"Did you find Saturn? What's the news?"

"It's not good," Astraea said. "The Mimics have taken over. They've copied Saturn, Hyperion, and Crius. But Zephyr found the originals."

"Where?" Darek asked.

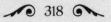

"In the Titus prison," Zephyr said. "Though I bet there are probably more in Tartarus as well."

"There must be." Darek pointed to the group gathered around him. "Everyone here believes their parents are Mimics."

Two fawn-colored centaurs clopped forward. A girl a bit younger than Darek had her arm protectively around a much younger centaur. Their eyes were wide with fear. "Our parents have been behaving so strangely lately. They don't care about me or my little brother anymore. We have to take care of ourselves now."

"That's because they're not your real parents. But don't worry. We'll get them back." Astraea turned to Darek. "We have a problem though. My grandfather supervised the building of the prison and says the keys are the only way to open the cells. The Solar Stream won't even work in there. The trouble is, Mimic Hyperion has the keys to the cells. We're going to need to get them. I suggest we pull a small group together and go after them."

"I'll go after Mimic Hyperion," offered a student.

"Me too," said another.

Before long there were loads of volunteers offering to help get the keys to the prison.

"Whoa, whoa, whoa," Zephyr said. "We can't all go. We must be careful or we'll alert the Mimics. We need a plan."

"I might have one." A winged Olympian stepped forward. He was much older than Astraea, although he looked to be only a few years older than her. He was tall with multicolored feathers on his wings and was known as the most handsome Olympian ever born.

"Cupid?" Astraea gasped. She had only ever seen him from afar but had had a big crush on him for years. All she knew about Cupid was that he was a good friend of Emily Jacobs and was very close with his mother, Venus.

"Cupid?" Zephyr repeated.

Cupid stood before them. "I am so glad that you are here and that Jupiter and the others are free. I had been noticing strange things happening around here for some time, so I broke the rules and flew to Xanadu to warn Emily. But when I got there, everyone was gone. Those creatures, the Mimics and the Shadow Titans, took them. They tried to catch me, but I got away and flew back here. They've taken my mother and everyone I care for. I've been searching for them, but it is difficult with the Mimics looking for me."

"They're after us, too," Astraea admitted. "Which is why we need to find a way to get the keys off Mimic Hyperion without the others finding out."

"As I said, I might have a plan," Cupid said. "The Mimics are smart, but they don't see younger Olympians or Titans as having any value."

"We already know that," Darek said. "Believe me, we've been fighting them a lot longer than you have."

"So do you know what would happen if one of these young Titans were to knock on Hyperion's door?" Cupid asked.

Astraea frowned. "He wouldn't care about them or why they were there."

"Exactly," Cupid said.

"What?" Zephyr said. She looked at Astraea. "Have I missed something here?"

Astraea considered what Cupid said. Then she understood. "So while the kids are distracting Mimic Hyperion with a question or something, some of us could sneak in the back and search for the keys."

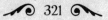

"That is the plan," Cupid said.

"It's dumb," Darek said. "What if Hyperion is keeping the keys with him?"

"Then we melt him with Belis or one of the other snakes," Zephyr said. "The other Mimics will feel it, but we should have time to get to the prison and get everyone out."

"So when do you want to do this?" Darek asked. He looked up at the sky. "It will be light soon."

"I know it's not ideal, but we should do it now," Astraea said. "Otherwise we have to find somewhere to hide all day, and that will be difficult."

"No, we must do this now," Cupid insisted. "If my mother is in that prison, I want her out immediately."

Everyone around them was nodding, and the little-boy centaur started to cry. "I want my mommy and daddy."

Astraea looked at the gathering and then over to Zephyr. "So we do it now."

Two volunteers were selected to be the ones to knock on Hyperion's door while Astraea, Zephyr, and Cupid would break in the rear and search for the keys.

At the same time, Darek would lead all the others to the monument that contained the secret entrance to the prison. If everything went to plan, Cupid would fly the keys to Darek and they could start to empty the prison.

That was the plan. It was dangerous, it was untried, but they had no choice. Time was against them, and they had to succeed before the sun rose and the Mimics came out in full.

After brief good-byes, Astraea and her team headed back to Hyperion's house.

"Do you really think this is going to work?" Zephyr asked.

Astraea was walking beside her with her hand on Zephyr's neck. "It has to. You didn't see inside the prison. I did. It was awful."

"I cannot imagine my mother in there," Cupid said softly. "It horrifies me."

"It should because what I saw horrified me." Astraea had heard that Cupid was a bit of a coward, a troublemaker, and liked to use his good looks to cause mischief. That might have been true of him at other times, but it wasn't tonight. This Cupid was brave and determined to save his mother and the others from the Mimics.

Along the way, they had to hide as a few Mimics moved around. Astraea was growing used to relying on Belis. At the first sign of him changing colors, she warned the others to hide. This worked all the way back to Hyperion's house.

When they reached the street of their target, Astraea looked at the two volunteers. They seemed so young and innocent. She wondered if that was how she'd looked not so very long ago. She had changed so much. She wasn't the same Astraea that dreaded going to school. This new Astraea was now a fighter. Would it be the same for them?

Their new team members were a girl and a boy. Angitia was a bit younger than Astraea, and then there was Picus, who was her age. They were selected from the group of volunteers because of their special talents. Angitia was known to charm snakes. Considering how important snakes were against the Mimics, anything she could do would help.

Picus had the best vision Astraea had ever encountered. She thought *she* could see well in the dark, but for Picus, night and day were the same. He even saw in full color at night, down to the tiniest details. This was probably because his mother was a day Titan and his father was a night dweller. Though he was pale like a night dweller, Picus could go out in daylight without injury from the sun. He also had all the night dweller vision talents. This extended to not only seeing well at night, but also seeing across vast distances. His talent became evident when they were at the end of Hyperion's street.

"Stop," Picus called. "Hyperion and Theia are outside their house talking to someone. I can't tell if the other one is Titan or Mimic. He is waving his hands and appears to be shouting at Hyperion."

"Can you tell what they are saying?" Cupid asked.

Picus shook his head. "No. They are talking too quickly. But Hyperion looks angry."

"No change there, then," Zephyr said. "Hyperion is always angry."

They stayed where they were and waited for the argument to end. Finally Picus said, "It's all right now. We can move. The other one has gone, and Hyperion and Theia have entered the house."

As they made their way down the street, Astraea said to Angitia and Picus, "So you know what you're going to say when you get there?"

"Yes," Angitia said. "We're going to ask Hyperion for help because he's the head of security."

"And what are you going to say?" Astraea made them repeat what they'd already rehearsed.

Picus responded. "That our parents are acting strangely and that we need him to speak to them so that things can go back to normal."

"Perfect," Astraea replied. "The hard part is going to be for you not to look scared. But, if it helps, know that Mimic Hyperion looks exactly like my grandfather, so while you're talking to him, imagine it is the same person."

"I'd be terrified if I were speaking to the real Hyperion," Angitia said.

"He's really scary," Picus added. "I try to avoid him."

"Astraea, let them show fear," Zephyr said. "They're right. Hyperion is intimidating. If they weren't afraid, it would look suspicious."

Astraea nodded. "I keep forgetting. For me, he's

just my grandfather. But to others he can be a bit scary."

"A bit?" Zephyr teased.

"Okay, a lot scary," Astraea said.

"We know what to do," Picus said. "Just be sure to get in as quickly as you can. We don't know how long we can distract him or your grandmother."

"We will," Cupid said. "And if we can't find the keys, I promise that Mimic Hyperion and his Mimic wife will be turned into puddles."

Before they parted to go to the front and rear of the house, Astraea pulled off one of her bracelets and handed it to Angitia. She showed her how to open the secret panel to reveal the two snakes hidden inside.

"Keep this with you. If things turn bad, use the snakes against the Mimics. It's horrifying to watch, but they melt into goo. You must get the snakes out of it because it's just as dangerous for them as for you. Just remember not to touch it."

"We'll remember," Picus said.

Angitia cooed at the snakes and stroked them lovingly. "They're so adorable. We'll be careful."

Zephyr leaned closer to Astraea. "Adorable? Not the word I would have chosen."

"I'm sorry, Zeph, but I agree with her," Astraea said. "These snakes are cute."

"Oh, please, I think I might be sick . . . ," Zephyr said.

"Can we go now?" Cupid said impatiently. "The sun will be up soon."

Astraea nodded. "All right, let's go. Angitia and Picus, please be careful. We're counting on you."

"We will," Picus said. "You be fast!"

They separated and made their way down the street. Astraea, Zephyr, and Cupid headed toward the rear of the large property. As they moved, Belis paused and turned back to look at Angitia.

"Come with us, Belis," Astraea called. "If you go with her, Hyperion might see you and he'll hurt her."

Belis lingered a moment longer and then followed Astraea.

"She really is a snake charmer," Zephyr teased. "Belis has only just met her and he's already taken by her. I think you're losing your pet."

Astraea looked at the snake and realized she felt a

tinge of jealousy that Belis was drawn to Angitia. It was petty and small, but she couldn't help the way she was feeling. The fact that Zephyr noticed made it even worse.

"I'm fine," Astraea said. "Belis can like whomever he wants. I don't own him—no one does."

Zephyr looked at Astraea and did the best she could to raise her brows. "Oh really . . . ?"

They made it to the rear of her grandparents' home and found the back doors open as a gentle breeze set the sheer curtains billowing.

"Stay here a moment," Cupid said. "I'll fly up onto the roof and see how the kids are doing." Without waiting for a reply, Cupid opened his large wings and took off.

"Kids?" Zephyr said. "He's not much older than us!"

"Actually, he's a lot older," Astraea said. "He just looks young. I don't think he ages anymore. My mother says he's almost as old as Pegasus. . . ." Astraea paused. "Sorry, I said the 'P' word."

"It's all right. He doesn't really bother me much anymore. Even though I've lost my blaze and look more like him."

"That's a relief!" Astraea said. "Not about the blaze, I mean. It's funny seeing you without it. But I mean how you feel about Pegasus. It makes things much easier, especially now with all of this going on."

Moments later, Cupid returned. "They are doing great. Both Theia and Hyperion are talking to them about their parents."

"Let's go," Astraea said.

They dashed through the garden and across the long lawn, then climbed the marble stairs and entered the house through large double doors.

For Astraea, everything looked the same as it always did. There wasn't a thing out of place. It was hard to imagine, as her grandmother was the tidiest person she knew, but the house looked even cleaner.

"Does Hyperion have a private room where he might keep the keys?" Cupid asked.

Astraea didn't know. She realized that despite being related to him, she knew very little about her grandfather. "I'm not sure."

Cupid gave her an exasperated look. "That is just great. You search in here. I'll try some of the other rooms."

When he left, Zephyr said, "I don't think I like him very much."

"He doesn't like us, that's for sure," Astraea said. She was darting around the room, searching every drawer, bookshelf, and desktop she could for the keys. "They're not here."

Belis slid up the stairs and entered the room. His scales were jet-black as he moved around a long sofa.

"I know there are Mimics here," Astraea said softly to him. "But stay there. We have to keep looking."

"Looking for what?" Mimic Hyperion said as he entered the room.

Mimic Theia was behind him, prodding Picus and Angitia along with a walking stick.

Astraea's heart leaped and she caught her breath. "Grandfather, Grandmother, it's so lovely to see you!"

"You may drop the act with us, Astraea," Mimic Hyperion said coldly. He looked over to Zephyr. "You too. You know who we are, and we certainly know you. The question is, what are you doing back on Titus?"

30

"POLICE?" TRYN SAID.

"Yes," Jake cried, watching the line of police cars driving down the road toward them. "They are the authorities. It means we've been discovered and they're coming to get us!" He looked back at Tryn. "How did they find us?"

Tryn's eyes went wide. "Maybe they followed Aurora and the others when they were out scrounging. If they find us, they could call the CRU!"

"Dad said the CRU were gone," Triana said.

"Groups like them are never gone," Tryn said. He looked around the room at all the Titans and Olympians. "This is bad. Really, really bad."

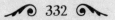

Word of the police spread through the gathering, and tension was growing. Jake looked at them and saw determination. They weren't frightened. They looked like they were preparing to fight.

"This is going to turn ugly," Jake said. "If they start to fight, the police will call in the army!"

Tryn looked down at his ring. "It won't get that far. If we must, we'll use the ring to get out of here."

"And go where?"

"I don't know. This is your world, not mine. Where could we go?"

Before Jake could answer, a centaur standing at the window on the opposite side of the room called, "They are here. If they want a fight, we shall grant them one."

"Please don't." Jake ran across the room to the windows overlooking the parking lot. The police were pulling up to the locked gates. An officer climbed out of the car, reached into the back, and retrieved a large set of bolt cutters.

"Uh-oh," Jake said. "That locked fence isn't going to stop them."

The centaurs readied their weapons, and one called,

"I am sorry, Jake, but we heard what happened to Chiron last time he was here on Earth. We will not let that happen to us."

Tryn looked at Jake. "Chiron told me what they did to him in Hawaii. It was terrible, so I understand how they feel. I hope we can avoid violence."

"Me too," Jake agreed.

Moments later the gate's lock was cut away and the cars were entering the disused parking lot. They followed the progress as the officers climbed out of their cars and, holding up flashlights, approached the loading dock.

Jake looked around the room at the fighters preparing for battle. "Wait, stop, I have an idea."

"What is it?" Tryn asked.

"Those police might think you're all intruders that have broken in. If I go down there and tell them that this is my family's steel plant and we're working together, they might leave without trouble."

"If you do that, they may take you away because of your family," Triana cried.

"If it means protecting you and saving Titus, it is a risk I'll have to take."

"But we need you," Tryn said.

Pegasus nickered and trotted over.

When Jake looked at Tryn, he translated. "Pegasus says it is a kind offer, but he agrees with me that we need you here."

"But I'm not needed. Not really. I'm just a human. I'm not strong like you guys, and I can't fight well. All I can do is talk to Nesso and she talks to the snakes. But you don't even need me for that now that they're learning to understand you."

"You're not leaving me here, are you?" Nesso hissed. *"I mussst ssstay with you."*

Jake stroked the snake at his neck. "No, I'm not leaving you. We're going to stay together, always."

"Thank you." Nesso sighed.

Cylus climbed up from his resting place on the floor and clopped over. "Yes, you are human, and I'll admit, I didn't like you when I first met you. But everything has changed. You have earned my respect. All our respect. You are one of us. You have to stay."

Jake had been stunned that Pegasus wanted him to stay because he barely knew him. But he was ever more stunned by Cylus because the centaur hated him. "Thanks, Cylus, but it's because I'm one of you that I might have to go."

There was the sound of someone running up the stairs. Aurora arrived on the third floor. She was carrying a torch as she ran over to the group. Her wings were covered in long rags, and unless you knew they were there, you'd never notice them. "Jake, we need your help. People have entered the plant and don't believe we have permission to be here. You must speak with them and explain."

Jake looked at Tryn and shrugged. "See? I told you so."

"Jake, don't let them take you away!" Triana threw her arms around him and nearly crushed him with a fierce hug.

"I'm sorry, but I might have to." Jake looked over at Tryn. "In case I have to go, I want you to know, you'll always be the best friend I've ever had. When the war is over and you've beaten the Mimics, please come to Los Angeles and find me." Jake ran across the room to his bed and grabbed his backpack and winged skateboard and carried them back to Tryn. Going through his pack, he pulled out a pen and a piece of paper and started to write.

"This is my address and phone number in California. The Solar Stream ring should bring you right here. Please, Tryn, come. Bring Astraea and even Zephyr. Then you can tell me how it all went."

Tryn accepted the paper. "I will, I promise."

Jake caught hold of Tryn and gave him a firm hug. He felt his throat constrict with emotions. Leaving was the last thing he wanted to do.

"Jake, please," Aurora said. "I am sorry, but they are waiting."

Jake sniffed. "I'm ready." He pulled away from Tryn and walked backward toward the stairs, looking at the strange and wonderful assortment of Titans and Olympians. Jake realized he'd found more of a home with these aliens than he'd ever had here on Earth.

"Please tell Astraea and Zephyr I'm sorry I couldn't say good-bye face-to-face."

"I will," Tryn said.

Jake finally turned away and entered the stairwell with Aurora. "I know they're gonna take me away."

"I hope not," Aurora said. "You mean so much to my daughter."

Jake stopped. "Will you tell her that I'll really miss her and that I thank her for everything she's done for me? Thank her also for being my friend."

Aurora nodded. "You do not have to thank her for her friendship; you've earned it naturally. But you can tell her yourself how you feel when she comes to see you again."

Jake nodded, but he remained silent.

As they walked down to the lower level, he said to Aurora, "I won't tell them about you. I mean the truth about Titus and all that. They probably wouldn't believe me anyway, but I promise not to betray your secret."

Aurora reached for Jake's hand. "Thank you, Jake. You have been a good friend to all of us."

They emerged from the stairwell and started to walk through the plant. The forge was untended, but the glow lit the room enough for Jake to see that all the Titans and Olympians were gathered together in a large group with at least twenty police officers standing before them, their weapons drawn.

One of the officers approached Jake and pointed back to Jupiter. "This man claims you are Jake Reynolds, the son of the owner of this place."

"Yes, sir." Jake looked at all the police officers. Their expressions were stern. "Please, don't hurt anyone. They're my friends. I gave them permission to be here."

"We've spoken with your family. They are very concerned about you and claim you ran away," the officer said. "It is time you went home."

Jake paused and frowned. "How could you reach my family when Jupiter just told you my name?"

"That is unimportant." The officer turned to another one. "Take him out to the vehicle. The rest of you get ready. . . ."

Jake started to back up. He looked at Jupiter. "Something's not right here. . . ."

"Ready for what?" a young officer at the back called.

A female police officer wearing thick gloves came forward and grabbed Jake roughly by the arm. She hauled him forward. "Come with me."

"I'm not going anywhere with you!" Jake tried to pull his arm free, but the grip tightened.

"Quiet," the officer said. "Or I'll put the cuffs on you."

"Why?" Jake demanded. "I haven't done anything wrong. These are my friends. We're just working here. You can't just come in here and take me."

"We are in command. We can do whatever we like."

"Actually, I do not think so," Jupiter said slowly. He took a step forward and raised his hand. "In fact, I think you should release the boy right now. He does not wish to go with you."

The other Olympians and Titans stepped forward. In response, the line of police officers raised their weapons.

"Jupiter, no, please, don't do this for me," Jake cried. "You have other things to worry about. Bigger things. I'll just go with them and that will be the end of it."

Jupiter paused, but before he could do anything, one of the officers came forward and shoved him back with the barrel of his weapon. "Stand back, Jupiter. This is over now."

Pluto moved faster than Jake had ever imagined

possible as he caught hold of the officer's arm. Jake was about to shout "no!" because Astraea had once told him that Pluto had the power to kill with a touch. But when Pluto grabbed the officer's arm, nothing happened.

"How is this possible?" Pluto asked curiously. Before he could say more, a tendril shot out of the police officer and wrapped abound Pluto's hand. He fell to the floor, unconscious.

"They're Mimics!" Jake screamed as he tried to pull free of the arm gripping him. "Everyone, run! They're Mimics."

"You are not going anywhere, spawn," the officer holding him said coldly.

Jake watched in horror as an all-out war started on the main floor of the building. Jupiter fired blazing lightning bolts at the line of police, but they passed right through the Mimics, hit the wall of the building, and blasted holes right through them. In response, some of the Mimics shot their tendrils at the Titans, while others fired their weapons.

Looking at the mayhem, Jake realized that a few of the police officers were human, as their terrified eyes watched the unearthly battle raging before them. One was struck by a tendril and instantly went down. The others ran for cover behind the forge.

"No!" Jake tried harder to pull away, but the Mimic's grip was too tight. Before he could reach for Nesso, a tendril shot out from the Mimic's torso and touched his bare hand. The effect was immediate. He was paralyzed and felt the sickening weakness start. As his vision faded, he watched more Mimics arrive through the loading dock doors and charge at the Titans.

31

ASTRAEA FELT SICK AS SHE STOOD BEFORE
Mimic Hyperion and Theia. The expressions on
Angitia's and Picus's faces revealed their absolute
terror. But that was nothing compared to what she
felt.

"I came back to find my brothers," Astraea answered
defiantly.

"And you thought you might find them here?"
Hyperion asked.

"I hoped that my *real* grandparents were still
here. But I was wrong. You've taken them. You've
taken everyone."

"Not quite everyone," Theia said. "But soon we

will. Soon we will no longer need these uncomfortable disguises and all of Titus will be ours."

"Titus will never be yours. We'll fight you!" Astraea cried.

"You can try, but you won't win," Theia said. "We are already in the final phase. When that is complete, our queen will divide and increase tenfold and we will spread through the known and unknown universe."

Hyperion moved closer. "But you will not live long enough to see our glorious rise. Your part in this struggle ends tonight."

Behind Hyperion, the front door of the house opened and was slammed violently shut. "I'm not through with you yet!" called the voice.

Astraea recognized the voice long before she saw the short, stocky man. Tibed, her grandfather's assistant, stormed into the room. When his eyes landed on her, he frowned. "Astraea, what are you doing here?"

"Me?" Astraea said. "What are *you* doing here?"

Tibed shuffled on his feet like a child that had been caught doing something very wrong. "It's none of your business. Why have you come back?" He looked at Hyperion. "I had nothing to do with this."

"We are aware of that," Hyperion said. "This young spawn has caused us much grief in many places. But that ends now."

"You might kill us tonight, but that won't end the fight. We'll stop you," Astraea challenged.

Tibed looked at her and took a step closer. "Astraea, we cannot win against them. The only hope is to join them and gain as much power as you can."

Astraea could hardly believe what she had just heard. There were beads of sweat breaking out on Tibed's brow, and Astraea realized he wasn't a Mimic. He was real, and he knew about the Mimics.

"It's you, isn't it?" Astraea cried. "You're the Titan traitor! How could you do it? How could you help them defeat your own people? Look, they've already replaced my grandparents."

"Why should I care," Tibed said, "considering how Hyperion has treated me? Is it any wonder that I turned against him? I want him and his brothers to suffer the same way they've made me suffer."

"What have they ever done to you—nothing!"

"It is not nothing!" Tibed fired back. "If they were

so good, why did Jupiter and his brothers turn against Saturn and the others?"

"That was in the past. It happened a long time ago. Jupiter was never mean to you, and yet you betrayed him, too!" Astraea cried.

"True, but Hyperion and Saturn were. They're all the same. Same family, same ruling elite. It's time for something new, and I'm going to be the head of it. I will rule the survivors of Titus. If we serve, we will survive."

"You foul little man!" Zephyr cried. "I should stomp you into the ground right now. You caused all this? You betrayed us?"

"It was going to happen anyway," Tibed said. "They were already moving in here when I found out. Why shouldn't I profit from it?"

"And profit you will," Hyperion said. "But not tonight. I told you, go back and await our command."

"Hey," Tibed said. "You do not command me. We have a deal."

Mimic Hyperion rose to his full height. "You are wrong. We do command, and you will obey or you will suffer the same fate as everyone else." A tendril shot out of Hyperion's torso and wrapped around Tibed's neck. The traitor's eyes rolled back in his head, and he collapsed to the floor.

"Do not kill him yet. We still have a use for him," Theia warned.

"It would be such a pleasure," Hyperion responded. Then the tendril pulled back in. "But you are correct. Now is not the time to dispose of this Titan. . . ." He turned and looked at Astraea. "As for you and these other spawn, on behalf of all of those that you have destroyed, I am going to enjoy this. . . ."

As Hyperion approached her with his hand outstretched, Astraea darted away from him. Flapping her tiny wings, she leaped over the sofa and landed beside Belis. She reached for her dagger. "Everyone, run!"

Across the room, Angitia let out a strangled cry as Theia caught hold of her and Picus. When they both collapsed, Belis responded and rose up hissing. Before Theia could react, the snake was on her and biting her in the leg.

When Belis turned to attack Hyperion, the Mimic started to run. Charging after Astraea, he cried, "You will die before that thing gets me!"

A tendril came out of Hyperion's hand and shot at her. Reacting on instinct, Astraea sliced it away from herself with her dagger. Hyperion stopped and looked at her quizzically. Before he could speak, he started to melt. Soon all that was left of him was a gray puddle.

"Way to go, Astraea!" Zephyr cried. "That's two more Mimics down, only a million more to go!"

Across the room, Belis was lifting Angitia up in his large mouth and carrying her away from the dangerous Mimic residue.

Cupid entered the room and caught hold of Picus and pulled him away from the danger. He looked around. "What happened in here?"

"Things didn't quite go according to the plan," Astraea said.

"You could say that." Zephyr snorted. "Or you could say it all went wrong and Belis turned into a crazed snake when Theia touched Angitia and Picus. He attacked the Mimic and melted her."

"Wait," Cupid cried. "Your snake did that to Theia? Is he dangerous?"

"No more than Astraea is," Zephyr said. She threw

back her head and cried, "Astraea, the Great Mimic Melter!"

Astraea shook her head at Zephyr and said to Cupid, "Belis is only dangerous to Mimics, not us. But he's not my snake. We are helping each other." She looked down into the Hyperion residue and saw keys and a Solar Stream ring. Pulling a cushion off the sofa, she knocked the keys and ring free, then wiped them off with the curtains.

"Here." Astraea handed the keys to Cupid. "Fly these over to the prison. We'll take care of Picus, Angitia, and Tibed."

"Hey, Astraea," Zephyr called as she crossed the room. "Where's Tibed? He was right here."

Astraea looked over to where Tibed had fallen. "He's gone! He must have awakened when Belis was attacking Theia and run out of here."

"What was Tibed doing here?" Cupid asked.

"He's the traitor!" Astraea said. "He's the one who brought the Mimics here."

"Tibed is a traitor?" Cupid cried. "How? Why?"

"Catch up, Cupid!" Zephyr shot. "Tibed is a traitor and brought the Mimics. Belis is an intelligent snake from a hot jungle world that is filled with monsters that nearly killed us—oh, and he really likes Astraea and Angitia. The Mimics are invading Titus and Xanadu and are imprisoning everyone. Jupiter and the others are hiding on Earth and waiting for us. . . ." She paused and looked over to Astraea. "Have I missed anything?"

"Loads," she said. "But there's no time." She looked back at Cupid. "Tibed hates Hyperion and wants to see us all enslaved. But now that we know, there's nowhere for him to hide. We must let the others know it was him."

"We will." Cupid clutched the keys. "I am going now. Follow me to the prison as fast as you can." Cupid ran through the doors and leaped up into the sky.

"Thanks for all your help, Cupid," Zephyr called after him. "We couldn't have done it without you!" She looked back at Astraea. "All he cares about is himself and freeing his mother. I bet he heard the Mimics come in and he stayed hidden until it was all over."

"Forget him," Astraea said. "We have to get moving before more Mimics come here."

Zephyr stepped up to Astraea. "If you can lift Angitia and Picus onto my back, we can leave here before they arrive."

By the time Astraea and Zephyr made it back to the monument in the park, there were prisoners emerging from the secret tunnel. Astraea scanned the crowd, but her brothers, grandfather, and great-uncles weren't out yet.

Angitia and Picus were awake and still on Zephyr's back. "Look how many there are!" Picus said. "I can't see my father yet."

"I can't see my parents, either," Angitia said.

"Zeph, would you stay here with these two? I'm going in to see what's happening. We've got to move faster. The Mimics must know about Theia and Hyperion by now. That will lead to here."

"I will. You be careful!"

Astraea smiled back at Zephyr and started to run. She wove her way through the growing crowd. Belis was right behind her. "Belis, please, this time will you stay here? If the Mimics come, these people will be in terrible danger—including

Angitia. Please stay and protect them."

Belis hesitated but stopped following her. Astraea wondered if it was because she asked him to, or because Angitia was still aboveground. Whatever the reason, she was able to dart into the monument, squeeze around prisoners, and get into the hidden passage.

Going down the stairs, she saw the long line of prisoners waiting to get out. She recognized some from the cells from her first visit. Seeing her, they thanked her for their freedom.

"This isn't over yet," Astraea called. "When you get above, stay near Belis—the large snake. He will protect you from the Mimics."

Making her way through the long tunnel, Astraea was amazed by the number of people that had been taken. Titans and Olympians and humans. They were all together, all helping each other.

Once inside the prison, Astraea ran down to where her grandparents were being held. She saw Theia directing others. "Grandmother, are you all right?"

Her grandmother embraced her tightly. "I am so proud of you! Thank you, Astraea. You have saved us."

"Not yet," Astraea said. "Where is Grandfather? I must tell him that Tibed is the traitor."

"Oh my," her grandmother said. "Hyperion and Crius are going through the prison freeing the others."

"I'm going to find him," Astraea said. "Please get everyone out of here as soon as you can. We don't have long before the Mimics come."

Astraea had heard that her sweet grandmother was once a fierce fighter. When Theia heard this, it was as though all the years that had passed since her last battle washed away. Astraea was now facing a formidable warrior.

"Go," Theia said. "Go find Hyperion. I'll get everyone else out of here."

As Astraea started to run, she heard her grandmother's voice ringing out loud and clear, warning everyone of a possible Mimic attack and organizing them to get out.

Reaching the end of the corridor, Astraea pushed through the door to the wing that had contained all the strange animals, including the Titan-eating rock and the large blue cat. But the moment she arrived, she noticed the change. These cells also contained Titans in the process of getting out through the open doors. She looked at the cell that had contained the deadly rock, but it was now empty.

Directly across from it was the cell with the two-headed worm, Finan and Nanif. They were still there. Astraea noticed how much they had changed. The last time she'd seen them, their red body had a sheen and was plump. Now it was turning gray and looked dried out.

"Astraea, you have returned!" the two heads said as one. "Will you free us?"

Astraea approached the gold bars. "Of course. I need to find my grandfather. He has the keys."

"Hyperion went that way," the two heads said. "But he would not open our door. We begged, but he only opened the cells containing his people. You promised you would free us."

"And I am going to keep that promise," Astraea said. "I will get you home. I just need to find my grandfather." Out of curiosity, she asked, "What happened to the others in here? That rock that tried to eat me and the big blue cat."

Both heads lowered. "The rock creature died of

starvation. And the cat, well, it sickens us to say, but those creatures ate it. They have eaten all the animals in here except us. I fear we are next and then perhaps your people."

Astraea shook her head. "They will not eat you or anyone else because you are getting out of here. Just give me a moment and I'll be right back."

"Please, don't forget us . . . ," Finan and Nanif called.

"I won't!" Astraea ran down the corridor, asking the Titans and Olympians she met if they'd seen Hyperion. Each time she was sent farther and farther away. From the outside, the prison seemed big, but on the inside, it was much bigger than she'd imagined and most of the cells had been filled.

Finally she reached the opposite end of the building and found her grandfather. He was putting the key in a cell door and opening it to release the prisoners.

"Grandfather!" Astraea called.

Hyperion turned. "You're back!" He embraced her tightly. "You did so well."

"Not really," Astraea said. "The Mimics must

 355

know about us now because we killed the Mimics that looked like you and Grandmother. They feel it when one of their own dies. So they know. It's only a matter of time before it leads them here."

"Let them come," Hyperion said. "We are finished. This is the last cell. We'll get to the surface and head to Earth."

"Grandfather, listen to me," Astraea said. "Tibed is the traitor. We just saw him with the Mimics. He said he was angry at how you and Saturn treated him, and he wants you to suffer. He thinks the Mimics are going to put him in charge. He's betrayed us all."

"That wretched little man," Hyperion cried. "If he did not like how I treated him before, he is going to be especially unhappy the next time I see him. Come, it is time to go."

Astraea held out her hand. "May I have the keys, please? There is one more cell to open."

"I am certain I opened all of them."

Astraea shook her head. "No, there is one more that holds a creature that looks like a two-headed worm. They are Nanif and Finan. They said they begged you to release them, but you refused."

"I had to worry about our kind first," Hyperion said. "I told them if I had time, I would come back for them."

"Last time I was here, they saved my life from another creature that tried to eat me. I promised them I would help them get home. Please, may I have the keys so I can keep that promise?"

Hyperion handed over the keys. "Of course. One must always keep their word."

"You came back," Finan and Nanif said as Astraea ran up to their cell door and inserted the key.

"I said I would." She pushed the door open and the two-headed worm slid out. But as they moved, they slowed down.

"What's wrong?" Astraea asked.

"We are too weak," they said. "It has been too long since we ate or drank anything. We are failing. Leave us, child. Just go."

Hyperion came up behind Astraea. "I am sorry if I led you to believe that I would not free you. Please, allow me to carry you."

"We would be grateful," the two heads said.

Astraea helped drape the long worm around her grandfather, the way Astraea draped a towel over her shoulders after bathing. They joined the long lines of people pouring out of the prison.

When everyone was at the surface, there were more Titans and Olympians and humans than she'd ever expected. Her eyes landed on Cupid as he supported his mother. Venus was pale and weak looking. But then again, everyone from the cells looked the same. They needed food. But there wasn't enough back on Earth.

"Astraea," Zephyr called as she trotted up. "I didn't think they would ever stop coming out." She looked back at the sky. "The sun is rising. I've seen Mimics start moving around, and Belis is black. If we're going, now is the time."

Astraea relayed the message to her grandfather. "We should go. The Mimics are waking."

Hyperion looked at the weakened prisoners. "I do not like the thought of taking everyone to Earth, but we have no choice."

Behind him, his brother, Crius, was carrying Saturn. He was still unconscious and limp in Crius's arms. Everyone else around them was weak but grateful to be free.

Darek pushed through the crowds to reach Astraea. He looked at her and Zephyr. "You did it! Now let's get everyone back to Earth, and then we can really go after the Mimics."

32

JAKE AWOKE TO THE SOUND OF SQUEALING brakes and a loud siren. There were two police officers in the front seat of the cruiser. At first confused, Jake remembered what had just happened. The two police in the front weren't police. There were Mimics on Earth!

He sat up and looked around. The cruiser was tearing down the streets of Detroit. Despite the snow, there were loads of people out. He realized if one walked into the street, there would be no way the car could stop.

They turned to the left sharply and he was thrown against the right-side door. When it lurched right, he slid across the back seat and smashed into the left-side door.

"Stop the car!" Jake screamed.

The Mimic in the passenger seat turned and looked back at him through the protective metal cage wire that separated the prisoners in the back from the police up front. "Silence, spawn!"

Nearing panic, Jake searched for a way out of the car. But this was a police cruiser. There were no door handles on the rear doors, and the window glass looked thicker than normal car glass.

As the cruiser tore down the street, Jake became aware of the people on the pavement. They weren't looking at the speeding cruiser; instead, they were looking up and pointing—many were holding up their cell phones and taking photos.

Jake looked out the back window and gasped at the sight of Pegasus and Aurora flying side by side, right behind the vehicle. They were out in public, showing themselves for all the world to see. He started to pound on the back window. "Aurora, Pegasus!"

Pegasus flapped his wings harder and passed over the top of the car. Jake spun around and gazed out the front windshield. The winged stallion was above them and moving faster down the street. When the road ahead cleared at an intersection, he landed on the street and turned to face the approaching police cruiser.

Pegasus reared high on his back legs and came slamming down to the ground. The power from the stallion's strike cracked the road surface, and the shock waves forced the approaching cars to swerve and lose control. One topped the sidewalk and crashed into a building, while others smashed into one another.

The Mimic driving the police cruiser uttered loud and angry words Jake couldn't understand. It struggled to keep the vehicle under control as they started to skid. The cruiser hit the curb and then struck a fire hydrant, causing a whoosh of water to come shooting up.

Despite the crash, the cruiser kept going, tearing along the sidewalk and forcing pedestrians to flee. There were obvious signs of damage caused by the hydrant as the front wheel started to wobble and large chunks of rubber flew into the air. Sparks were flying from the front end, as part of the car's bumper had broken free and was dragging on the road. Yet with all the damage, the Mimic managed to steer the cruiser back onto the road and drove it straight at Pegasus.

"Fly!" Jake shouted at the stallion. "Pegasus, fly!"

Pegasus reared again and tried to strike the police cruiser. But just before he hit it, the Mimic turned the wheel and they screeched away. Another large chunk of car tire broke free and struck Pegasus in the chest.

Jake looked out the side window and saw the long black skid mark on the stallion's white chest. There was rage on Pegasus's face as he launched into the air again.

Out the back, Aurora was nearing the car. She swooped close and motioned for Jake to cover his head and get down.

When he did, he could no longer see what was happening, but he could hear it. Loud pounding started on the roof. Ignoring Aurora's warning, he peered through the back window and saw Pegasus was now hovering low and kicking the roof with his golden hooves. With each strike, the car bucked and swerved on the snowy road. The flashing lights were soon torn off the cruiser's roof. On the inside, Jake could see deep dents appearing.

"You have to let me out before he wrecks the car and kills us!" Jake shouted.

But the Mimics ignored him and would not stop. The driver maneuvered the vehicle like a Formula One pro. With each blow from the powerful stallion, the Mimic was able to maintain control and keep driving.

As they turned down another busy street and headed into the heart of the city, more police vehicles joined the chase. With their lights flashing and sirens blaring, things became surreal.

"Please," Jake cried. "Let me out before it's too late!"

But no matter what he said or did, no matter how much damage the cruiser sustained, the Mimics refused to stop the car.

Jake looked out again and saw Aurora sweeping close. With her powerful wings, she was able to land on the top of the unstable car. She leaned over the back window and called to Jake, "Cover your eyes!"

Doing as he was told, Jake covered his eyes.

Moments later, there was a loud thud and the sound of cracking. Unable to stop himself, Jake peeked and saw that Aurora had punched the window and it was starting to crack.

A second punch put a fist-size hole in it. Jake reached up and started to pull at the edges of the broken safety glass. It was coming apart in tiny pieces— but with the car wobbling on its damaged wheel, his arm and wrist were knocked against the breaking safety glass and cut to ribbons. But Jake didn't feel the pain or care about the blood. All that mattered was getting out.

Aurora reached through the hole. "Jake, take my hand!"

Just then the Mimics in the front started shouting in their own language and the driver turned another corner sharply. Aurora's arm was badly cut as she was thrown to the side. But despite her wounds, she held on to the car.

"Aurora!" Jake cried. He increased his efforts to break the glass. Lying down on his back, he used his legs to start kicking at the window.

Pegasus was just above the car and swooped in

close to keep Aurora from falling off. When she was righted again, she reached in for Jake.

Just as she touched him, the Mimic in the passenger seat turned and pressed its hand against the cage. A tendril shot past Jake's head and struck Aurora's arm. The reaction was instantaneous. Aurora's eyes rolled back in her head and she collapsed.

When the car turned another corner, her limp body rolled off the trunk of the car and onto the street.

"Aurora!" Jake cried.

The police car directly behind them was able to swerve to avoid hitting Aurora, but the car behind it didn't have time and struck Aurora, running her over, before it crashed. The third car continued its pursuit.

Above them, Pegasus looked back at Aurora in the middle of the road and hesitated, then turned back to Jake again.

"Pegasus, go to Aurora!" Jake shouted through the hole in the glass. "Save her!"

When Pegasus hesitated again, Jake renewed his efforts to break more of the glass and get out. When

he put his head and then shoulders through, he heard the Mimic call, "You are not going anywhere, spawn!"

Moments later, a tendril touched him, and the weakness struck. Jake couldn't move, couldn't speak. His last sight was of Pegasus flying behind the police car before his vision faded to black.

33

THERE WERE TOO MANY TITANS AND Olympians to safely enter the plant at once. Instead Astraea held up the ring and called, "Take us to the large parking lot outside the Reynolds Specialty Steel plant in Westward Junction, Detroit, Michigan, Earth—nighttime." The Solar Stream opened, and the large gathering of prisoners started to run into it.

Astraea traveled beside Zephyr. Darek was on Astraea's other side, and Belis was directly behind her. When Astraea looked back at the snake, she was surprised to see Angitia sitting on Belis and riding him the same way she rode Zephyr. She tapped her friend on the wing and pointed to Angitia.

"There is something seriously wrong with that girl!" Zephyr shouted into Astraea's ear.

Astraea laughed and patted Zephyr's neck. She looked around at the immense gathering of Titans and Olympians around them. She realized that Finan and Nanif were still draped around her grandfather's neck. When they arrived at the plant, she planned to use the ring again to get them safely home.

Looking at everyone, Astraea felt a profound sense of relief knowing that they had so many fighters ready to take on the Mimics. Her eyes scanned the large gathering, searching for her brothers. But she couldn't see them as there were just too many people blocking the way.

Arriving on Earth, Astraea stepped free of the Solar Stream to discover the ground had changed completely. It was covered in white and the air was much colder. Just ahead of them, there were many vehicles with flashing lights. The loading dock doors to the plant were wide open.

Shouts and screams were coming from inside. Astraea looked back at the others and immediately noticed Belis. The snake was black and hissing. That could mean only one thing. . . .

"Mimics!" Astraea shouted. "There are Mimics inside!"

Despite not having weapons, the Titans and Olympian prisoners charged forward and into battle.

Astraea saw that some of the humans that had been brought against their will to Titus were charging forward with the Titans—joining the fight. Others were running away from the area.

"Wait, please!" Astraea cried after the departing humans.

"Astraea, leave them be. They are home!" Hyperion shouted. "Come!"

Following behind her grandparents, Astraea, Zephyr, and Darek ran forward to the building, and into a nightmare. Inside there were Titans and Olympians holding weapons and charging at what looked like humans in strange uniforms. But when a centaur struck one of the uniformed humans with an arrow, they started to melt.

Across the plant, Shadow Titans were fighting with other Shadows. While behind them, the Solar

Stream opened, and more Mimics and Shadow Titans arrived.

Belis was sliding through the gathering, biting any Mimic he came upon. Angitia was still on his back, struggling to hold on to the snake's slippery scales.

When a tendril shot out of a Mimic and struck her, Angitia went down. This enraged Belis further, and he became unstoppable. Astraea watched in disbelief as the snake moved quickly through the plant, able to distinguish between Titan, Olympian, human, and Mimic. Everyone but the Mimics were spared the snake's rage.

Just in front of her, a middle-aged woman in a black uniform was holding up a weapon, but her hands were shaking as she watched the battle unfold. A Mimic charged at her, and just as a tendril shot out of it, a Titan knocked the woman away and took the tendril in her place. He went down before her.

Astraea drew her venom-covered dagger and joined the fight. Entering a run, she sped past Mimics, slicing them lightly with her blade. That was all it took to bring them down.

Across the floor, she saw Tryn and his sister. They

were each holding armfuls of venomed swords and were distributing them to the new arrivals.

As the fight intensified, the floor became slippery with Mimic goo. Some Titans that were still wearing sandals slipped in the residue and were instantly rendered unconscious when they fell. Others would then pull them free.

Astraea was unsure how long the fight went on. But eventually the Solar Stream closed, and no new Mimics or Shadow Titans arrived. With only those left in the plant to fight, the Titans and Olympians were able to quickly dispatch them and pick up their controllers for the Shadow Titans to stop the ferocious hollow warriors.

A hushed silence filled the room when the last Mimic fell. Those left standing helped moved the unconscious Titans and Olympians away from the danger of touching any residue. Others gathered whatever they could to start clearing away the dangerous mess.

The Detroit Titans and Olympians greeted the new arrivals loudly and with much emotion. Some families were reunited, and there was excitement in the room.

After a few minutes, the human police officers emerged from their hiding spots. Their eyes were wide as they stared at the assorted Titans and Olympians. Each officer had a radio on their side that was blaring information.

Finally the female officer who was nearly downed by a Mimic came forward. Her eyes were wide with fear, but she had put her weapon away. "Excuse me," she said with authority. "Would someone please tell me what just happened here? What are you? Where did you come from, and what were those things that looked like police officers?"

Tryn came forward first. "My father is human and from Earth. He was a CRU agent."

There were gasps from some of the officers who recognized the name of the secret government agency. Others didn't react at all.

The officer came up to him. She frowned as she inspected his silver skin. "What are you?"

Tryn sighed and looked back at the large gathering. "Well, unless you know mythology, you won't understand. But these are Titans and Olympians. And me? I'm what you might call an alien. But we are not hostile. However, those creatures that looked like your officers are very hostile. They are spreading throughout the universe and are invading and taking over worlds. We are here"—Tryn swept his arm back to include everyone—"because we are fighting them. We call them Mimics. They have plans to invade Earth once they finish the takeover of our worlds."

Another officer came forward. It was a young man with a mix of fear and anger on his face. His wide eyes were staring at everyone, including the large gathering of centaurs. Then he saw Zephyr and gasped. "You're Olympians?"

"And Titans," Tryn said.

"So—so you came here to invade us first?" he demanded.

Tryn frowned. "No! We are here to regroup, so we can go back to our worlds to fight them. We are not your enemy. We are going to defend Earth as much as our worlds."

"This is insane," the officer said. "Why should we believe you?"

A voice that Astraea recognized called from the group. It was the clown. "Because I'm Jason Carpenter from

Brooklyn, New York. I'm also known as the Great Mr. Bo-Bo the Clown, and I've seen what those monsters the Mimics can do—up close and personal. They've been abducting people from Earth and taking them to their world, Titus, to distract the Titans while they took over. It was working too, until this kid figured it out." The clown pointed to Astraea. "Come here, kid." When Astraea did, the clown put his arm around her. "She's the reason I'm back home. Why a lot of us humans are home again. Believe me, I wanted to hate these people, and at first I did. That is until I saw what was happening and what they were up against. What we're all up against. These Mimics are bad news—really, really bad news."

"Why should we believe you?" the younger officer demanded.

"What? Are you blind?" the clown cried. "Didn't you see what just happened here? How that unconscious Titan just saved this cop from the Mimics?"

They all looked over to the Titan who had taken the tendril for the policewoman. He was slowly coming around and holding his head.

Then the clown continued. "Those Mimics

looked like cops. But to do that, they gotta touch the original cop to copy them and learn what they know. Somewhere out there"—he pointed through the loading dock doors—"your police buddies have been hurt by them. If I were you, I'd start looking for them and stop worrying about the Titans in here. Trust me, those creatures ain't our friends. Now that they're here on Earth, we're in trouble big-time!"

Astraea started up at the clown in disbelief. She'd guessed he would be one of the first to run away when they made it back to Earth. Instead, he'd charged in here to fight the Mimics.

"Thank you for staying," she said to him.

"Don't sweat it, kid. Those Mimics really got me mad. Now that they're here, too, we gotta work together against them."

Astraea looked around the room. She could see Tryn and Triana. Her father was among the unconscious who were slowly recovering. Not far away she saw Cylus and Render with their bows. But she didn't see her mother or Jake.

"Tryn," she called. "Where are Jake and my mom?"

"They took him," Tryn said. "When the Mimics

got here, they looked like them—" He pointed to the police. "They said they were going to take him back to his family. After that, the Mimics were exposed, and things went crazy. By the time I got downstairs, he was already gone." Tryn looked at the officers. "Was it your people that took him?"

The female officer shook her head. "I don't think so. We were called here to find an abduction victim and his captors. We were told to expect trouble, but I never expected any of this."

"Somehow the Mimics arranged all this," Jupiter said to Astraea. "They are more clever than I imagined possible—which makes them much more dangerous. We tried to fight them, but they got away with Jake. Your mother and Pegasus flew after them, but we haven't heard anything since. That was some time ago. I fear something might have happened. We must organize a search party."

Astraea's eyes went wide with fear. Jake taken and her mother and Pegasus missing? "Wh-why? Why would they take Jake? We have to find them!"

"We do not know why, but we will find them," Jupiter said.

The female officer held up her radio. "Pegasus. I know that name from stories. Aurora, too. Are you saying that is who is out there?"

Astraea nodded.

"Wait," another officer called. "What about that horse?" He pointed at Zephyr. "That's Pegasus right there, isn't it? It's white and has got wings just like the stories say."

"What?" Zephyr cried furiously. "Did he just call me Pegasus? Everyone stand back. I'm going to stomp that dirty human into a puddle!"

"Zephyr, calm down," Astraea said. "This isn't the time. Mom, Jake, and Pegasus are missing!"

An officer at the back of the group came forward. "I've been listening to reports on my radio. There's been a big police chase through the city. They said there's a flying horse and a winged woman chasing a police car. It's turned into a battle with a lot of property damage. The woman was struck by a car. Now the winged horse is fighting anyone who comes near her."

"What?" Astraea cried. "That's my mother. She's been hurt?"

The officer turned up the radio, and everyone could hear urgent voices calling updates and asking for orders.

Suddenly a voice over the radio shouted, "Unit forty-nine, stand down, stand down. That stallion is destroying everything! We need backup. Someone call in the military before that crazy horse brings down a building!"

Zephyr pushed through the gathering and ran up to Astraea. "Get on. We've got to rescue Aurora and save Pegasus!"

"I am coming too," Jupiter said. He looked at the officer. "We are here to help Earth. But have no illusions: if your people harm Pegasus or Aurora, you will have me to answer to! Now tell your people to leave them be."

"They won't listen to us over the radio," the female officer said. "But they might if we take you there."

Jupiter nodded and turned to Astraea. "You and Zephyr head out first. We'll be right behind you."

When Astraea climbed up on Zephyr, she asked the policewoman. "Please tell me, which direction do we fly?"

379

"Uh, um, downtown," the officer said. Then she pointed. "It's that direction."

"Wait, I'm coming too!" Tryn called.

Astraea looked at him. "Where's your skateboard?"

"Upstairs. There's no time to get it." He looked at Zephyr. "Can you carry us both?"

"Yes. Now shut up and climb on!"

34

THE GATHERING PARTED AS ZEPHYR CHARGED forward. She was barely out the loading dock doors when she leaped up into the air and spread her wings.

Tryn was seated behind Astraea with his arms tightly around her. Behind them, the police were running out of the building and to their cars. Astraea looked back and saw Jupiter and Pluto among them.

"They're all coming with us!" Astraea called.

"I don't trust the police," Tryn said. "Their duty is to Earth. They have Jupiter and Pluto now. If they try to keep them as well as Aurora and Pegasus, it will turn into a deadly battle."

"They wouldn't dare," Zephyr said. "But if they

do try it, I will stomp everyone there. This time I mean it!"

"Me too," Astraea agreed.

They flew in the direction the officer had directed. But with the snow coming down heavily, visibility was limited, even with their Titan vision.

Zephyr was flying at top speed and keeping low as they flew over the rooftops. Ahead was the blazing glow from the lights of the city. Astraea had never seen anything like it before. But even the beauty of the city didn't matter, as fear for her mother obscured every other thought.

"She'll be all right," Tryn said reassuringly. "Your mother is strong."

"But what if they've hurt her?"

"Then I'll stomp them for that, too!" Zephyr called.

Astraea turned and looked back at Tryn. "Why do you think they took Jake? What do they want with him?"

"I don't know," Tryn said.

"Maybe Jake wasn't their only target," Zephyr called. "They might have wanted Jake and Nesso together to understand their relationship and discover how Jake and Nesso communicate."

"Why?" Astraea called.

"How should I know," Zephyr replied. "It was just an idea."

Zephyr's words sent a chill down Astraea's spine. She was horrified to imagine Jake and Nesso in the hands of the Mimics. What would they do to them? The thought was too terrible to consider.

"There!" Tryn called. "Look at those blue and red flashing lights. Those are the like ones that came to the plant. They are the police."

"Look how many there are!" Astraea cried as she saw a whole long street filled with flashing lights. A lot of people stood around watching what was happening. Astraea strained to see her mother in the madness.

As they got closer, the crowd stared in shock. "There's Pegasus!" Zephyr cried.

Pegasus was on the street, rearing high with his wings open. He was surrounded by police. Their weapons were drawn and pointed at the stallion.

"There's Mom down on the ground!" Astraea

cried. Her mother was lying on the wet snowy ground in front of Pegasus. One of her wings was at a bad angle, and there was red staining the snow. The stallion was kicking to keep the humans away from her.

"Mom!" Astraea choked. "She's not moving. Why isn't she moving?"

"She must be hurt," Zephyr called. "But we're going to save her."

"How?" Astraea called. "Look how many people and police officers are there. How are we supposed to get her?"

"I have an idea," Tryn called, then pointed. "Zephyr, please land on that roof over there."

Half a block from where Pegasus was rearing over Aurora, Zephyr touched down on a large, empty roof. Tryn and Astraea slid off her back.

"If we plan this right, it will work," Tryn said.

"What?" Astraea begged. "Please tell me what you're thinking."

Tryn walked over to the ledge and pointed. "If I go down to the street—I'll pull down my hat and bring up my collar so no one notices me—I'll get as close to Aurora as I can. After that, you two swoop in. I'll run forward, grab Aurora, and throw her high in the air. We must time this perfectly, and you must be ready to catch her. Then I can ride Pegasus out of there."

"That's not much of a plan," Zephyr said.

"Do you have a better one?" Tryn asked.

"No, I guess not," Zephyr said. "But is sounds dangerous. Those humans have weapons."

"Yes, but you're a Titan. My father told me that it takes a lot of bullets to really hurt you."

"Why doesn't that make me feel any better?" Zephyr said.

"Come on. Every moment we waste could bring the military, and then no one gets out. Let's go." Tryn looked around the roof. Then he jogged over to a door. It was locked. But he pulled out his lockpick kit and had it open in no time.

"Keep an eye on the street and watch for me. When I wave, I need you to fly down. Then I'll go for Aurora."

"Be careful," Astraea said.

"You too," Tryn agreed. "And be prepared for Aurora's weight when you catch her. Don't let her pull you off Zephyr. Remember what happened with Cylus on Zomos."

Astraea did remember how Cylus holding on to her leg had nearly pulled her off Zephyr. It was only Tryn gripping her from the other side that had kept her from falling. "I will."

Tryn vanished into the stairwell.

Astraea and Zephyr went back to the ledge and waited. A few minutes later Tryn appeared out the front doors. He looked up to the roof and nodded. Pulling up the collar on his tattered winter coat, he entered the crowds that were watching Pegasus.

"This is a weak plan," Zephyr said.

"I know, but look at it down there. If we just barge in, they'll start shooting. Tryn was right; it takes a lot of bullets to stop us. But I've heard that getting shot really hurts."

"Who told you that?"

"Diana," Astraea said. "When she was here on Earth with Pegasus, they were both shot many times."

"Great, so now I've got that to look forward to."

"Not if we're fast," Astraea said.

She kept her eyes on Tryn as he wove his way through the crowds. A couple of times she lost him, but then she saw him turn and nod back to her.

As Tryn made his way closer, there was a line of police officers blocking access to Pegasus. Tryn tried to get through without lifting his head, but an officer pushed him back. When he tried again, he was knocked to the ground.

"This isn't going to work," Zephyr said. "Tryn can't get close to Aurora." She looked at Astraea. "I've got an idea. Get on my back."

"What are you planning?" Astraea asked as she climbed up on Zephyr.

"We're going to cause a distraction. Everyone says I look like Pegasus. Well, let's confuse them and show them two Pegasuses! Hold on tight to my mane; this is going to get crazy."

"You're not going to land down there, are you?"

"Heavens no. We'll do a low flyby, just enough to distract the humans and let Pegasus know we're here. Then Tryn can run forward and grab Aurora." Zephyr looked back at her. "Are you ready?"

"Absolutely. Let's go get Mom!"

Zephyr trotted deeper onto the roof and then charged forward. She spread her wings wide and then leaped over the ledge. "Here we go!"

Astraea felt the exhilaration of soaring with Zephyr again. As they flew lower over the crowds, Zephyr started to shriek. "Pegasus, we're here! Tryn is going to grab Aurora and throw her to us!"

On the ground, Pegasus looked up and whinnied, "Get out of here! They have weapons. It is too dangerous!"

But it was too late do to anything other than stick to their plan. The crowds and police officers turned and gasped at the sight of Zephyr and Astraea gliding above their heads. The officers turned their weapons away from Pegasus and were now pointing at them.

Astraea couldn't see which officer fired first, but soon they all opened fire. Astraea felt the bullet strike her arm. It stung like nothing she had ever felt before. Zephyr was struck several times and shrieked in pain and anger. "I'll stomp all of you!"

They soared over the line of police and past Pegasus. Astraea looked back and saw Tryn break through their line and run up to the stallion. Just as he scooped

Aurora up, one of the officers trained his weapon on Tryn.

Before he could fire the weapon, a great explosion sounded at the end of the street. Astraea looked back and saw Jupiter and Pluto standing in the middle of the wet road. Jupiter held both his hands high above his head as lightning sparked between his fingertips. As he clapped his two hands together, a massive peal of thunder sounded and shattered windows. This was followed by a lightning bolt that shot forward and struck a building with an explosive force that sent bricks and mortar flying everywhere.

"Astraea, get ready. I'm turning around," Zephyr called.

Holding tight to Zephyr's mane, Astraea could feel her friend's powerful muscles work as she did a tight turn in the narrow street. Ahead, Tryn was crouched on the ground and holding on to Aurora. He was looking at them.

"Get ready," Zephyr called.

Astraea was already prepared. She tucked her feet under Zephyr's wings where they joined her body and braced to catch her mother. Closer . . . closer . . .

"Tryn, now!" Astraea shouted.

As the police split their attention between Jupiter, Zephyr, and Pegasus, only a few weapons opened fire on them. Astraea was struck again, this time in the chest. She cried out, but she didn't move or let the pain distract her. Zephyr flew lower to the ground just as Tryn hoisted Aurora higher and leaped up. Then, as Zephyr and Aurora zoomed past, Tryn threw Aurora high in the air.

Astraea reached out and caught hold of her mother by one of her limp arms. Locking her hand around her mother's wrist, she pulled her up onto Zephyr. "Got her!" she cried. "Zephyr, go!"

Astraea settled her unconscious mother across Zephyr and held on to her tightly. She felt for any signs of life and cried with joy when she felt her mother's heart pounding.

"She's alive!" Astraea cried. "Zeph, she's alive!"

"We won't be if we don't get out of here!" Zephyr shouted as she zoomed over Jupiter's head and climbed higher into the sky.

Astraea stole a look back and saw Tryn was already on Pegasus. Just before the stallion took off, Pegasus reared and then slammed his hooves to the ground. The force knocked everyone down and cut huge, spreading cracks in the road. Soon water burst from the cracks and rained down on the fleeing crowds. Astraea had heard he had the power to draw water from the ground, but she'd never seen it before.

"That's amazing," Zephyr called. "I've got to learn how to do that!"

"Ask Pegasus to teach you when this is over."

"I might just do that," Zephyr agreed as she climbed higher in the snowy sky and headed back to the plant.

Zephyr and Pegasus landed together outside the loading doors and charged into the building. Once they were safely inside, Astraea handed her mother down into her father's waiting arms. "Dad, she's really hurt. Her wing is broken, and she won't wake up. She needs ambrosia."

"We're out of it—and nectar, too," her father said as he held on to Aurora. There was pain on his face as he looked at her. Finally he turned back to Astraea. "I am so proud of you both and grateful. Thank you, Astraea. Thank you, Zephyr. . . ."

"Astraea, you are bleeding!" Darek cried when he clopped up to her.

She looked down at her chest and to her arm. There was blood trickling from her bullet wounds. "I'll be all right."

"You're injured too," Cylus said to Zephyr. "What happened out there?"

"They shot us!" Zephyr complained. She looked up at Astraea. "Diana wasn't kidding about being shot. It stings!"

Astraea slid off Zephyr's back and looked over at Pegasus. She hadn't had time to notice before, but Pegasus was covered in wounds. From bullet holes to large scrapes. There was even a black tread mark on his chest.

Astraea looked back at Zephyr, whose own black blaze had gone. Now Pegasus had one right were Zephyr's once was. She wondered how long it would be before Zephyr noticed. She also saw just how many times Zephyr had been struck by bullets. Her friend had taken many more than she had.

"Are you all right?" Astraea said to her.

"I will be," Zephyr said. "Once I eat a bucketful of ambrosia. How is Aurora?"

"I'm not sure," Astraea said. "I think she's really hurt."

"She will live," Themis said as she approached. "Thanks to you." She looked back and included Tryn. "That was very brave of you."

"Or foolish," Cylus said. "You should have waited for us."

"I'm sorry," Astraea said. "But there was no time."

"Where's Jake?" Cylus asked, looking past them.

Astraea turned to Pegasus. "Please, tell us what happened to Jake. Where is he? Do the humans have him?"

Pegasus clopped forward. "Aurora and I tried to stop the Mimics from taking him. We pursued them through the city and even damaged their vehicle. But when Aurora nearly had Jake out the back window of their vehicle, the Mimics touched her, and she fell. She was then struck by a police vehicle. I was so torn." Pegasus dropped his head. "Do I stay with Aurora or try to reach Jake? I had hoped to achieve both. But when I was about to disable the Mimics' car, they opened the Solar Stream and drove right into it. I dared not follow them—Aurora needed me." He sighed heavily. "I am sorry. I failed Jake the same way I failed Emily when the Mimics came to Xanadu."

"You did not fail them," Jupiter called as he entered the plant. He turned back and waved at the police car that had dropped him and Pluto off.

"Jupiter, you're all right!" Astraea cried. "I was so scared they would capture you."

"Pluto and I are quite unharmed." He looked at the gathering. "That kind policewoman who was here helped us escape and brought us back. She said she was going to try to stop the others from coming after us, but now that they know we are here, they will find us. We must leave here, now. Everyone gather your things. We don't have a moment to waste."

35

WITH THE FEAR OF THE MILITARY'S OR THE Mimics' possible arrival, everyone set to work preparing to leave as quickly as they could. All the snakes were put back in their containers and carried downstairs. Astraea looked at the snakes and felt a great weight resting on her chest that had nothing to do with her wound. Jake and Nesso were gone. Her mind was spinning with all the terrible things the Mimics could be doing to them right now. She was hardly able to function through the fear she felt.

Zephyr tried to help by suggesting that the Mimics might have taken him to Titus or even Xanadu

and that when they took it back, they would find him. This was the thought that kept Astraea moving.

In the center of the main floor, Jupiter, Juno, Hyperion and his team, along with Pegasus and Cylus's mother and several others, were gathered together to plan their next move. A large map of the area around the Temple of Arious had been drawn on the floor.

"So, this is the Xan lake, where we'll land," Jupiter said as he pointed to the circle drawn in the center of the map. "From there, we can break up into teams and take different routes toward the Arious encampment."

Tryn cleared his throat and approached the gathering. "Forgive me for interrupting, Jupiter, but you must know, right before we left Xanadu, the Mimics were surrounding the lake and sending Shadow Titans onto it to get us. They couldn't walk on it and were lying down so others could crawl on them. If they know that we know it's a safe place to land, they may have posted sentries there."

Jupiter rubbed his beard. "A very good point, but I do not believe we have much choice. Though Themis gave us hope for Aurora, her recovery will be quickened by getting her to Arious for treatment."

Astraea frowned. "So why don't we just order the Solar Stream to take us inside the temple to Arious directly? That way we can get my mother there quicker. Even if the Mimics are in there, we have enough weapons and fighters to defeat them."

Jupiter looked at the map and then to Astraea. "Because . . ." He paused and scratched his head, looking at the others. "Why don't we?"

"Because," Themis said as she joined them. "It does not take a seer to know the Mimics will have attempted the same thing. Arious would be a great prize for them. I have no doubt that she has protected herself against a Solar Stream incursion."

"The same way we fortified the Titus prison against such break-ins," Hyperion added.

"Perhaps the main area that holds Arious," Pegasus offered. "But the first time Emily and I ventured there, the Solar Stream deposited us on the lowest level of the temple. It is vast chamber and has many areas around it for us to hide in and start our assault against the Mimics."

Cylus's mother looked at the map. "Landing within the temple itself is the best option. We can arrive with our bows, swords, and daggers ready. The Mimics will not be prepared. We should be able to clear the temple before anyone outside knows about it."

"I can shoot," Cylus called.

"And me," Darek and Render said as one.

Jupiter turned and raised his eyebrows at everyone who had gathered behind them to hear the council's discussion. "Normally these discussions are private," he started. "But in this case, it is only fair that you should all hear this, as it involves all of us. Our next move against the Mimics will be crucial."

"I agree that we land in the temple," an older night dweller called. "Might I also suggest that we land at night in case we chase them out of the temple? I for one want to fight all the way but can only do so at night."

Astraea nodded. "Nighttime would be best because the Mimics don't see well in the dark. It helped us in Titus."

"I agree. We will land at night." Jupiter drew the discussion to a close. "Now we must hurry.

Take up your arms. The time has come to move."

By the time they were ready to leave, the sun was up and glistening on the thick layer of snow. So far, they hadn't been found by the authorities, but they were all feeling the pressure of time.

Astraea stood with Zephyr, watching Vulcan with his team. They were shutting down the forge and extinguishing the flames. There was a look of sadness on Vulcan's face as he patted the old machine. "You have served us well," he said softly.

Weapons were being distributed, but despite the large number Vulcan had made, with the newly released prisoners from Titus, there wasn't enough to go around. Those who didn't get swords were given daggers. As the centaurs were the best archers, they were given all the bows and arrows.

When Vulcan handed Astraea a dagger, she thanked him and said she already had one. But he ruffled her hair. "Take it anyway, in case you lose your other one. You've earned it."

Astraea stored her second dagger under her belt just as Tryn and her father arrived with two night dwellers who were carrying her mother on a cot. Since arriving back, she had yet to regain consciousness.

"Dad, has there been any change?"

He put his arm around her. "Not yet. But your mother is strong. Once we get her to Arious, she will recover in no time."

"What if we can't get her to Arious?" Astraea asked as she watched her mother's still face covered in cuts and bruises. "What if there are too many Mimics there?"

"If there are, we will get her ambrosia. Do not fear. Your mother will be fine."

Two night dwellers smiled warmly at Astraea. One said, "We are getting ready to leave. Do not fret, Astraea. We will take special care of your mother."

Jupiter approached one of the plant walls. He looked back at his people with a grim expression on his face. "It is time to move. Forward teams to the ready?"

"Yes," Hyperion called. He was standing before a large group of his security team.

"Secondary team?"

"Ready," called a tall, midnight-black centaur who was leading all the centaurs forward.

When all the advance teams were ready, Jupiter

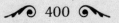

looked around the plant one more time. "Are the Shadow Titans ready?"

"They are," called a Titan. She and her group all had the controllers that worked the Shadow Titans.

"Excellent," Jupiter said. He turned to the wall and held up his hand with a Solar Stream gem. "Take us to Xanadu, lowest level inside the Temple of Arious, nighttime."

The wall exploded in a swirling vortex of light. "For Titus!" Jupiter called as he raised his sword and charged into the light.

36

ASTRAEA WAS BESIDE ZEPHYR AND HOLDING on to her wing as they took the long journey through the Solar Stream. Tryn was standing on the opposite side of her, and her father was beside him with his sword drawn. On the other side of Zephyr were Cylus, Render, and Darek. Astraea looked back and saw Belis behind her. Once again, Angitia was on his back. She had been given a dagger and was holding it ready.

Astraea and her team had been positioned at the very back of the large group, working as escorts for all the snakes. Around them were some of the Shadow Titans, carrying the containers.

Just ahead were the night dwellers with her mother. Themis had said that she was going to recover, but so far there had been no signs of it. Her mother hadn't moved once during the seemingly endless journey.

Finally, the masses in front of the group stepped clear of the Solar Stream. When it was Astraea's turn, she emerged into a raging battle. Titans and Olympians were engaged in fights against many Mimics.

They were in an immense, high-ceilinged chamber in the lowest level of the Temple of Arious. The same containers they'd seen beneath Arcadia Two were stacked along the walls. Astraea realized the Mimics were using the chamber to store all their food. They arrived just as a large number of Mimics were eating.

Astraea was ready to fight. But with so many Titans and Olympians in front of her, she didn't think any Mimics could reach her. Especially as they were at the very back of the large group.

She was wrong.

A long tendril caught hold of Darek and spun him around. He was unconscious before he struck the floor. As he went down, Cylus reacted and fired a poisoned arrow at the Mimic. Astraea turned and gasped when she saw a wide line of Mimics charging forward from their place along the back wall of the spacious chamber.

Moving on instinct alone, Astraea used her dagger to slash the tendril that reached for Zephyr. The creature howled and pulled it back. Soon it started to melt.

Behind her, Belis was black and already moving toward the line of Mimics, biting anyone that was within the large snake's reach.

Everything became a blur of time and movement as Astraea fought against the Mimics in the chamber. She thought she was prepared to face them again, but seeing the mass of bulbous gray creatures charging at her was almost more than her mind could take in.

As the fight intensified, the floor became slippery from melting Mimics, and half the Titans and Olympians went down just from touching the residue. The night dwellers came into their own as heroes as they pulled their fellow Titans away from the dangerous goo.

Astraea was swinging her dagger at one Mimic when Belis rose up in front of her. His eyes were red, and she could see the fury within them. For an instant she wondered if all the fighting had turned Belis into a serpent like Lergo. But when he charged, he flashed past her and went for the Mimic running at Astraea from behind.

Two other Mimics were advancing on Zephyr. Unable to defend herself, she called out for Astraea. But Belis was already moving, and before they could touch Zephyr, Belis had them both down and melting.

"I guess you want me to thank you," Zephyr called to the snake. "So, thank you!" She looked over to Astraea. "How many Mimics are down here?"

"Too many," Astraea replied. Ahead of her, she saw a sword from a fallen Titan. Casting aside her dagger, she picked up the sword and was able to fight the Mimics from farther away.

The sights and sounds around them were beyond Astraea's imagining as a hoard of Mimics were still fighting the Titans and Olympians. It was overwhelming, and she had to focus on each Mimic alone if she wanted to keep from screaming.

As the endless fight continued, Astraea searched the masses for the night dwellers holding her mother.

It was then that she saw her mother had been put down in the same area where the night dwellers were dragging the unconscious Titans and Olympians. The area was unguarded.

"Zeph, look!" Astraea cried. "Mom and the others are alone!"

"We have to protect them!" Zephyr whinnied.

With the crowds of fighters all around them, Zephyr flapped her wings and tried to fly over the top of the fight. But as she rose, a tendril shot out and caught her by the back leg. Zephyr howled once and crashed down to the floor.

"Zephyr!" Astraea cried as the Mimic kept hold of Zephyr's leg, trying to kill her.

Astraea's heart was in her throat as she attacked the Mimic and cut off the tendril gripping her best friend. The Mimic cried out and started to melt. The first danger was over, but Zephyr was down on the floor in the middle of the worst battle Astraea could ever imagine. There were puddles of goo everywhere from the fallen Mimics. One of the puddles was spreading toward Zephyr's tail.

Astraea ran up to Zephyr's front hooves. She put

down her sword and caught hold of a leg, starting to haul her heavy friend away from the danger. She had gone only a few feet when a Mimic caught sight of her. "Astraea!" it shouted. "I will end you now!"

Astraea realized she'd put her sword down to drag Zephyr. The Mimic knew it too. But what it didn't know was that Vulcan had given Astraea an extra dagger, which she'd hidden in her belt. When the Mimic came closer, she drew the weapon and threw it. Though it passed through the creature, the poison on the blade did its work, and the Mimic gurgled and started to melt.

Now unarmed, Astraea reached for Zephyr's hooves again and continued to drag her away from the fight. With each step, she realized just how big and heavy Zephyr really was. Her arm muscles were quivering, and she felt winded. Just when she thought she couldn't drag Zephyr any farther, Tryn and Triana arrived.

Without speaking, Tryn caught hold of Zephyr's other front hoof, while Triana grabbed a back leg, and the three of them pulled Zephyr over to one of the walls where the large group of unconscious Titans and Olympians were being taken. They laid Zephyr beside Astraea's mother.

Astraea looked at all those that were down. "We must protect them," she panted. "But I don't have a weapon."

"I do." Triana held up a sword.

Tryn also had a sword. His haunted eyes revealed the pain he was suffering from the battle he was witnessing and being part of.

Astraea dashed back into the fight and retrieved her own sword, and together the three of them stood watch over Zephyr, her mother, and the other fallen. They attacked any Mimic that came near them.

Despite the fight seeming endless, eventually the defenders got the upper hand. What amazed Astraea was how, once again, the few remaining Mimics didn't try to run or escape. Instead they fought right to the end.

Finally, it was over and all the Mimics in the food chamber had been reduced to puddles.

Jupiter looked around the room with his sword held up, ready to take on more. When he realized there were none left, he walked to the corridor outside the chamber and looked around. Then he turned back to his people. "The corridor is clear. I want an advance team to move forward and clear a path to Arious."

"We will go," Hyperion called as he, Crius, and several other security Titans charged forward into the corridor.

Astraea's father came up to her and saw what she, Tryn, and Triana had done for the unconscious fighters. He nodded at Astraea and smiled weakly. Then he reached for her mother.

When he carried her forward, he called, "Will someone please tell me how to get to Arious? I must get Aurora there."

Pegasus came forward. "I will show you."

Astraea was torn. She wanted to stay with Zephyr, but she needed to be with her mother. A night dweller came over to her. "Go, child. Stay with your mother. We will keep watch over your friend and the others."

Astraea nodded and reached down to touch Zephyr. "I'll be right back, Zeph. You're safe now."

Tryn put down his weapon and, saying nothing, walked beside Astraea. Triana also followed, but like Astraea, she kept her sword at the ready.

Finally Tryn spoke in a hushed voice. "I have killed. It goes against everything my people stand for. Everything I believe. What does that make me?"

"It makes you a hero," Cylus said as he, Darek, and Render joined them with their bows held at the ready.

Astraea touched Tryn's arm. "I know you don't feel it right now, but because of what you and Triana did down there, Zephyr is safe. So are a lot of others."

"I understand that, but . . ." His words trailed off.

Astraea had no words of comfort or encouragement to give him. She felt the same.

Everyone was silent as they made their way through the temple. No one needed to speak. They all understood that the fight had been more dreadful than they'd ever dreamed.

Along the way they encountered several more Mimics. These were quickly dispatched by Cylus, Darek, and Render with their bows. When the group finally arrived on the level of the supercomputer, Pegasus clopped up to the stone wall that hid the door. He kicked it with a golden hoof.

"Arious, we have returned to free Xanadu from the

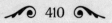

Mimics. . . ." Pegasus barely finished speaking when the hidden door slid open.

Tryn's parents rushed out, and his mother ran up to him. Triana embraced them both.

"I am so glad to see you all," Ben said as he invited them into the chamber. The door closed tightly behind them. "We've been trapped in here for days. . . ." His eyes trailed over to Astraios carrying Aurora. "What happened?"

"She was hurt on Earth," Astraios said. "She has broken bones and I fear more injuries that we cannot see. There was no ambrosia left to give to her. She has not awakened since it happened."

Arious called, "Bring Aurora forward. I am ready to receive her." A drawer slid open in the wall. "Place her here."

Astraea's father carried her mother over to the drawer and placed her inside. Then the drawer slid silently closed. Moments later Arious said, "Scans reveal that Aurora does have many broken bones. As well there is internal bleeding. I am starting treatment immediately."

Astraea could barely speak as she looked at the closed drawer. "Will she . . . ?"

411

"Aurora is young and strong. She will recover," Arious answered.

Tryn was still with his mother. He lowered his head. "Forgive me, Mother. I have fought and I have killed. It was not what I wanted, but the Mimics left me no choice."

"So have I," Triana said.

Their mother's face was filled with loving compassion. "Do not fret. I understand. We all do. When the Mimics attacked us, they killed many Rheans and took others away. They are a species we have never encountered before. They are a living horror, and we must all stand against them."

Tryn's father embraced him. "None of us want to fight. But we must." He looked around the room. "Where's Jake?"

Tryn dropped his head and told them the events of Earth. "We hoped they might have brought him here."

The lights on Arious flashed. "I am sorry, Trynulus," the computer said. "Scans reveal there are no humans on the surface. The Mimics did not bring him here."

"Don't worry," Ben said. "We'll get him back. We'll get them all back."

"We brought the snakes with us," Astraea offered. "They are giving us a lot of venom. Plus Belis is here. He's a giant snake that really hates Mimics." It was then that Astraea noticed the two snakes around Ben's neck and remembered Tryn telling her that his father had wanted to be bitten by the ones Tryn brought back from Zomos. "Can you understand them the way Jake understands Nesso?"

Ben nodded. "These two are real characters," he said. "They are going to help us all they can."

"That's good," Astraea said. "With Jake . . ." She couldn't finish the sentence, as it was still too painful.

"I understand," Ben said. "Arious has analyzed their venom and, unfortunately, she can't duplicate it."

The computer agreed. "The venom contains an organic compound unique to the snakes. I cannot reproduce it. We need our snake friends if we are to defeat the Mimics."

"But can they give enough?" Pegasus asked. "There are a lot of Mimics, and they do not care if they die in battle. They sacrifice themselves easily."

"That is because they are part of a hive society," Arious explained. "Individuals are unimportant and dispensable. Only the hive and their queen matter."

"How can we fight an opponent like that?" Cylus asked.

"One at a time," Ben answered.

Tryn walked up to Arious. "Can you feel when someone arrives by the Solar Stream?"

"If it is within the temple, yes," Arious said. "I have sensors throughout. I was aware of your arrival. It was unfortunate that you picked the busiest chamber in the temple to arrive in."

"That was my fault," Pegasus said softly. "That chamber is where Emily and I first arrived. It was on the lowest level. I believed it would be safest."

"Your reasoning was logical," Arious agreed. "Unfortunately, that level is also the coolest place on the planet, and the Mimics needed it to store their food."

"Not for long," Render said. "A team is down there now destroying their supplies. If they can't eat, maybe they'll leave."

"I fear it will take more than that to discourage them," Arious said. "But it is a start."

Astraea walked over to the wall where her mother was being treated. She could see the outside of the drawer, but not her mother inside. She laid her hand against it, wishing she had the power to heal her. "How long will my mother be in there?"

"Not long," Arious said. "She is already responding to treatment."

Moments later, there was pounding on the chamber door. It slid open to reveal Jupiter and Juno. "How is Aurora?" were Juno's first words as they entered.

"Recovering," Arious called.

"Thank the stars." Jupiter approached the consul. "Arious, are there any more Mimics in the temple?"

"No, Jupiter. Your people have destroyed them all. Thank you."

"Will you tell us if more arrive?" Jupiter asked.

"Yes. I have set up a central alarm to sound if there are any Solar Stream incursions into the temple. It will announce where they are. But I do not know about outside it."

Jupiter nodded. "We have been to the entrance and have seen a good number of them out there." He looked back at Astraea. "You are right about their night vision. They are all carrying torches and other sources of light. That gives us a small advantage. But we need more."

Astraea looked at the computer. "Arious, if you can sense when the Solar Stream opens, can you stop it?"

"I wish I could, but I cannot. This chamber is the only place that is magnetically sealed against the Solar Stream."

"Themis was right," Juno noted. "She said it was likely this is the only place you could protect."

Ben came forward. "At least with the central alarm, we'll know when and where more arrive." He approached Jupiter. "Now that you have cleared the temple, I believe it is time we set up patrols on every level to deal with any new arrivals."

Jupiter nodded. "I have teams out, but we could use your help to better organize them. Your CRU experience would serve us well in this matter. May I count on you for support?"

"Of course," Ben said. He looked back at his wife, Tara. "I'm going to get started."

"Not without me you aren't," Tara replied.

"But, Mom," Tryn started. "Rheans don't fight."

Tara nodded. "In the past we did not fight. But the Mimics have changed that. They have killed our kind and taken others. We have no option. I will stand beside your father and I will learn to fight."

Just as they prepared to leave, Arious sounded a shrill alarm. "Solar Stream incursion in the lower food chamber. Mimics and Shadow Titans!"

"They're back!" Tryn cried.

Jupiter charged out of the room. "Come, we must get there."

Astraea held her sword at the ready as they charged into the chamber. It was deadly silent. The Solar Stream was closed and there were no Mimics around them. Several Shadow Titans lay sprawled in pieces on the floor. It was impossible to tell which ones were under their control and which ones were from the Mimics.

Over to one side, they saw that the stacks of Mimic food had been reduced to ash by Pluto. But there was no sign of him.

"What happened here?" Jupiter turned in a circle.

A Titan warrior was climbing slowly to her feet.

She had a deep wound in her side. "It was Mimics and Shadow Titans. They struck so quickly. We managed to melt several Mimics, but the Shadow Titans are almost impossible to destroy."

"Where is my brother?" Jupiter demanded, looking around. "And Vulcan?"

"Taken," the warrior said. "Though I do not think they were the real target. I think the snakes and the containers of venom were."

"They got the venom?" Cylus cried.

The warrior nodded.

"Astraea," Zephyr called. She was across the chamber and offering her wing to a wounded Olympian to help them up.

Astraea ran over and helped the Olympian stand. He had a head wound and looked unsteady on his feet.

"You must get to Arious," Astraea said. "She can heal you."

Juno came forward. "Allow me to help you." The Olympian looked stunned at who was offering. He bowed his head. "Thank you, Juno."

When they were gone, Astraea focused on her best friend. "Zeph, are you all right?" She checked around

Zephyr's body and under her wings. "Did they hurt you anywhere?"

"I'm fine," Zephyr said. "But they took Angitia, two containers of snakes, and the jars of venom. They hurt Belis and now he's going nuts!"

Across the chamber the immense snake was slithering around and smashing into the wall. There was blood coming out of several deep wounds on his head.

"What did they do to him?" Astraea asked.

"The Shadow Titans went after him. I think they were trying to capture him or even kill him. When Angitia tried to protect him, they grabbed her and took her through the Solar Stream. Maybe they wanted him to follow, but he was too hurt. Where he's smashing his head against the wall is where they came through and left. He's either brain damaged or doesn't understand that he can't follow them."

Ben gasped. "Look at the size of that snake!"

"That's Belis," Astraea said. She looked at the snakes around his neck. "Would you come with me and tell him to stop? He's going to hurt himself more. He can't follow them, not that way through the wall."

The snakes hissed, and Ben said, "They'll tell

him." He hesitated. "It is safe, right? I mean, that's a really big snake."

Astraea nodded. "He's very gentle."

"To us," Tryn said. "To Mimics he's their worst nightmare."

Ben looked at his son. "Then we must find more snakes like him!"

37

THE ATTACK IN THE LOWER CHAMBER WAS quick and well thought out. The Mimics knew their targets and moved quickly to secure them. But how they knew who would be in there remained a mystery.

With nothing more to do, everyone made their way back to the control room. The remaining snakes were also brought up for their protection.

Belis had been more wounded than they realized, and it took Pegasus, Zephyr, and several strong Titans to help get him up to Arious for treatment. The snake was now lying down beside Astraea and taking up more than half the space in the control room.

"I don't like seeing him like that," Zephyr admitted.

"He may irritate me at times, but I'd never want him hurt. I didn't even think he could be hurt. But those Shadow Titans nearly killed him."

"I know," Astraea agreed as she stroked Belis's head. "The Mimics must be very scared of him."

"Too bad we can't get Lergo on our side," Zephyr said. "That would be all we'd need to defeat the Mimics."

Jupiter and Juno came in to check on Belis and heard the comment. "Do you know of another serpent like Belis that could help us?" Jupiter asked.

"Not Lergo," Zephyr said. "That's the one that's ten times bigger than Belis. It bit me and wanted to eat me. It's way too dangerous."

"That is unfortunate," Jupiter said. He and Juno approached Arious. "Please, Arious, what can you tell us of these Mimics? Even those Titan blobs that brought about the end of Olympus were nothing like these. The Mimics use the Solar Stream as adeptly as the Xan."

"That is because they are a race as old as the Xan," Arious said. "I fear with all the powerful beings they have taken—especially Riza and Emily—when the queen spawns, a new race will rise that is more powerful and destructive than ever before. If they go unopposed, there is nothing to stop them from overrunning the universe."

"They have taken my children, my brother, and Vulcan, and so many others from here," Jupiter said. "Believe me, they will not go unopposed. We will get our loved ones back."

"If they haven't killed them already," Arious said softly.

Astraea gasped. "They took Jake and—and Angitia and—and everyone. Please tell me they aren't going to kill them!"

"I am sorry, child," Arious said. "We do not know their reasons for taking prisoners. It may be for a deadly purpose."

Ben was shaking his head. "We've just engaged the Mimics again in one of the corridors. They are still trying to get in here. We had bows, swords, and daggers, but they just aren't good enough against the Mimics' tendrils. They managed to kill two more Titans."

"Those weapons are all we have," Jupiter said.

"My powers are useless against them. As are all of our powers. Are you suggesting we return to Earth to acquire guns and such human weapons?"

Ben shook his head. "No. Guns won't work, either. I've tried that already. I got some venom from my two guys and bathed bullets in it. But when they're fired from a gun, the heat destroys the potency of the venom. Then I tried putting the venom inside the bullet, but they just passed through the Mimics and did no harm. We need something else."

"Like what?" Jupiter said. "If you have a suggestion, please say it now."

"Well, there was something I was thinking of before we were locked in here after the second wave. It's an old Earth toy most kids played with. That is, until computers and mobile phones took over. It's called a slingshot."

Astraea frowned. "A what?"

"Slingshot," Ben said. "They are easy to make." He went on to describe how to create them. "As kids we used slingshots to knock cans off fence posts from quite far away. I'm hoping it will work if we coat rocks in the venom and shoot them at the Mimics. Even if the rock passes through them, the venom might do the trick."

"That sounds very much like a sling," Juno said.

"Almost," Ben said. "If we could make some here, it would give us more weapons against the Mimics that can be fired from farther away. They're smaller than bows and arrows and easier to carry."

"It sounds perfect," Astraea said. "I would like to try it."

Cylus and the other centaurs all nodded.

"And me," Tara agreed.

"If this works, we will all have them," Jupiter agreed. "We just need to reach some trees to use their branches. I will organize some teams now. We will charge out of the temple and take back the area."

"Your plan will not work," Arious said. "By my estimate, there are too many Mimics outside the temple. By now they know you are here and will no doubt be planning another assault against you."

"What else do you suggest?" Jupiter demanded.

"The Solar Stream," Arious said. "There is a continent here on Xanadu called Willow's Lay. There you will find trees that I believe will suit your needs perfectly. Also, there are vines there that grow with great elasticity. But you must not harm the trees. Riza would be devastated if you did, especially if it was to save her."

"Of course not," Ben said. "This is Xanadu. Nothing living here must ever be killed—except for Mimics. All we need are some branches and pieces of the vines."

"Perfect," Jupiter said. He looked around the room, and his eyes landed on Astraea and Zephyr. "Your team worked well going to Zomos. I am asking you now to go for the branches we need. As Arious suggests, I have no doubt the Mimics will be launching an attack on us soon. We will stay to fight them. Please hurry. We need those weapons if we are to succeed."

"Of course," Astraea said. She looked up at Zephyr. "Right?"

"Um . . . yeah, sure," Zephyr said unenthusiastically. "I'm not worried that there are more Mimics out there than in here. Not the least bit worried. Another trip. Great . . . it'll be wonderful."

"We'll come too," Cylus offered, looking at Darek and Render.

"Count me in," Tryn said.

"And me," Ben said. "I know what we're looking for."

"Perfect," Jupiter said. "We will start to gather more venom from the snakes and be prepared for your return."

Astraea looked back at her team. "Tryn, let's go out in the corridor and use your ring. We can't waste a moment."

38

THE TRIP THROUGH THE SOLAR STREAM was instantaneous. In less than the blink of the eye, they were emerging in a forest that was just waking with the first rays of dawn. As Astraea looked around in the increasing light, she thought it was unlike anything she had ever seen before. It didn't even look like Xanadu anymore. The trees were unbelievably tall, and their blue-leafed branches were swirling, waving, and bending toward the rising sun.

As the group walked around, the trees responded to their presence, trembling and lowering their branches and making a pleasant hushing sound.

"Wow," Zephyr said. "These trees are amazing. There's no wind, but they're waving as though there is."

"They remind me of weeping willows from Earth," Ben said. "But they're so much prettier." He approached a tree and patted the trunk. The tree actually sighed.

"They're alive?" Cylus said.

"Of course they are. They're trees," Astraea said.

"No, I mean alive, alive, like us. You know, conscious. You touch them and they respond." He drew his sword and approached a tree. "I'm sorry, tree, but we need to do this." When he raised the sword, the tree branches shied back.

"Cylus, stop!" Ben ordered. "Don't touch that tree!"

"But you said we need branches."

"We do," Ben agreed. "But it's obvious these trees are sentient and aware of us. We promised we wouldn't harm them, and we won't. Look around you. There are plenty of fallen branches. There's no need to cut new ones."

Tryn's father was right. As Astraea and Zephyr walked closer to the tree trunks, they saw many fallen branches. While they were looking down, one of the branches bent down and stroked Zephyr's neck.

"Whoa!" Zephyr cried as she jumped clear of the tree. "It just touched me!"

"This is Xanadu," Ben said. "Why wouldn't the trees be curious?"

"But . . . I mean . . . it touched me!" Zephyr cried. "It reached out and petted my mane!"

"That's because you're so pretty," Astraea said. She looked over at Ben. "So, what kind of branch are we looking for?"

"Come here and I'll show you." Ben walked to the nearest tree and searched beneath it. As he did, more branches reached down from above and one touched the top of his head. He reached out and grasped it gently. "Nice to meet you too. We need to borrow some of your fallen branches. Xanadu is under attack, and invaders have taken Riza and Emily away. Your branches can help us save them."

The trees all around them visibly shook in reaction. They lifted their branches to allow everyone to walk closer.

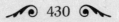

Cylus looked up and frowned. "This is wrong. Trees shouldn't move like this."

"This is their home," Tryn finally said. "They can do as they wish."

"When we get Jake and Angitia back, I really want to see more of Xanadu," Astraea said.

"But you said you wanted to see more of Earth," Zephyr said.

"I want that too. Jake promised he'd show me . . ." Astraea's voice trailed off as she thought of Jake as a prisoner of the Mimics.

"We'll get him back," Cylus promised.

"Yes, we will," Ben agreed. He reached for a fallen branch. "Now, the slingshots need to be like a big *Y*. So, look for that."

"What's a *why*?" Cylus said.

Darek and Render shrugged.

"This is a *Y*," Ben explained as he tried to break the dried limbs off the branch, but they wouldn't give. He handed the piece to Tryn. "You're much stronger than me and know what a *Y* is. Would you break this for me?"

Tryn received the branch and soon broke away the

needless pieces until it was shaped like a large *Y.* He handed it back to his father.

"Thanks," Ben said. He held up the *Y.* "You see, we attach a piece of elastic or vine, as Arious suggested, between the two top branches. Then you hold on to the lower one like a handle. You would load your rock and pull back on the vine and then fire."

"Oh," Cylus said, nodding. "I understand. It's like a small bow."

"Exactly," Ben said. "But with a bow, the rod bends. With a slingshot, the elastic is pulled."

Now that they knew what they were looking for, the search went quickly. Much to Astraea's surprise, the trees started to shake, causing larger and more useful branches to fall to the ground. "Thank you!" she called up as she gathered them.

Before long, they had a large pile. As Astraea and the centaurs gathered more, Tryn used his Rhean strength to break them into shape.

Next they went searching for the vines. Just as Arious suggested, they were very elastic. Pieces were cut from the ends of the vines and put with the other supplies.

"Now let's see if this works," Ben said. He tied a length of vine to the slingshot and then reached for a pebble. When he loaded it and fired, the rock shot across the area and landed a good forty feet away.

"I don't believe it!" Cylus said. "Let me try!"

Ben handed over the slingshot and showed Cylus how to use it. When the centaur fired it, the rock traveled even farther. "This is perfect!" Cylus cried. "The Mimics won't be expecting this!"

"Now all we need are some stones and we can head back to Arious," Tryn said.

They worked quickly to gather as many small stones as they could carry. When they had all the supplies they needed, Ben pulled off his shirt and laid it down on the ground. He made a sack of it and put all the stones inside. "This will get us started so we can clear the area around the temple. Then we can gather more there."

"I'll carry the sack," Zephyr offered. Ben handed it to Zephyr, and she bit down on it. "I'm ready," she muttered.

Everyone else gathered up the shaped branches and

pieces of vines. With his arms full, Tryn struggled to hold up the ring, but he managed it and gave the command to take them back to the corridor outside Arious. The Solar Stream opened, and everyone walked through.

39

THE CORRIDORS OUTSIDE THE CHAMBER of Arious were filled with Titans and Olympians working to create a large supply of slingshots to Ben's specifications. They then learned to fire the new weapons and were gaining in accuracy with each attempt.

While everyone practiced, Astraea, Tara, Triana, and several others started to coat the rocks in venom. When they dried, they were handed to the advance team, which prepared to go outside the temple to test the new weapons.

Ben was leading the assault. "Remember, keep low and hidden. Don't let them see you. These Mimics learn fast! Let's not show them what we're using. I'd rather keep them guessing."

Astraea had her own slingshot ready and was prepared to go, but Jupiter stopped her. "But we can shoot," Astraea insisted.

"Yes," Cylus added. "You know how accurate we are. You can't ignore us because we're young."

"I am not ignoring you," Jupiter insisted. "You have earned my respect. But while they are outside, who is going to protect those inside the temple? What if the Mimics use the Solar Stream again? We must keep this stronghold if we are to have a hope of freeing Titus."

Astraea wasn't happy, but she had no choice but to obey. She, Zephyr, and Tryn remained with Arious while Cylus and his herd joined the patrols throughout the temple.

While she awaited word on the success of the new slingshots, Astraea stood beside the door to her mother's healing chamber. Belis was finally awake and was pressing against her. She was absently stroking his head and wishing she were outside with the others.

After what seemed an eternity there were excited

shouts outside the chamber of Arious and the silver door slid open. Ben ran in and embraced his wife. "It worked! We got them! They didn't even have time to turn their Shadow Titans against us. We've got a small army of them now."

"Really?" Tara cried. "The Mimics are gone?"

He nodded. "The entire area around the temple is clear."

"What if they return through the Solar Stream?" Tryn asked.

"We're ready for them," Ben said excitedly. "The night dwellers are patrolling inside the temple, and we've set up perimeter guards outside it. The Shadow Titans have been ordered to attack any that come through. Come outside. Jupiter is calling everyone together to discuss our next move."

While Ben, Tara, and Triana left, Tryn, Astraea, and Zephyr lingered behind. Astraea looked at the drawer containing her mother.

"Go now, you three," Arious said softly. "I am taking good care of Aurora and all the wounded. If anything changes, I will send word. Go out and see what Jupiter has to say."

"We have to stay with the snakes," Astraea said.

"I'll take care of them too," Arious said. "Including Belis, who is recovering nicely but needs a bit more time. I shall tell him to stay."

Cylus and Render trotted past the control room and called in, "Come on, you guys, they're waiting for us."

Astraea, Zephyr, and Tryn reluctantly left Arious and followed behind the centaurs.

"Hurry up!" Cylus called. "We don't want to miss this."

Making their way to the surface, they shielded their eyes against the bright morning sunshine as they left the dark entrance of the temple. Everyone was there except for the night dwellers, who remained in the covered safety of the temple.

Outside, the strongest among them formed a large circle around the encampment with their new slingshots held high.

As they approached, Astraea was stunned to see Pegasus rearing and then slamming back down to the ground before Jupiter. "No, Jupiter, you are wrong!" the stallion insisted. He shook his head and snorted furiously. "We must rescue Emily, Riza, and Jake first. We do not know what the Mimics are doing to them. I must save my Emily!"

"I am sorry, Pegasus," Jupiter said. "I, above all others, know how important Emily is to you—to all of us. But going to the Mimic world right now is impossible. Titus is in great danger, as the number of Mimics there has increased. Now that we have a way of effectively fighting them, we must free our world first. Only then will we have the strength and resources to go after Emily, Riza, and the others. Remember, my own children, Diana and Apollo, and my brother are there too, but they would understand this decision. Titus must come first."

"Please, Jupiter," Pegasus begged. "Let me go after them alone."

"No, Pegasus, not until Titus is free. Then we shall all go after them."

"That could be too late!" Pegasus shrieked. "I cannot imagine what they are doing to Emily right now. It is tearing me apart. We must go *now*!"

"I am sorry, my nephew, but we cannot."

"That is not good enough." Pegasus snorted. "All

my life, I have done everything you have asked of me. Never once questioning your decisions, never once saying no. This is the one time I am begging you for something. Please, Uncle, please help me save my Emily!"

Jupiter shook his head. "I am truly sorry, Pegasus. No. Titus must come first."

Pegasus reared and shrieked again. He flapped his wings furiously and took off into the sky.

Astraea stood in silence, watching the stallion fly away.

"Wow, he's really angry," Zephyr said. "I didn't think Pegasus could get angry. Especially at Jupiter."

"I've never heard him raise his voice before," Tryn said. "But he's right. Jupiter is a fool for not going after Jake and the others first. Riza and Emily are powerful. They could help us clear Titus. If we don't go after them now, the queen may spawn, and then we're all doomed."

"What are you saying?" Astraea said. "You want us to go rescue them?"

"I'd go," Cylus offered. "I kinda like that stupid human Jake, and I miss him."

"Me too," Render and Darek said together.

Astraea looked at everyone and nodded. "Actually, I would go too."

"Are you crazy!" Zephyr whinnied. "You're saying you'd go to the Mimic world to rescue Jake? Jake the human, Jake the one who still smells funny? Jake the guy who really likes the snakes?"

"Are you saying that you don't want to rescue him?" Astraea asked. "What about Angitia? You like her, don't you?"

Zephyr paused. "Yes, I like her, and no, I'm not saying I wouldn't go. I'm just checking on you."

Tryn said nothing for a few minutes, then reached into his pack for his skateboard. "I'm going to go talk to Pegasus."

"About what?" Astraea asked.

"To ask him if he wants to come with us to the Mimic home world to rescue everyone."

40

"I'M COMING WITH YOU," ASTRAEA SAID TO Tryn.

"I guess you'll want a ride," Zephyr said.

Astraea stroked Zephyr's muzzle. "Zeph, I know you're still not comfortable around Pegasus. You don't have to come. I can travel with Tryn on his skateboard."

"Hey, if anyone is going to carry you, it's going to be me," Zephyr insisted. "Besides, he doesn't bother me *that* much anymore. . . ."

"Oh really?" Astraea said.

Zephyr nodded. "I've never seen anyone stand up to Jupiter like that. Pegasus is a lot braver than I thought."

Cylus approached Astraea. "If Pegasus agrees to go to the Mimic home world, promise me you'll come back for us. We're a team. We should stay that way."

Astraea nodded. "We will, I promise."

"Good," Cylus said. "Now, get going. We'll start to gather supplies here. If Jupiter asks where you are, I'll tell him you had to go to the toilet or something."

"Yeah, that will work," Zephyr said, "telling him we all had to go together. . . ."

"Just go," Cylus said.

Astraea walked beside Zephyr until they were away from the gathering. When they reached the side of the temple, Astraea climbed up onto her back. Zephyr entered a trot and then a gallop and took off into the sky.

Tryn flew up beside them and called down to his skateboard, "Take us to Pegasus."

They traveled across the blazing sky, over the dense jungle. Xanadu was lusher and more beautiful than Astraea could imagine. The trees were dense and full like Zomos, but somehow so much prettier. Although she didn't have time to appreciate it all. Her thoughts were only on finding Pegasus and rescuing Jake.

After a while the skateboard started to descend. They spied a small lake in a clearing. Pegasus was standing on the shore.

"Pegasus," Astraea called as they touched down.

"Go back to the temple, Astraea," Pegasus said sharply as he paced the area. "I need to be alone."

Astraea could feel the anger and hurt coming from the stallion in thick waves. She looked at the water and noticed that it was rising. She realized it wasn't a lake at all. Pegasus was drawing the water from the ground by slamming his hooves down in fury. He'd done it in Detroit, and now he was doing it here, too. The fast rate the water was rising showed just how angry he was.

"Jupiter was wrong," Tryn called as he stepped off his board.

Pegasus stopped and turned to him.

"He was wrong, and you were right," Astraea agreed. "We should be going after Jake and Emily, Riza and the others first."

Pegasus lowered his head and pawed the ground.

"How can I rescue Emily when I do not know where she is?"

"We know where she is," Tryn said.

Pegasus's ears pricked forward, and he charged at Tryn. "You know where she is?"

Tryn nodded. "We know the name of the Mimic's home world. That is where the queen is. If she is trying to steal Emily's and Riza's powers, it's logical to assume that they are there too."

"Tell me the name," Pegasus demanded. "I will go there now."

"No," Astraea said as she slid off Zephyr's back.

"What?" Pegasus cried.

"We're not telling you the name until you agree to let us come with you," Astraea said.

"That is impossible," Pegasus cried. "I cannot allow you to endanger yourselves. This is my mission."

"Pegasus, listen to me," Astraea said gently. "You are really powerful. I know, I've seen it. But, please forgive me for saying this, you don't have hands. I'm sorry, but you don't. How can you fire the slingshot or wield a sword? Even if we put venom on your hooves, you'd have to touch the Mimics to use them. Then you'd be hurt. Maybe even killed. Now that we have the slingshots, we can shoot more Mimics from farther away. There is no need to fight them with swords, daggers, or hooves. Cylus, Render, and Darek have already agreed to come with us to rescue Jake. The way Belis feels about Angitia, I'm sure he will come with us too. We're going anyway. Wouldn't it be better to go together?"

"You have discussed this?" Pegasus asked.

Astraea nodded. "Briefly, right after your argument with Jupiter, when we realized he wasn't going to go after Jake."

Tryn stood before Pegasus. "Jake is my friend. So are Emily and Riza. A friend doesn't abandon another friend just because it's dangerous. I'm not a fool. I know what could happen to us, and I know I will have to fight again. I am ready for that. But what I'm not ready for is finding out that something bad had happened to Jake while I could have saved him."

"Besides," Zephyr added, "we're going whether or not you join us."

Pegasus tilted his head to the side and looked at

Zephyr. "I thought you did not like Jake because he was human."

"Yeah, well, he's kind of like a fungus. He's grown on me."

Pegasus looked at the three of them. "And you are all set on this course?"

They all nodded.

Pegasus turned and looked at the water again. "This is madness. What am I doing, considering taking you with me? It is suicide."

"Look at it this way if it helps," Zephyr said. "You aren't taking us. We're letting you come with us."

Pegasus looked back at her and shook his head. "You may not be my daughter, but you are more like me than you realize."

"Hey," Zephyr cried. "There's no need to insult me!"

The stallion chuckled. "All right, let us go."

"Where?" Tryn asked.

Pegasus opened his wings to fly. "Back to the temple to collect the three crazy centaurs and that giant snake. Then we rescue my Emily, Riza, and Jake."

Astraea climbed back on Zephyr. She leaned forward and put her arms around her best friend's neck.

"You know, you and I are just like Pegasus and Emily. I would do anything to find you again. Promise me we'll always be together."

Zephyr looked back at her and nodded. "We will be. Even if we go to the Mimic world and face unimaginable horrors. If we go together, we'll be just fine."

"Are you two finished?" Tryn said as he climbed up on his skateboard.

Astraea nodded. "Yes. Now, let's go save our friends!"

ACKNOWLEDGMENTS

I know I say this all the time, but if it weren't for the help and talents of a lot of people, my books would never see the light of day. In the case of this book, there have been so many strange things happening—sorry, dear friends, that I can't go into details—but, trust me, this one has been a doozy!

So I am especially grateful that it has made it out of the abyss.

The ones who do deserve special thanks are my agent, Veronique Baxter, and my editor and very dear friend, Fiona Simpson. It's been quite a ride, hasn't it, Fiona?

For everyone else deserving thanks, you know who you are, and you do have my gratitude!

And finally, I know I'm repeating myself, but you, dear reader, are the future. Please treat our beloved Earth gently and with great love. It's the only home we have; we must protect her. Also, care for all the other nonhuman inhabitants of the world. I mean, wouldn't Earth be boring without all this wonderful wildlife?

"ZEPHYR, I'M SCARED," ASTRAEA SAID SOFTLY.

"Me too," Zephyr agreed.

They were standing on the edge of the jungle just outside the Temple of Arious. It was their turn to keep watch for any new Mimic attacks. So far, their shift had been uneventful, but things could change in an instant.

The massive snake Belis was beside Astraea, his tongue dipping in and out of his mouth as he tasted the air for Mimics. Every few minutes, Astraea would look at him. The moment Belis became aware of the deadly Mimics, his scales would turn from colorful stripes to black.

Around them the trees were filled with cheerful birdcalls, but they found no joy in the songs. The beauty of Xanadu was missed as they stood watch.

Since arriving on Xanadu and clearing the temple of the shape-shifting Mimics, everyone was on edge. There had been several more attacks, but now that the Titans had security patrols carrying slingshots with rocks covered in snake venom that killed the invaders, the Mimics were quickly driven back. It was the Shadow Titans controlled by the Mimics that proved to be the most dangerous. Their arrival was always brutal and was happening more often. It was obvious—the deadly Mimics were fighting back.

"Do you think Jake is with my brothers?" Astraea asked as her keen eyes watched the jungle. "You don't think the Mimics killed them?"

Fear for Jake and her missing brothers had been pressing down on Astraea like a lead weight. Despite her best hopes, her four brothers hadn't been in the Titus prison, while Jake had been abducted from Earth by the Mimics and had vanished without a trace.

Not long ago, she, Zephyr, Tryn, and Pegasus had decided to go to the Mimic home world to try to rescue Jake and the others. But that was before the attacks had become bolder and more intense.

Zephyr snorted and shook her head. "Of course they're not dead. If the Mimics wanted to kill them, they wouldn't have bothered taking everyone. I think Jake was taken because he can talk to the snakes."

"Why would they care? All Mimics want to do is kill the snakes. Look what they did to Belis." Astraea looked along the snake's body to all the scars from the Shadow Titans' swords. "Every time they attack us, he seems to be their main target."

The snake could now understand them completely and raised his head higher for Astraea to stroke. "But we won't let them hurt you again," she cooed.

"I still don't get it with you two," Zephyr said, and snorted in disgust. "But it seems that's the only reason the Mimics would go for Jake. I mean he's human. Why else would they care, if not for Nesso?"

Zephyr looked slyly at Astraea, then winked.

Astraea chuckled softly. Zephyr was still making a show of not liking Jake because he was human, but she was ready to go on the secret rescue mission to save him. "Maybe. But I'm just so worried about him."

"I'm worried about all of us!" Zephyr said. "Seriously, I never imagined we'd ever be going through anything like this. Our lives have been turned upside down. Titus is overrun with Mimics, and they want Xanadu as well."

"They want our worlds, but not us," Astraea said.

Tryn appeared out of the temple and flew over to them on his skateboard. "How's it going?"

"So far it's been quiet," Astraea said.

"Quiet?" Zephyr snorted. "I can barely hear myself think with all the jungle sounds around us."

"I'm glad for the sounds," Tryn said. "Haven't you noticed how it goes quiet when the Mimics are here? It's as though everything in the jungle is frightened of them."

"Does it?" Zephyr said.

Astraea looked at her friend in shock. "Seriously, Zeph, you haven't noticed?"

"Hey, I'm too busy trying to stay alive to notice stupid things like that."

"Those stupid things could help save your life," Tryn said.

Astraea was about to say more when Jupiter, a

herd of centaurs, and several other Titans ran out of the temple. They were followed by multiple Shadow Titans being controlled by Tryn's people that were racing behind them. Everyone vanished into the jungle behind the temple.

Triana ran out of the temple and up to her brother. "We all have to go back inside right now!"

"What's happening?" Tryn asked.

"They're back!" Triana cried.

Astraea looked all around and saw only the calm jungle. She looked at Belis, who was still striped. "Where are they?"

"They're attacking the nectar orchards," Triana cried. "Jupiter says they are going after our food."

"That's low!" Zephyr cried.

"That's war," Tryn said.

Triana caught hold of her brother's arm. "Come on, Mom says we have to get inside. This is a big attack."

It didn't take more prompting to get them running. They entered the temple just as more fighters rushed out. Hercules and Mercury, the messenger of Olympus, were among them. Hercules paused long enough to call, "Get to Arious and seal yourselves in."

"Maybe we should help them," Astraea said.

Belis was still at her side and hissed loudly. When Astraea looked at him, the snake was jet black.

"Uh-oh," Zephyr said. "That isn't good."

Moments later, a blaring siren sounded. It was Arious, the mainframe computer, warning of Mimics arriving within the temple.

"This is huge!" Tryn cried. He pulled out his slingshot and opened his pouch of venom-covered rocks. Astraea and Triana did the same as they ran deeper into the temple.

"I wish I had hands," Zephyr cried.

"You don't need them," Astraea called above the siren. "You can stomp the Mimics' Shadow Titans into oblivion. That's way better than hands."

"Yes, but I can't stomp Mimics."

"We'll take care of them; you just go after the Shadows." Astraea entered the stairwell going down toward the entrance to Arious and looked back at Zephyr. "Be careful here."

"How?" Zephyr complained as she followed behind. "Would you please tell me how I'm supposed to be careful on stairs? And why are there always so many of them? Here, back on Earth, Tartarus, even Titus—they're everywhere. Don't architects think about those of us with hooves? What's wrong with ramps?"

"You can tell them when this is over," Tryn offered.

"Don't think I won't," Zephyr finished.

Tryn and Astraea linked arms while bracing against the stairwell walls to keep Zephyr from slipping down the long flight of stairs. When they reached the bottom, Zephyr neighed, "Thank you."

The siren was still blaring as they moved deeper through the cavernous corridors of the temple. Belis was directly beside Astraea and still as black as night. She held her slingshot at the ready but knew that the snake would move on any Mimics long before she could fire it.

With each step, Astraea felt more and more on edge. Perhaps it was the blaring siren, or the confines of the temple. But the fear that she'd felt earlier was now turning into terror as she kept looking all around. It wasn't a question of *if* there were Mimics in the temple—it was a question of where. It was not knowing that was making her terror worse.

When they approached a junction, Zephyr's ears sprang forward and she stopped. "I hear something."

Belis didn't stop. The snake lunged forward, hissing loudly as he slithered down the corridor. Just then, a group of four Shadow Titans rounded a corner. The large warriors were bright green and looked like walking sea turtles. Standing side by side, they formed a large, impenetrable wall blocking the corridor.

When they saw Astraea and her team, they paused. But then a gray, blubberous Mimic appeared behind them. Seeing Belis, it raised a small silver cylinder to its mouth and gave the command "Kill that snake!"

Belis hissed again and slithered toward the Shadow Titans.

"Belis, no!" Astraea cried, but the snake wouldn't stop.

"We have to have a serious talk with that snake!" Zephyr whinnied as she charged forward behind Belis. As the Shadow Titans whacked at the snake with their swords, Zephyr arrived, spun around, and started to buck. "It's stomping time!"

"Zephyr, be careful!" Astraea shouted.

"Go for the Mimic!" Zephyr called. "Get the controller!"

As the Shadow Titans focused only on killing Belis, Zephyr managed to kick the first one to pieces.

Astraea, Tryn, and Triana took aim with their slingshots and started to fire on the Mimic controlling the Shadows. But the Mimic was blocked by the large fighters. It held up the controller and shouted, "Kill the snake *and* the winged horse!" Two of the Shadow Titans stopped hitting Belis and focused on Zephyr. They charged forward with their swords held high.

"Winged horse?" Zephyr spun again and reared high, kicking out with her front hooves. "I'll show you a winged horse!" With her rage focused, she kicked at the attacking Shadow Titans and drove one to the ground. Zephyr slammed down on it, stomping it to pieces.

The second Shadow slashed at her, grazing across the chest and knocking her to the ground.

"Zephyr!" Astraea screamed.

"I'm all right," Zephyr called. "Keep going for the Mimic; get his controller!"

The Shadow Titan advanced on Zephyr as she struggled to regain her feet on the slippery stone floor. Standing above her, it raised its weapon high.

"Leave her alone!" Tryn sprang forward and used his skateboard like a bat to knock the Shadow Titan's descending sword away. Then he struck the massive Shadow in his armored head.

With only one Shadow Titan left trying to kill Belis, Astraea had a clear shot at the Mimic. She drew back her slingshot and fired. The small rock passed right through the Mimic's gelatinous body, but the poison covering the rock worked. As the Mimic cast out its deadly tendrils, it started to melt.

There was just a puddle on the ground by the time Belis arrived from his fight with the Shadow Titan. But the snake didn't stop; he charged forward and slid around the next corner.

Triana ran forward past the broken Shadow Titans and reached the melted Mimic. She kicked the controller out of the goo and cleaned it off with a piece of fabric torn from her top.

"Stop fighting!" she called into the controller.

The turtle stopped just as Tryn gave it a final whack.

"Belis!" Astraea cried as she watched the tip of his long tail vanishing around the corner into another corridor. Running after him, she made it to the junction and was met with four more Shadow Titans with drawn swords.

"There are more here!" Astraea shouted.

Belis was braver than she'd imagined, but the snake was being struck and cut by the relentless Shadow Titans. She feared by the time the others arrived, he would be dead.

"This is dumb, Astraea," she muttered as she charged forward. She approached the tail of the snake and threw herself down on the floor. Loading her slingshot, she drew back the elastic vine and waited for a clear shot at the Mimic controlling the Shadow Titans.

"Astraea, what are you doing there?" Zephyr cried as she charged around the corner.

Astraea heard her friend but didn't look back. The Shadow Titans were weaving back and forth as they attacked Belis. But with each movement, there was a moment when she had a clear shot.

Astraea fired. The rock struck a Shadow Titan

and bounced harmlessly off its arm. Cursing silently, she pulled out a second rock and loaded it.

Tryn arrived, threw himself down on the ground beside her, and raised his slingshot.

"Astraea, Tryn, get away from there!" Zephyr whinnied. "Belis might crush you!"

"Just a moment more," Astraea called. "Belis, move a bit!"

Belis finally moved, and for the briefest moment, Astraea and Tryn had a clear shot. "Please . . . ," she uttered as she took aim.

They both fired at the same time, and two rocks shot between the Shadow Titans and straight through the Mimic.

With a double dose of venom, the Mimic melted quicker. But that didn't end their troubles. The Shadow Titans were still trying to kill Belis.

Astraea sprang to her feet and looked at the wall of fighters before her. There was no way through.

"Astraea, come here and get on my back!" Zephyr cried.

Astraea leaped onto Zephyr's back. Without pausing, Zephyr turned and ran down the opposite corridor. Then she turned again and galloped toward the Shadow Titans. "Tryn, move!" she shouted.

When Tryn stepped back, Zephyr spread her wings wide in the confines of the corridor, leaped into the air, and flew awkwardly over the heads of the Shadow Titans.

Zephyr and Astraea touched down on the opposite side. Sliding off Zephyr's back, Astraea peered into the puddle of dead Mimic and saw the silver controller. She knocked it out of the goo with her foot and cleaned it off. Pressing the button, she shouted, "Stop fighting!"

The four Shadow Titans stopped immediately. Two were midswing with their swords, but now stood stone-still as though they'd been turned by Medusa.

Astraea ran up to the snake. Belis raised his head and looked at her. His eyes were clear, but there was an angry wound running the length of his head.

"He's a mess," Tryn called as he approached. He reached out and patted the snake. "Belis, I know you can understand me. You must stop doing that. You're the one they're after."

"Yeesh, I think I'm going to be sick," Zephyr said

as she looked at the snake's wounds. "They really wanted to kill him."

"You're not much better," Astraea said as she approached Zephyr and inspected the slice on her chest. "This is deep."

"It looks worse than it is," Zephyr said. "It will heal quickly. But Belis is hurt badly."

"We have to get him to Arious. He needs treatment," Tryn said.

Astraea nodded and lightly touched the snake's snout. "Come on, Belis, let's get you taken care of." Belis closed his eyes briefly; then his body tensed and started to slowly turn around in the corridor.

When they were halfway to Arious, the grating siren stopped and the whole temple fell into overwhelming silence.

"Thank you!" Zephyr said. "That alarm was really getting on my nerves."

"At least it means there are no more Mimics inside," Triana said.

They heard footsteps in the corridor next to theirs. Soon a large group of armed night dwellers arrived. Several were wearing pieces of armor taken from destroyed Shadow Titans. They approached Belis.

"How is he?" a woman Astraea knew as Paye asked. Her long white hair was tied back, and she had a deep wound on her cheek.

"He's alive," Astraea said. "But the Shadow Titans hurt him. We're taking him to Arious."

"How bad was the attack?" Tryn asked.

"Bad," another night dweller said. "Really bad."

Paye sighed. "I fear they are attacking us here to keep us occupied while they go after the nectar orchards."

"We were ordered to go to Arious," Astraea said. "But I'd rather go to the orchards to help. We can fight from the sky." She looked at Zephyr. "Are you well enough to do that?"

"It's not a question of whether I'm well enough," Zephyr said. "It's if I want to."

"Do you?" Astraea asked.

"Not really, but we're going to go anyway, aren't we?"

When Astraea nodded, Tryn stepped forward. "We're coming too."

"The trouble is Belis," Astraea continued. "He needs help. We should get him to Arious first."

An older night dweller came forward. He also had several wounds. "Go join the battle for the orchard. We'll take care of Belis."

Astraea nodded and patted Belis again. "I know you want to stay with me, but please go to Arious with Paye and the others. We'll be back soon."

Belis lifted his head weakly and leaned against Astraea.

"Please, Belis, do this for me," Astraea coaxed.

Finally he started to turn around in the corridor and move toward Arious.

Astraea looked at her friends. "Come on, let's go. They need our help."

From KATE O'HEARN, the author of the Pegasus series, comes a new adventure featuring Freya, a Valkyrie out of Norse myth. Normally, Valkyries reap the souls of lost warriors and bring them back to Valhalla to live in luxury, but Freya may well be the first of her kind to save lives rather than take them.

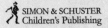